SPIRITS OVER TIME AND OCEANS

Demons in the Deep

First Published in 2022 by Echo Books

Echo Books is an imprint of Superscript Publishing Pty Ltd
ABN 76 644 812 395

Registered Office: PO Box 997, Woodend, Victoria, 3442

www.echobooks.com.au

National Library of Australia Cataloguing-in-Publication entry.

Creator: King, Suzanne, author.

Title: Spirits Over Time and Oceans: Suzanne King

ISBN: 978-1-922603-27-2(paperback)

A catalogue record for this
book is available from the
National Library of Australia

Book and cover design by Andrew Davies.

Spirits

OVER TIME AND OCEANS

Demons in the Deep

Suzanne King

CONTENTS

The Eternal

When you look upon the mountain
Shining bright in morning dew
Do you feel the eternal
Beyond here and now
Beyond you?

When you look to the river
So startling blue
Do you see with your heart
Spirits
Transcended above you?

If you lean close and listen
To the land and the sea
Your life will glisten
Pure serenity

Artemis Awakens

The deep blue beckoned
Down, down to the sea floor
She endured like no other
Enticed onwards
To the sacred below the shore

Entranced
Heart enraptured and bold
She endured like no other
Enticed onwards
To be immersed in an aura of gold

Behold cried Her Grace
For I am you and you are me
My golden aura
Will embolden
For we are Artemis; you will see

Spirits Over Time and Oceans

The author lives in lutruwita / Tasmania overlooking the Derwent River, which was the inspiration for this story.

Dedication

To all the wild, verdant places in the world, my loving parents (Arthur and Dene King) who inspired my love of nature and my darling husband Alan, my best friend and great love.

Acknowledgements

Thank you to the tireless support of my husband Alan who wondered over seven years when, or if, I would ever emerge from the study with a completed manuscript in my hand! I have cherished your infinite encouragement and support, and our years of intense and often hilarious plot discussions. Thank you also to my life-long friend Lindy Genovesi, for her unwavering support and for reading the draft chapters of this book. I am also grateful to the excellent mentors who I had the privilege of working with at the Sydney Writers' Studio over a three-year period, in particular Robin Shaw. You were a highlight of my writing journey, and our rapport allowed me to explore my creativity, resulting in many laughs and an early draft. I would also like to thank the crew of the 1874 James Craig Heritage Tall Ship who provided an understanding of the layout of the deck of a barque, crucial for the chapter entitled 'Master and Commander'. I also very much appreciated the assistance of Victor Manawatu, Educator at Waihōpai Rūnaka, New Zealand, who helped me with Māori words and culture. I am also thankful to Dr Alison Dean, Station Leader, Macquarie Island (2018), and Lyne Kelly who kindly put me in touch with Pete Pedersen, Station Leader, Macquarie Island (2022). Also, I am exceedingly grateful to Simone Ford, Professional Editor, whose brilliant feedback worked to lift my writing to new heights and shape my final draft. Finally, a massive thank you to all friends who have supported my endeavours over many years and have given me confidence to go forth and write with all my heart.

Legend – The Mermaid of Mykonos

Mykonos, Greece, 1772

'Uncle Nicos! Viasýni! He is right behind me today!' Zana's bare feet landed with a thud onto the deck of the ketch. Within seconds she had taken up her usual hiding spot between the wire baskets, long fishing lines and floats and drawn her shawl over her long black hair.

'You will get me into trouble, girl – you must do your chores!'

She giggled at the way he always sounded gruff, but his stained-tooth grin gave him away. They were so alike, never happy unless the cobbled streets and whitewashed walls of Chora were at their backs.

She felt the ketch shift away from the harbour wall just in time.

'Eh! Uncle Nicos! Is Zana with you?'

'What's that, Spiros? I'm old and deaf!' Nicos yelled to the dark shape that was fading from view in the pre-dawn light.

She forced herself to not laugh out loud. It felt so right here, huddled beneath her shawl, listening to the creak of the ketch, the lap of the waves against the hull, feeling the pull of the sea. She was free to dream her dreams and let her faith and courage converge and propel her onwards to the mystical beyond the shore. So what if she couldn't cook moussaka and the stone floors went unwashed. The need to follow her calling was too great. Her eyes had always looked upon the sea as if it was Heaven. Her body told her that it was, the first time the great aquamarine of the Aegean lapped at her thirsty skin.

Always she carried the need in her to be with the sea. Always she stifled her unspoken wisdom that there was something out there bigger than herself, her family, the village. She just needed to dive deeper. The answer was down there, way beyond the schools of *lavráki* and the boggle eyes and tentacles of the *htapodi*.

Like any other dawn, they waited for the other ketches to race ahead then turned towards the uninhabited island of Delos. For years they'd watched as others chased the fish in deeper waters, eastwards towards Ikaria or to the south near Naxos or Paros. Their secret sheltered cove off the sacred island served them well, providing plenty of fish for her uncle and blessed freedom for her to be as unruly as she wanted.

She crawled from her hiding spot. 'So my little *gorgóna,* you help me catch some *lythrini* and *lavráki*, then you go diving, eh?'

'What? Not without the best diver in all of Greece?' The long-running joke was snatched up by the light breeze. She pulled the shawl around her neck and tried to pout at his daily retort.

'Ah, I'm too old, and you, my little one, go too deep for me now.'

She leaned into him for a moment, happy to bask in his love and feel the rising sun warm her face. Was this the last time she would feel so safe? She tossed the thought into the vessel's wake and resumed her position between the wire baskets to mentally prepare for the dive.

Was it wise not to tell him that today was the day? All those times she could have told him about the channel between the rock-ledges, but never once had she mentioned the thousands of fish, the way they glided through the space in trance-like, languid formations. So how could she tell him that today was going to be like no other, swimming far beyond the channel, going deeper and further than she had ever gone before?

She closed her eyes and visualised herself launching off the ketch, slipstreaming down through the shards of light, and merging with the thousands of fish. She could see her body converge in the crowded space of coral red and silver scales and strange liquid bubbles of gold. She'd be through the other side, below their underbellies, in ten to twenty seconds.

What if I panic, like I did before? The twinge of doubt that had been pricking at her heart seized upon the opportunity to strike. She could see herself flail for a moment, the fish absorbing her terror, darting away before she managed to climb up to the surface. She placed a hand over the pain in her chest and reminded herself it had been at least a year since that awful day.

You've learned to quieten your mind. All you need to do is surrender to the beauty and embody the peace of the depths.

The instant she made a conscious decision to reject panic, the pain in her heart started to subside.

She commenced her breathing exercises and visualised the golden bubbles floating in the light current. Only a peaceful mind, a courageous heart and a strong, willing body could ever have found the bubbles of gold in the first place. They were barely discernible amidst the mass of scales and fins and watchful eyes. Now all her training had led to this day, to go beyond, further than she had ever gone before. This was her moment, her calling, a journey like no other, when her faith would be tested, to follow the gold to its source.

After fishing, the swan dive allowed her to leave the hull of the boat and the silver surface far behind. Her strong arms pulled against the weight of water. Down, down, through the aquamarine coolness into the deep chill. Red and silver bellies slid past her ears and weaved through her long black medusa hair.

Always here, in the channel, she felt more scale and fin than human. Immersed in the mass of fish and their trance-like journeys, she would normally float here, content. How many times had she floated blissfully in this space, allowing the tentacles of golden bubbles to entwine her body?

Today though, truth drove her onwards. Zana pulled herself further down, below the mass of a thousand bellies. There was the ancient misshapen pillar, smashed on the seabed, just as she had spied before. And there was the boulder-strewn entrance of a cave, swarming with fish. Strings of golden bubbles, like an immense underwater harp, danced in the current. They beckoned like magical, magnetic fingers to come closer, to follow her heart. Truth was there, knowledge of all that is and will ever be lying just inside the entrance. Her heart told her so, and her body willed for it to be true.

She slid with the current over the weed-covered rocks into the cave. At once, a wall of scales and gel eyes engulfed her body. Somewhere back there was the entrance, lost in darkness.

Trust your intuition. Feel your skin – the water is warmer.

Her lungs were screaming now. This journey would surely be her last. The press of fish and jagged edges of rock scraped at her thighs.

Keep going – there is light up ahead.

She pushed her body towards shafts of light that penetrated the water. With her body screaming for oxygen, she tried with all her will to fight off the compulsion to gasp.

Swim to the rays of light. Swim!

At the edges of survival, with her final seconds and courage spent, she burst past the press of fish into a cavernous space. Sea mist and shafts of sunlight licked her floating form. She took a desperate gasp, floated, eyes closed, sucking in precious air, while waiting for the pain in her chest to dissolve.

Where was she?

At that moment, she cared not. She had followed her heart, journeyed to where she must and survived. The lapping sound of water on rock and the healing warmth of sun on her cheeks teased the trauma from her body and soothed her soul.

Feeling calmer, she squinted through golden tinged sea mist and dazzling columns of light and past sheer cliffs to a patch of blue sky way above. Here was a sacred place, blessed, timeless.

Something started to push with urgency against her bare legs, the water churning in a frenzy of tails and gills. She flipped over and touched the seabed with her tip-toes. *Something's changed.*

The golden amorphous sea mist cleared a little to reveal she was standing in a cavern, surrounded by rock-ledges. The walls ahead were covered with algae-covered broken tiles. She moved forward, feeling the incline of the seabed, until she found a resting place next to a ledge. From here she could sit in knee-high warm water and see sections of intricate mosaic tiles. There was a leopard's eye and another, of loin-clothed warriors holding high their bows and arrows.

'*You have come – so brave to enter from the sea.*'

The startling crystal-clear words seemed to erupt from within her chest. Startled, Zana clasped hold of the rock ledge.

'Who's there?' She squinted through the golden sea mist. There was nothing, no-one. Only the sound of water sloshing on rock reached her ears.

She waited, straining to hear footsteps. Was it a trick? Was the calm of this cavern protected by some unknown force?

A prism of light beamed through the haze, warming her forehead with gentle radiant heat. She closed her eyes and averted her head from the glare, but even then somehow she could see a distant yellow light, a flickering candle. She breathed in the peace of the ages and felt her heart pound with faith and love, while focusing on the light. Warmth from the glow infused her veins, radiance filled her being, white light seeped from her tingling skull and merged with the sacredness of the cavern.

She felt the beauty of this place, a pureness so profound. Her heart and mind burst wide open. This was truth. This was Heaven. Visions erupted in a cataclysmic flash of bright light, leaving her gasping and wondrous. She'd become at once bliss and the colour blue of the sea. She could feel her eagle-eye scanning the earth from up high and yet, at the same time, she could feel her dolphin tail propel her high above the water. She was the roots of trees entwined into the earth and a lofty canopy for birds to nest.

The voice full of compassion once again flooded her being. '*You cannot see me, dear one, for I am now inside you, breathing as you breathe.*'

'Who are you?'

'*I am you and you are me. We are Goddess Artemis – you will see.*'

'I feel like …' Zana pulled herself up on to the rock-ledge, placed her hand on her heart in wonder, 'It's like I'm full of sunshine and rainbows but … it's like I've breathed in the earth and the sky … I can't explain it.'

What was real? She was forever changed, infused with a universal truth she did not understand.

'The strength and love you feel for the earth and all its creatures will forever flow in your veins and the veins of your children and your children's children. You will carry my essence through the ages and protect the earth and all its creatures through the ages. Go forth my little goddess, my brave one.'

Zana clambered barefoot over rubble and broken tiles, stopping for a moment to pick up a turquoise stone next to a shattered clay pot. She took one last look around the tiled walls of the cavern, marveled in the direction of her perilous entry, before ascending steep stairs inset within the cliff-walls. Up and up she climbed, making sure to lean in towards the rock, lest she'd topple over the side to her death.

She crawled through a space between boulders, emerging into the light atop a barren, windswept hill. There was her uncle's fishing vessel, anchored just off what she knew to be the channel of a thousand fish.

Zana was now part goddess-eternal, her grace's essence captured in a mortal yet courageous body. With the rapture of peace coursing through her veins, she saw her surroundings with new eyes. The Aegean had taken on an indescribable sapphire blue, melding on the horizon into a lavender sky. Even the barren earth at her feet pulsed with life.

With her eyes reflecting nature's beauty, she knew she had found her calling – to nurture all corners of the pulsing earth, the wild verdant places, wondrous beings, thriving sea. Let no man harm the vibrant beauty that lay before her. Her muscles tensed, veins flushed with adrenalin, heart pulsed with the love of a warrior mother.

* * *

From that day on, she took her place next to a white-washed wall of a windmill. With the sparkling Aegean reflecting the passion in her eyes, she pointed to the infinite blue. 'You see the crystal-clear water here?' Her muscular arm motioned towards the sea. 'You must protect it. Only use a simple line. Take only the fish you need.'

She spoke of the medicinal properties of plants, the shade-giving trees, the thriving earth and wondrous beings, the spirits that lay nestled beneath mountains, forever enticing the rain to fill life-giving streams.

From that day on, the legend of Zana has been handed down from generation to generation. Little fingers smudged the glass-frame containing the family tree, depicted on yellowed parchment-like paper. There was proof alright, that a Zana Kakoulis had lived and breathed, born in 1756 and died in 1804. She had borne a daughter, Katania in 1784. Who the father was? No-one knew. Was the legend true? No-one knew.

The only other proof that she had existed at all was stored in an historic dust-covered tome within the Chora library. The near illegible scrawl proclaimed that a Z. Kakoulis had owned a small, yet prestigious stone villa overlooking the harbour of Alefkandra. Perhaps this was the only clue to her standing in the community. A prime site, with uninterrupted views of the azure Aegean, complete with a tiny paved courtyard adorned with purple bougainvillea.

These days tourists just weaved their way past, climbing higher, making their way to the sun-bleached walls of the nearby windmill. Perhaps they just presumed the crumbling old villa once belonged to the house of a rich merchant or a seafarer of old. The question remains – did the legendary Gorgóna, 'mermaid of Mykonos' really live there or was truth as hard to grasp as the stars?

CHAPTER 1

Snowy Mountain Bound

Piraeus Port, Greece, 1961

Melia placed her hand on her belly and felt the shape of a tiny foot. 'Stop kicking me, little one. I know. I don't want to leave either.'

Once again she saw in her mind the tiny paved courtyard, the pond adorned with purple bougainvillea and the view of the Aegean beyond. The foot kicked again, as though furious at being forced to leave the homeland of their famous ancestor, the legendary Gorgóna, 'mermaid of Mykonos'.

'Don't worry, my precious one, I won't let you forget where you came from.'

She wiped an angry tear from her cheek, clasped hold of the suitcase and pushed her way through the crowd lining the port.

'It's the land of peace and prosperity.' The voice of her olive-skinned beloved beckoned from a million miles away across the ocean.

'Please, I need to get through!' The sea of hats parted as if on cue, revealing the crowded decks of the *Stratheden* just ahead. Already it looked heavy in the water, sagging with British migrants, rust marks at the waterline. And this was to take her across the vast Indian Ocean?

Invisible fingers brushed her cheek. *'We'll be together soon.'* The memory of his caress made her stride with more purpose towards the edge of the wharf.

Her feet looked alien on the ramp, her tears tasted bitter, yet still she began the ascent. There was no arguing with destiny. One step, two steps, her heart squeezed with effort. There was no blood pumping, just picture albums in her mind filled with cobbled streets, whitewashed walls and windmills. She turned and looked one last time across the chaos and farewelled her homeland.

What would life be like, living in the Snowy Mountains of Australia? As if to make sense of it all, she whispered 'Your Papa is building a dam so you, my little one, will be born in a mysterious land.'

After finding her cabin in the place of the damned below deck, she curled up on her bunk and sobbed. She held the heirloom turquoise stone so tight, that its engraved markings penetrated her skin.

Days and nights merged. Dark ocean troughs taunted her body in a monotonous, bile-filled, sideways dance. Creak, lurch, roll, rise, fall. She had nothing left to vomit yet still her stomach squeezed its wretchedness. She willed herself to think of the promise of land and slumped into a fitful sleep, drifting on dreams of leopards with hungry yellow-slitted eyes and loin-clothed warriors.

Finally, the blare of the ship's horn forced her to join the throng of passengers in the corridor. A force-field of heat had already seeped below deck. Air, she needed air. She ascended the stairs and just like all the other ladies, placed her handkerchief up against her nose. The heat pushed down on her head, the stench accosted her nostrils. She pushed her way forward to the railing, eager to find some air and stared down at the port teaming with people, rickshaws, taxis and wandering cows. She swayed a little. *Was it wise to disembark?*

'Now, ladies, stay close to me, eh.' The craggy old farmer in the big hat beckoned for the women folk to band around him.

Melia struggled down the ramp in the searing heat, hoping the sickness in her swaying body and belly would soon subside after setting foot on solid land. They walked in a regimented group; handkerchiefs held to noses to fend off the assault of Bombay's spices and sweat. The haphazard market stalls and walls of humanity soon closed in around them. *Is there no air in this place?* She sidestepped iridescent saris and vivid sacks of spices and backed away from toothless stall-holders. The crowd pressed, the smells and heat crashing down upon her as the path between the stalls became narrower and narrower.

A bejewelled hand clasped her wrist, a voice beckoned 'come look.' She lurched to her left and glanced at the array of turquoise and silver displayed before her, leaning against the stone side of the stall for support.

A change of mood rippled its way over the crowd. The sea of faces parted to reveal a loin-clothed *sādhu*. His presence rippled through the press of bodies and lapped at her feet. How could someone so old move with such grace? He seemed to glide forward, propelled by an unseen energy. She looked again at his naked dust-covered torso and the painted markings on his face and found herself trapped in the pure whiteness of his eyes. She felt a force connect her, reel her in. She tried to drag her eyes away, to look again at his long braids brushing the dust, but she was entranced, under his spell.

Alien words washed over her head like tumbled stones as she half slid, half melted into the stone wall at her back. All the while she remained transfixed on the whites of those eyes. The crowd pushed back even more to make way for the holiest of holy, those at the front swaying and crumpling to the earth. Her heart hammered. She felt cornered, out of her depth, as he came closer. Where were the farmer and the women off the ship? Why had they left her so?

Yet even as she thought to scramble away, a feeling of bliss rippled through her body and tears fell upon her hot cheeks. Why had she thought to run a second ago when his luminous eyes were upon her? When he exuded such pure love?

Ancient words continued to caress her soul. She was lost in the magnetic pull of his eyes, caught in his field of vibration. Was she even breathing now that his long fingers were spread across her swollen belly?

Soft, sacred words hung in the air and dissolved. The heat of the day smashed into her forehead and the warmth from his palms swelled within her. She was bound by a euphoric glow; a bliss so immense that it threatened to blow her mind wide open.

'Miss, Miss ...' The stallholder's words penetrated her thoughts. 'He's saying your child, she is special. She will in turn give birth to a modern-day *sādhu* who will be able to feel nature as it truly is. Your grand-daughter of the future is waiting to arrive in the era of most need but ...'

The hennaed hand gripped, the crowd murmured. Melia glanced at the woman's sari-draped face, unsure why she had stopped translating.

The stallholder's brown eyes flickered with empathy. 'She will be faced with a true, formidable enemy and ...' She placed her bejewelled hand on Melia's heart. 'And you will be unable to protect her. Your child,' she looked to Melia's belly, 'will be unable to protect your future grand-child. She will have friends, but far away, as far as the stars. It will take all of her courage, she will need to overcome her mortal emotions and fight.'

It felt like barbed wire was twisting around her heart, the air too thick to breathe. She felt the large hands slip from her stomach, saw a flash of bright scarlet, a ringed toe, and then blackness.

When Melia opened her eyes, there was the bunk above her head, her suitcase by her side. She lay there, struggling to think beyond the sharp kick inside her belly. Just like the leopard eyes and the loin-clothed warriors, it had all been a dream. Sick and exhausted, that's what she was. The brain was curious, conjuring up a fantasy like that. All she needed was rest and to keep blessed land beneath her feet.

She heaved herself up and out of her bunk, checking her image in the mirror. Lank black hair, flushed skin, dull eyes. She yanked at her sweat-stained dress to put on something clean and gasped in shock at the imprints seared into her skin, each finger a fateful branding of her belly.

CHAPTER 2

Alone

Foothills of Majestic Sleeping Beauty, Tasmania, December 1992

'You can't take me! I'm not going!' Delia ripped her hand from the giant's clutches and fled down the corridor. Instinct told her to run, run like the wind into the long golden grasses of the top paddock but her little bare feet sped towards her Mummy's bed instead. She dived under the doona, pulled the lavender-scented cocoon around her and heaved a deep, ragged sob.

Her fingers found the protective obsidian stone lying beneath the pillow. 'Mummy needed you today,' she whispered. Maybe it was all a nightmare. That thought made her squeeze her eyes shut. She'd just block it all out so those men in blue would just go away.

Heavy boots shuffled on the floorboards beyond the bed. Hushed words dipped in poison seeped through the doona. 'We'll have to take her with us – poor kid. Grandmother just died too.'

'No-one's ever gunna want her', whispered another male voice. 'Not when they see,' the voice trailed off.

'Oh for God's sake Gavin – get out the way!' huffed a female voice.

Delia felt the roof of her protective cave lift a little. 'Hi sweetheart, look, this will make you feel better,' the woman's voice cooed. 'You'll feel closer to your Mummy if you put this on.'

Delia watched the turquoise stone swing on a golden chain, back and forth, back and forth.

'That's it, sit up for me sweetheart so I can put it around your neck.'

Faces leaned forward in Delia's peripheral vision. 'See what I mean', said a grave male voice.

Storm clouds crossed the woman's kind brown eyes. 'Can you lot go and pack Delia's clothes please.'

'Now, Delia, can you promise me something. It's very, very important.'

Delia held on tight to the stone at her chest and tried hard to stop the quiver in her bottom lip.

'Promise me that you will always remember that your mummy and daddy loved you and that you are beautiful. Don't ever, ever forget. Don't ever let anyone tell you different. Ok?'

Delia nodded but the pain in her heart meant it was pointless to pinky promise.

CHAPTER 3

Treasures of Sleeping Beauty

Hobart, Tasmania, April 2009

A surge of anticipation ripped through Delia's veins. She stood on tip toe and craned her neck to peer over the counter. *There he was!* She caught sight of the Frenchman's salt-and-pepper hair and straight-backed form just before he turned into the fromagerie. Somehow her hands continued to wrap ham while she thought of last week's strange encounter.

'Ah Miss Drakos. The great artist – we meet at last,' he'd said.

Caught in the spotlight of his piercing aqua eyes, tumbling back in time to the ruins of her past, she'd just stood there blinking like a deer in a spotlight.

'Your landscape – it was – magnifique!'

Why had she refused his offer of a drink? *Because it's best to stay in the shadows, that's why.*

'We shall see, *ma chérie*.' Those words had clanged inside her head like a mantra ever since.

Back to reality, she shoved a distorted package of ham towards a customer and edged around the side of the counter.

'Delia! Where a-you-a going?' Tony's heavy Italian accented words lassoed around her like a snare, grounding her to the spot. She tucked a long tress of hair, the colour of juicy watermelon, behind her ear and looked back to see his jowls jiggling with annoyance. 'Um ... I just need to speak to a gentleman in the fromagerie for a second.'

'Chitty-chat later; this lovely lady here, he gestured to a woman in a fur-lined puffer jacket, 'needs you now.'

Delia fluttered a well-practiced hand up to her scarf and retraced her steps, while polished fingernails tapped a morse-code of impatience on the counter. *God-damn it!* He was so close, yet here she was, lugging a ham haunch instead of finding out the answers to her hundred questions.

'Excuse me!' Delia snapped to attention and handed Ms Impatient her items.

'Delia! Come over here.' Tony's hands swished through the air like swollen samarai swords. 'We need to have-a chat. Why don't you pay attention – huh? There is too much competition. We must be known – no, renowned – for our customer service.'

'Yes Tony,' she muttered, while eyeing the exit.

'And would it hurt to not be so – so – in your face?' he grimaced at her hair. 'Look at Sandi and learn, eh! Always she dress nice, always a smile.'

Delia's eyelid twitched. *Yes, yes – the flirt with the big bazookas.*

Smash! The sound of glass on concrete amidst a woman's scream pushed Delia into a run.

Thankful for the diversion, she snatched at a dustpan and brush and pushed her way through the throng of shoppers towards the sound of calamity.

'*Stupido*! Look at them – my prize Venetian trousers!'

Delia rounded the olive oil aisle and skidded to a halt just beyond a pasta-sauce catastrophe. 'You must be more careful, *ma chérie.*'

She gasped and swept her eyes over his perfect posture and black cashmere jacket, and the way he managed to exude an aura of regal detachment. She noticed a twinge of movement at the corner of his mouth, just above grey, virulent whiskers while a coiffured woman flicked globules of thick red sauce from her fawn-coloured suede trousers. 'Ruined, just ruined!' she muttered.

'Um – let me help you.' The woman shoved Delia's arm out of the way and yelled '*stupido*!' With that, she wheeled around and crunched her way through the crowd, leaving imprints of sauce in her wake.

'Au revoir!' he called, loud enough for everyone to hear, before turning his full attention back to Delia.

'So, *ma chérie*, I meet the famous 'D. Drakos' yet again'.

She lost herself for a moment in his eyes, the colour of a coral atoll, before bending down to brush shards of glass into the pan.

He crouched down beside her, while still managing to maintain his military precision, rigid form.

'It's nice to meet you again, Miss Drakos.'

His words were softer than she expected, intriguing coming from a man who looked like he could command an army. The incongruence made her look up for a moment but, feeling herself blush, jerked her head down again. Even in that instant, his eyes seemed to bore their way into the crevasses of her soul.

'Delia – my name's Delia. Yes, we meet again.' She addressed the floor and willed her shaking hands to work.

'Well, let me tell you Delia, you are worth more than this.' He motioned to the sauce lapping at his polished black shoes.

She frowned and flicked him a frustrated look.

'I can still remember the moment I saw *Treasures of Sleeping Beauty*. The way you captured flowing water and dark mystery beneath the ferns; I see it even now.'

In an instant his words transported her back through time. She could see her child-like hand applying the final touches to what would be her last painting. She blinked back tears and said 'how do you know about my early work?' Her voice sounded shrill, odd. She cursed herself for not being able to look him in the eye.

'Ah, *Treasures* was hanging in the Long Gallery. It would have been ... mmm, let me see, 1992. I had just returned from France. I needed something bold, something that conveyed ... shall we say mystery, but also truth.'

'I was about to purchase another painting, but when I saw your work, you could say I had an out-of-body experience. You had captured every element – *c'était la perfection*! An interplay of beauty, darkness and mood. Your painting was, luminous. Non – more than that, it was near breathing.

I felt pulled towards it, connected. I dearly wanted it but,' he sighed 'it was not to be. I have yearned for that painting ever since.'

Delia's hand dropped the steel dustpan to the floor. It clattered, jarring the moment of connection.

'My name,' he said, standing up 'is Ronan St James, by the way.'

She felt his hand under her arm, guiding her upright. 'Now *ma chérie*, I ask again, would you do me the honour of accompanying me for a drink?'

'But … I'm working.' The words tumbled out, awkward and cold.

'Ah, I can see I have taken you by surprise yet again. We shall see then. Just remember,' he motioned to the sauce splattered floor 'you are worth more than this.'

Delia felt her throat constrict. By the time her hands patted down her scarf, he'd melded back into the crowd.

She jostled her way back to the small-goods counter aware that her carotid artery was pulsing out of control. The hairs on the back of her neck prickled a warning that Tony had her under surveillance once again.

She started serving a man with overgrown eyebrows when the sound of a French-accented voice made her hand stop. The spoon quivered, olives teetered.

'Back again, sir? How can I help you?' Sandi cooed.

'Merci but *non*, I am just waiting for Miss Drakos here to end her shift.'

The spoon she was holding clattered to the concrete floor. Luscious black olives rolled under the cabinet to meet their dusty fate, forcing Tony to desert his covert post.

'Is there a problem?'

'Ah, you are the owner of this fine *épicerie*? Just the man I need to see.'

Delia watched Tony's eyes bulge. Here was a man who reeked of power and prestige. Other customers, sensing a disturbance, gave the man in the long black cashmere jacket a wide berth.

'You run a fine operation here. He swept his arms across the counter. Your girls are why I come here instead of the shop up the road. Now, Delia has a prior engagement with me, so perhaps efficient Sandi can assist with this patient gentleman's olives?'

'But, her shift...?' Delia cringed as she felt Tony's possessive hand clamp down on her shoulder.

'Ah, but Sandi here has it all covered, haven't you, Sandi?'

'Of course,' she said, her words sounding flat.

Delia felt Tony's hesitation and edged out from beneath his hand. Backing away, she noticed his confused expression, weighing up the pros and cons of keeping this imperious man happy.

Delia took advantage of the moment, peeled away her apron and trance-like, felt herself guided out to the carpark towards a ruby-red convertible.

'So, Delia. Never have I met an artist so talented. I want to know everything about your latest works.'

She gulped, aware that fate was swirling around her, as real as the cold air smacking at her face. Did she want this man to drive her towards the truth of her empty life? Panic bubbled in her throat while her long pink tresses frothed in the breeze like flotsam on the tide.

How was she going to converse with a man like him? She felt her cheeks flush at her imposter status. Soon her swan-dive from the great height of his star-studded pedestal would be complete.

Just go along for the ride' whispered her dark side.

CHAPTER 4

The Promise of Beautiful Tomorrows

Delia's world condensed to the smell of cedar and orange at his neck and the sight of his red tie grazing her jeans. She pushed herself deeper into the black leather seat while he reached across to pull an exquisite pashmina from the console.

'This is for you, *ma chérie*'. 'For me?' she exclaimed. The shroud of wool around her shoulders felt soft, warm and luxurious to her touch. 'It's beautiful. Um – so, Mr St James, where are we going?'

'Ronan – call me Ronan. Ah, but it is a surprise!'

He settled behind the wheel, pulled a woollen hat over his greying temples and pushed his hands into black leather gloves. 'Get ready for a thrilling ride!'

Her heart was beating way too fast. The sports car revved and edged towards the exit. 'Isn't it too cold to have the roof down?'

'I refuse to bend to the will of a grey day! Not when I finally have you, the great artist, at my side'! he yelled back.

The vehicle roared to life. She pressed the pashmina to her frozen cheekbones and thought of her lack-lustre life, back there in the Maserati's wake.

The riverside flashed by and a woman's startled face made her laugh out loud. Adrenaline ripped through her veins while all the suppressed parts of herself whooped and cheered for more. She tried to memorise every moment; the bare upper branches of a walnut tree, the brilliant crimson of rambling vines and mountains of leaves piled high in the gutter.

They passed historic weatherboard cottages wedged between modern architectural masterpieces on the edge of the café district before veering towards the gated sanctuaries of Larke Avenue. Within seconds the car slowed, crawling past mansions with impenetrable hedges, before coming to a stop outside a wrought-iron gate. At the press of a remote, the gate clanged into life.

'This is where we're going?' She cast a quizzical glance in Ronan's direction and saw a flicker of amusement beneath his focused façade.

'*Oui* – I wanted to treat you like the star you were born to be', he grinned. 'You will always be most welcome to my sanctuary Delia.'

He edged the Maserati through the gate, past a green and gold mottled plane tree standing in the centre of an emerald, leaf-littered lawn. A row of standard white roses nodded their greeting before they came to a stand-still.

'This is your home?' Delia swept her eyes up the sandstone steps to a portico and the most colossal timber door she'd ever seen.

'*Oui* – it's my haven from the mad world. Now, my Delia, you are freezing. You will soon warm up inside.'

Her thoughts fired like a scatter-gun. Unable to think straight, she pulled the protective pashmina close and succumbed to the feel of his guiding hand in the small of her back.

'But it's as big as a castle? You must have a big family?' She gazed up at the masterpiece door before it swung open on its central axis.

'No – it's just me.' Four words, so matter-of-fact, yet somehow his tone only made her heart race even more.

She stepped into an austere black marble foyer. The castle door swooshed close behind them. 'Oh wow – such an amazing space – your eyes go straight to the water.' She motioned to the plate glass and the river beyond, aware that her voice sounded unnatural, breathless.

'You are shivering *ma chérie*. Here, come and warm yourself next to the fire,' he called over his shoulder.

She followed his imperious straight-backed form through the foyer, stepped down on to a vast polished concreted space and gravitated towards orange flames behind glass.

'Just relax, while I make us a special drink.' He draped his jacket and gloves on the side of the single leather sofa furnishing the room, and moved out of sight, somewhere to her right.

Delia watched the flames lick the glass and waited until the warmth had penetrated her frozen limbs. Only then did she peel away the pashmina and turn to survey the room. What a clever illusion. From where she stood, the smoke-coloured polished concrete floor took on a liquefied quality so that it merged with the dark water flowing beyond the plate glass window.

Something large and red on the far wall to her left caught her eye. She walked closer to the vast, vertically hung triptych then stepped back in shock. The top two sections focused solely upon a suspended sliced heart, while globules of blood dripped down to the third section. She turned her back on the disturbing image and walked to the plate glass, feeling squeamish.

From her position at the glass, she could see that the property was surrounded by high convict brick boundary walls. The lower wall opposite the shore was topped with wrought-iron spears, presumably to ward off intruders entering from the river. To the far right, beyond the rusted roof of a boatshed, a rickety silver-wooden pier stood resolute against the elements, despite its dilapidation. All the while, the moody troughs of the Derwent bled greens and ink beneath leaden clouds.

His smooth voice called from a hidden room to her right which she presumed to be the kitchen. 'It's an incredible view isn't it', he called. 'I never tire of it – an artist's paradise.'

Her jangled nerves were soothed a little by the scene. 'Yes, I was just thinking the same thing.' A sudden wave of emotion, so peculiar, so familiar, washed through her body. She tried to discern the sensation, feeling the petals of her heart unfurl at the sight beyond the glass. She watched a cloud's effect on the water below, casting the river in charcoal and emerald hues in the changing light.

Emerald – the colour of her mother's eyes. For a second she heard her mother's voice cooing: '*You are my very own little goddess, Delia.*'

Seabird's floating past the glass morphed into a flock of white cockatoos. Delia closed her eyes to re-imagine making clumsy daisy chains in the bottom paddock, while way in the distance, her old friend Sleeping Beauty mountain reclined amidst blue hills. How she'd loved the defiant mountainous 'chin' aimed towards the heavens.

The sound of approaching footsteps and ice clinking against glass brought her back to reality. The edginess that had incapacitated her on arrival started to creep back. It was a curious thing, the way he walked so straight-backed and rigid. She could almost hear someone in his childhood yelling, 'Press your shoulders back, expand your chest!'

'Come sit on the couch, *ma chérie*', he cooed.

She focused on the glasses in his hands, the amber liquid, ice-cubes with sprigs of mint, and wondered what she would soon be drinking. As if reading her mind, he said, 'a surprise – let me see if you can discern the flavour.'

She settled on the edge of the sofa once again smelling wood and citrus as he leaned forward. Her hand accepted the glass. A silence enveloped them. She knew he was assessing her; she could feel his aqua eyes drilling, searching for something. She took a tentative sip, then another.

'Um, like a pinot. But, there's an orange after-taste. Mmm, yes it's nice.'

'It's a French aperitif called Dubonnet – an old recipe combining grenache, orange rind and spices. It's the English Queen's favourite, so a perfect drink for a star.'

Only the sound of ice against glass and a seabird screeching in the distance filled the void.

Ronan smiled and motioned towards the river. 'This is my favourite spot, right here. I can sit for hours, just watching the flow of the river, the changing light. You know, just two nights ago, the moon rose like a golden orb over those hills and cast a silver shadow across the water, straight towards me. It was extraordinary. I wish I could paint, Delia, but' he threw up his hands in despair, 'I cannot.'

Sitting ram-rod straight, it seemed to Delia that he never relaxed for a single moment. Still, she imagined women would find him alluring.

A thought sizzled at the corner of her mind. *Does he desire me?* She looked down at her pink Target jumper, hanging forlorn over her scrawny frame. *Surely not.* She'd keep an eye on his hands just the same though. Like him, she couldn't let herself relax until she knew what he really wanted.

He snapped himself out of his distant longings. 'So, Delia, it is frustrating. I have so much in here,' he placed a hand on his heart, 'but I am incapable of expressing what I feel. I must therefore turn to artists, like you, who can convey my thoughts on-to canvas. For example, what do you think of the triptych? 'Interesting, *non?*'

He thankfully gave her no time to respond. 'You know, of course, of my need to purchase a fine piece back in 1992. It should have been your masterpiece hanging there, but no, *Ache* has graced the walls ever since.'

'Um, well, it's quite different to my work ...' She averted her eyes from the image, aware, too late, of what her face conveyed.

'I see that you do not like it, but it speaks to me on many levels. Let us take ambience – the burgundy and black congealed forms, they offset the polished concrete, and the vertical placement is perfect for the space. It is bold, original, uncompromising. Ha!'

Delia's body jerked at his short, sudden outburst.

'It is a little amusing, like me, *oui?* But,' he pushed a hand through his salt-and-pepper hair, 'what I most respond to, is its truth.' She felt his piercing aqua eyes on her as she looked again at the paintings. 'Truth can tear at tender hearts. It is a constant reminder to walk my truth, follow my path.'

'Does that mean the 'tender ones' get left behind?' The words were out of her mouth before she could assess them.

'Ah, I am very happy with your response, Delia. It shows you have not only talent but potential for deep analysis on the subject of art. I look forward to having many conversations with you about art. In the meantime, though ...' He cast an arm around the room. 'Let me put it to you this way: do I look like I've been left behind? I have followed my own path and, I have to say, I have excelled in that.'

Delia's own tender heart squeezed tight. She felt herself squirm as his conversation swiveled to focus on her artwork, or as she well knew, lack of it.

'So my Delia, how lucky I am to have found you. You were a child prodigy, *oui*? How young to have painted such a masterpiece as *Treasures of Sleeping Beauty*. Your talent was exceptional. So, you must have perfected your skills even more now.'

Delia sipped her drink, unable to think straight over the deafening silence. She took another sip before replying 'That was my last painting.' She dared not look up.

'*C'est une tragedie, ma chérie.*' His quiet words seemed tinged with genuine sadness, yet still she could not lift her head to look him in the eye.

'Well, that perhaps brings me to why I brought you here. I have a business proposition for you.' He leaned in and clinked his glass against hers.

Delia jerked her head up and was lost for a moment in his startling eyes until the intensity of his stare made her look away. There was something; beyond boldness within them, and she tried to figure it out as she studied her drink. Then it dawned on her; 'desire'. The thought of it was so bizarre, so far beyond the sphere of her existence, that she immediately downed a swig of the amber liquid. *But he could have anyone!* Her face flushed hot.

'I have made you uncomfortable, Delia, but – hear me out. First, do you know who I am? You've seen me in the papers, pictured at the highest levels of society and influence, *non*?'

'Um, no – I mean, I should know obviously'.

'Here, this is my business card'. He rifled in his suit pocket and pushed a black card with embossed gold letters into her hand. Delia ran her fingertips over the beautiful lettering that revealed that Ronan was the 'CEO / Chief Projectionist' of *Future Projections*.

'Projectionist? I'm sorry, I don't understand.' She frowned 'something to do with the film industry?' *What were they filming?* She placed her drink on the floor ready to make a hasty exit.

'No, though it is a common misconception. My neighbour still thinks

I entertain movie stars; that I somehow smuggle them in at night. Ha! No, my job is far more important. I nurture people. People who have talent. And I project those people – people like you, Delia – to realise their full potential. They are, therefore, projected to a brighter, happier future.'

Delia frowned and tilted her head, unable to grasp how he or anyone or anything could 'project' her towards a happier life.

'You see', he continued 'I realised long ago that for people to believe in themselves, well, it is just so much easier if someone like me believes in them first. I can spot potential – I have a gift for recognising talent. Now, in your case, you are different. Of course, you know this, your work is extraordinary. This is why I would like you to live here, so I can make sure that your dreams are realised.

'But ... you can't be serious!' She launched herself off the couch and found herself backed-up against the glass. 'Me, live here?' her high-pitched, startled voice echoed off the concrete. Boggle-eyed and with her heart hammering like a bird in a box, she snatched at the mint laden drink and guzzled the last of it.

'I'm serious Delia. A better life is all about opportunity. And believe me, I can show you a much better life starting right here, right now, if you want.'

'But – you don't know me. I mean ...' His offer hung in the air like a teetering chandelier.

'I may have startled you Delia but, it is a great opportunity – *n'est-ce pas?*' Not waiting for her to respond, he added 'You are a star, Delia ... you just need to be allowed to shine. Living here, would give you time to focus on your passion under my patronage. We then exhibit your artwork and I take a modest commission. *C'est simple.*'

The taiko drumbeat of her heart pounded out a retreat. Without realising, she had edged around the sofa towards the foyer. She stopped herself for a moment and cast a wistful gaze over the river before turning back to Ronan.

'Thank you, Ronan, truly ...' Her words had lost any shrillness and were now filled with regret. 'It is an amazing offer but I would just be a disappointment.' She started to turn but already he was calling to her.

'Delia, come sit with me. Please, hear me out. It will only take a moment.' He patted the leather next to him.

Feeling obliged she heard her boots stomp their way back across the concrete. She sat down next to him, feeling all of a jitter.

'You want to live the good life, *non?* It is beautiful here, a paradise. It would be easy. I go to work, you paint. You would love it. Why protest?'

Oh God – don't do that! She watched him lift her limp hand and graze his lips upon her skin. French words washed over her ears like some sort of exotic spell. She was caught somewhere between panic and compulsion to just give in.

'Um ... I can't seem to think straight.' She pulled her hand away before continuing. 'I would need to, you know, assess ... things, like my job ...' she trailed off.

'Ah, yes, your 'job' ...' he said, reaching out to hold her hand once again.

She saw the disappointment in his face and gazed at her hand in his. The strangeness of it jolted her mind back to long ago, to a time when her parents filled her heart with love. Was this the place where she could emerge from her personal desert to once again find peace and happiness?

She dragged her eyes away from her tiny hand enveloped in his and looked around. *Could she live here?*

She tried to picture herself walking through the room like it was second nature, standing at the plate glass looking at the view. There she was, standing behind an easel, brush in hand, trying to keep pace with the ever-changing scene before her. A little thrill crept into her heart, as she contemplated it.

She could walk the little rocky beach below the house and be lulled to sleep by waves on the shore. Winter was coming and she could be here, luxuriating in this warm, dry, beautiful home instead of breathing in spores from her mould-ridden ceiling.

Delia edged her hand away from his grasp again and twisted a pink lock around her forefinger. He waited patiently, assessing every nuance of her response.

'Ronan, this is the most incredible, kind offer … an astounding opportunity.' She willed herself to keep eye contact and knew that her cheeks had flushed red again. She twisted her hair with greater urgency and found herself blurting, 'but I can't afford an easel or supplies, plus there's my lease and I still need my job …' Her words sounded flat, like they had been launched off the top of a skyscraper and fallen to their death on the polished concrete at their feet.

With a resigned sigh, he said, 'I understand, Delia. It is a big decision. Why, you hardly know me. How about you think about my business proposal then … get out of your lease. And why work when you can paint? It would be my pleasure – that is what a patron does – to support their protégé. You will want for nothing – that is my promise. What I am offering is a once in a lifetime opportunity.' He motioned at the view beyond the plate glass, one last time, before standing and reaching for his black cashmere jacket.

Delia looked out to the river, where sea-mist merged with low-lying cloud, and felt the suck of the tide. She could just keep drifting and float on the current of her lack-lustre life out to sea, or she could take a risk.

Already he was at the colossal door, standing rigid, while pulling on his leather gloves. There was an air of impatience about him now, so she dragged her eyes away from the river and made her way after him.

The sudden appearance of his black gloved hand around her wrist made her gasp. She looked up in surprise.

'You need not worry about your art supplies, by the way Delia. The cost – it is insignificant.'

She stared, mesmerized for a moment by his complete and utter faith in her, before stepping down to the gleaming Maserati. The colossal door thudded to a shut behind her.

Hand on the door handle, she stopped to contemplate if that thud was the sound of being locked out from a life full of beauty? Could she live here? She watched him descend the stairs, looking like a European prince next to his castle.

She tried to ignore the sudden buzz of excitement that spiked in her heart. Was she even capable of reawakening the child artist within?

'So, what ... I mean just to be clear ... I'd get my own room, I wouldn't have to work and you'd buy all my art supplies. All I have to do is paint, and you will be my patron ... is that it?' Delia touched her face, aware that her cheeks were flaming as bright as her hair.

'Exactly. *C'est simple*!' He threw his gloved hands in the air and grinned. 'It will be an honour to be your patron. You will be my star, my Delia. Now, that's settled then.'

CHAPTER 5

On a Wing and a Prayer

Delia slammed the front door behind her, forever smothering the old-fashioned wallpaper, pock-marked by rising damp. The sudden bang caused a currawong to screech. It stretched its glossy black wings wide as it flew towards the Rivulet. Somehow the bird's effortless flight mirrored her own feelings, uplifted and free. Never again would she have to face the mould and the cold.

She swung the satchel of old canvases across her body and stooped to clutch the handle of her battered brown suitcase and a rubbish bag full of clothes as she headed towards the waiting taxi. The great mauve mountain, etched against a darkening sky, bore witness to this major transition in her life.

She forced a smile at the olive-skinned taxi driver. 'Larke Avenue, miss?' he said, eyebrow raised.

'That's right.' The defensiveness in her voice left no room for questions.

He glanced from her flowing pink hair down to her meagre possessions, before pulling the boot closed.

The taxi slid past people scurrying home before dark. She could see herself amongst them, hunched and cold, but now they were like actors in another play. She was going to leave her dark chrysalis and emerge into the light, to live the life of a true artist.

The taxi weaved through the tight streets and turned into Larke Avenue. Her stomach did a little leap as poplar-lined driveways and tall clipped hedges slipped by.

'This is it!' They slowed and came to a halt. She spied the Maserati through the tall wrought-iron gates and smiled.

The driver flicked an incredulous look in her direction as she piled her belongings onto the pavement and bid him farewell.

She stabbed at the intercom button beside the closed gates and tried to push her nervousness aside, taking in the bright crimson Japanese maple on the nature-strip opposite. A golden Buddha sat serenely beneath it, atop a sandstone letterbox.

The next house up was fronted by an ostentatious circular fountain with a metal swan sculpture. The rest of the streetscape had a refined dignity, yet this fountain was jarring. *Just like you?* It was the barest of dark whispers, but once the thought had erupted, the words grew wings, circling like an angry bee. She looked down at her scuffed brown case and pressed the intercom button again.

A blackbird heralded it was time to return to the nest. She pressed the button hard this time.

'*Oui?*'

She jumped, wondering at the question in his voice. 'Ronan – it's me, Delia.' She tried to sound casual but her breathlessness made her sound like an anxious schoolgirl.

'Delia, *bonsoir!* Just come down the driveway and I'll meet you at the door.'

The gate sprung to life, allowing her to set foot on the driveway. Beyond the sound of her old case being wheeled along, she heard the wrought-iron gate clang shut behind her. Excited now, she increased her pace towards the regal, straight-backed man standing in the light of the foyer in the distance.

She passed by the nodding roses and the Maserati parked at the bottom of the steps and looked up to where he was standing in the doorway. Strange how he looked taller, more imposing than she had remembered. She took a deep breath and called 'So good to see you, Ronan. Thank you again ...'

'My Delia – welcome home! Come in, come in, out of the cold.'

The case bashed its way up the steps, a loud decree that she had arrived at the threshold of her new life. He stepped aside, allowing her to cross into the black marble foyer feeling like a mountaineer who had just arrived at a long-awaited summit.

'Welcome to my humble abode.' He closed the gigantic door, while chuckling at his own joke. 'Now let me show you to your room'.

*　*　*

Delia dragged a high-backed leather chair from the corner of her bedroom, across the polished floorboards to the spot in front of the sash window. She imagined she'd sit here for hours, just like this, propping her elbows on the large painted white sill, to just contemplate the view. Even with night approaching, she could make out yachts bobbing just offshore. What a room to wake up in every day! She felt like jumping up and down with glee on top of the double bed but not wanting to disturb the exquisite gold quilt, she decided to remain demure – for now.

She sighed with contentment and swept her eyes over the bedside table adorned with her heirloom turquoise stone necklace and precious childhood photos. There was her smiling dad working in the paddock, flannel shirt rolled up at the sleeves. And her favourite, the faded colour photo of the three of them leaning against the old cottage wall, took pride of place. She loved that one, the way his big protective arms wrapped around her. *How proud they would be.* She ignored the twinge of loss that squeezed her heart and moved across to the gilt-framed mirror hanging on the opposite wall.

She assessed her image, tucking a swathe of pink hair behind her ear and smiled. The vibrancy of her hair, her mint-coloured scarf, the way her long pink tresses lay against her favourite mottled-green and yellow jacket. For once she really did look like she'd stepped straight out of a Frida Kahlo print. On the inside, she could be anything she wanted to be. A bright toucan in flight; soaring towards a happier version of herself. Feeling uplifted, she walked towards the sound of plates being assembled in the dining room.

'Ah, Delia! I trust you have settled into your room?'

She accepted the long-stemmed wine-glass Ronan pushed into her hand. 'Thanks. Yes, it's lovely – so warm, and a view of the river. I feel very lucky.'

'Well, that is good to hear.' He clinked his glass of red wine against hers and motioned towards takeaway containers atop the large marble dining table. 'A celebratory dinner. I hope you like prawn risotto.'

'Lovely! So generous,' her voice shook and fell away as he hovered close reaching out to her neck.

'I like your scarf, by the way. It is so French, so feminine.' She froze as he glanced his fingers lightly over the Indian cotton fabric before gesturing towards the table.

Her thoughts slithered, collided and slipped away like eels. *Why did he just do that?* She fluttered a practiced hand up to her throat to check everything was in place and tried to settle her nerves.

He plated the risotto and set it in front of Delia before easing himself into a chair. '*Bon appetite.*'

Picking up a fork, she surreptitiously studied his clipped to perfection whiskers and the odd way he ate, bringing the food up to his unmoving head instead of looking down. She managed to swallow a few forkfuls of risotto and murmured her appreciation.

'So, my Delia, I have been thinking. You should know that this house, it is a springboard for your success. Here,' he motioned in an expansive gesture, 'you can learn about cuisine, wine, classical music. I want to nurture you, Delia, allow you to appreciate the good things in life, but of course, your artwork ... it is paramount. Everything is second to the importance of your art.'

Her last forkful of risotto hovered close to her mouth. She was transfixed by his words. A perfect future stretched before her, full of art and beauty.

'Thank you, Ronan, I hardly know what to say.' She smiled and wondered if this was the moment to ask about art supplies.

He pushed himself away from the table. 'Come, let me show you something, Delia.' His large hand encircled her wrist as he led her towards the triptych on the far lounge-room wall.

The risotto felt heavy in her stomach and in her mind's eye she saw herself looking down from the ceiling at their strange forms, the regal prince and the scrawny pink bird. She looked up at the grotesque, blood-dripping sea looming above her head and wondered how she could extract her hand from his grip without appearing rude.

'My hope is that, as much as I love this piece, we replace it with a masterpiece – your masterpiece, Delia. I want,' he motioned to the bare wall above the fireplace, 'to see your paintings come alive, right here. Let us fill the room with your work and then exhibit it! I want you to paint like you have never painted before.'

The way he tensed made her shift focus from the wall to his face. *What was that?* She frowned at a shadow, blood perhaps, at the edge of his nostril. He pointed his nose to the ceiling and inhaled deeply.

'You okay Ronan?' she said, taking the moment to extract her hand.

'*Oui* – but of course,' he said. He took one long, loud inhale before clearing his throat and turning to smile in her direction. 'Now, your art supplies my Delia. I have ordered everything *ma chérie* – you will have everything you need.'

'You're so kind Ronan. I want you to know I'll do my best for you.'

'Very well then, Delia, that is all settled. As I have work to do, I will bid you *bonne nuit.*'

'*Bonne nuit,* Ronan – and thank you again.' She heard his retreating footsteps and a faint bleep as he used the keypad at his bedroom door.

After clearing the plates, Delia luxuriated on the sofa, immersed in her thoughts. With the lounge-room light off, she watched the flickering lights of the far shore.

What if she couldn't paint? She let the bubbles of dread float in and out of her consciousness. She thought of the half finished canvasses in her bedroom. Why she'd dragged them around all these years, she didn't know. *But this is different.* Yes – this time she felt hopeful.

Through the plate glass, staring into night, she saw slide-show images that made up her heart's scar. The wreckage at the bottom of the old farm driveway, blurred faces of families she cared not, school-ground bullies tearing away her scarf, the dogged aloneness. *Could it be possible that she'd found a place to heal, a place to breathe, at last?*

And Ronan – was he sick? She'd seen blood ... hadn't she? Perhaps she was his last protégé? The more she thought about it, the more the idea resonated. She felt a surge of need to bring beauty and colour to the stark spaces in his life. Surely, if she really tried, she could move her hand like she used to; in time with an unseen force?

Feeling infused with a sudden spark of confidence, she got up and padded past the triptych down the passageway, leaving the fairy-tale lights of the distant shore to twinkle over the empty sofa.

*   *   *

Delia poured two glasses of wine and breathed in the aroma. She took a sip of the delicious red liquid, leaned up against the sink and contemplated her first blissful day.

She'd awoken to the call of gulls and the sight of a bright sequined river beckoning through her bedroom window.

After hearing Ronan call *'au revoir,'* she'd padded barefoot out to the lounge-room and stared at the river through the plate glass. Standing there she'd felt light-years from her past, far from prying eyes and bullies pulling at her scarf. Here was a place she could put all that behind her and move in time with nature.

By studying the water, she'd realised that the river was like a sentient being. Today the silken serpent had rolled over and exposed its belly to the autumn sun.

She'd studied the wheeling gulls and heard the echo of the yellow-crested cockatoos of her childhood, squabbling in the ghost gum in the bottom paddock. In her mind she had seen her young hands painting the craggy bark of a she-oak on a small canvas. Her childhood painting had pulsed with colour, a flame robin in the foreground and endless blue hills on the horizon.

The long-suppressed image had stretched out as real and bright as the sparkling water before her. She'd stood there for a long time, mulling over why she'd forgotten that painting – the one left behind – then scurried onto the back deck to escape the answer. Still the sepia movie had played on in her mind, laying out the old farm's dirt driveway lined with purple and white agapanthus, the eagle circling high above the cottage, the men in blue. She'd had to gulp in the sea air and feel the breeze on her face to help push the memory of that fateful day when they'd taken her away, aside. Delia gulped her wine and tapped her fingernails on the stainless steel. *Best check on the lasagna.* Her sudden movement toppled the glass on-to the marble floor.

How could she be so clumsy! She squatted down and started to gather the larger shards then gasped at the sudden vision of a black polished shoe in her peripheral vision.

'*Bonjour*, Delia! So nice to arrive home to this delicious smell. Ah, a little accident, I see.'

'Sorry, Ronan! I can't believe I did that!' She turned to find him towering over her like a colossus. Blood pounded in her ears as she looked up at his long black jacket, an expensive gold insignia belt and, way above her head, a red tie, dangled like a dagger. She eyed the two large bags in his hands and pushed herself up off the floor.

'Um, can I help you get anything from the car?' She glanced towards the open door where another large carry bag lay on the doorstep. A little bubble of delight floated up from the depths of her heart. Even from here she could see an array of sketch books poking from the top.

A sense of relief pushed past the embarrassment of her clumsiness, but even still the shadow of dark thoughts stalked her mind. '*You doubted, didn't you?*' She flicked her eyes over the parked Maserati and heard the leaves rustle within the internal garden before picking up the bag and closing the door, leaving any doubt to curl up and die out in the cold night air.

'I have your easel in the car, Delia.'

'I'm so grateful, Ronan – I can't wait to put all my ideas on canvas.'

She moved to the oven and removed a baking dish, passata oozing through béchamel sauce and golden cheese.

'We should have your delightful meal while it is hot,' he said. Let us celebrate your beginning,' he said, sounding a little breathless.

He walked ahead of her, carrying the bottle and glasses. She placed the lasagna beside a green salad she'd prepared earlier and took her place on the other side of the rectangular dining table.

'À ta santé! To new beginnings!'

Looking into his intense eyes, she held up her glass in silent celebration. In the flickering aqua and shadows she saw a flash of something – fear, loss? She wondered again at his past and the prospect of a present illness. For a moment she felt their bond, an intimate wave of silent knowing that they had found something unlikely yet precious.

The twinge of a smile teased the corners of his mouth as he rubbed his whiskered chin. 'To you, my Delia.'

CHAPTER 6

Dragons and Demons

Delia spread a rug out on the back deck, leaned up against the house and sighed with contentment. Nursing her coffee, she revelled in the feeling of her body uncurling to the rhythm of a new life. The luminous silver water before her made her feel like a seal, basking on a warm beach. She kept her face aimed towards the heavens, the delicious autumn sun on her bare throat. Out of habit, her hand floated up to her throat, but for once, its rough surface only made her grin. *'This is what freedom feels like!'*

The spray pluming off rocks below the house, signalled a change in weather. She drained the last dregs of black coffee, tucked her long pink tresses inside the old fleece jacket she was wearing, and zipped it up to her chin. *Time to begin.*

Waves crested, frothed and fell away, and seabirds glided past while the petals of her heart started to unfurl like an exotic peony facing the sun.

She picked up a brush and held it poised above the canvas for a moment. *Breathe, relax, you can do it!* The mantra gave her strength to apply the first tentative brush-strokes on-to the burnt umber prepared surface. It felt good, liberating even. Each brush-stroke gave her confidence to keep going. The more brush strokes, the more she could breathe, the freer she felt. She started to paint with a sense of urgency, wanting more than anything for the rippled dragon-skin river to come alive on canvas.

Her painting would depict a mythical river, the rush of water flowing out to sea taking up two thirds of the canvas. The key was to show the river as an ancient, wild and effortless creature, breathing in, breathing out. She stepped back and cocked her head to one side. *Perhaps she could add a whale diving within its depths to enhance the feeling of timelessness?*

A sudden sound made her jerk her head towards the house. Did she imagine it? She strained her ears. There – the sound of slow, heavy footsteps.

Frowning now, Delia walked across the deck and slid back the glass door. She pushed her head into the passageway and called 'hello, is anyone there?' but the words fell flat at her feet.

The male form standing at the end of the passageway, close to the edge of the lounge-room, took a step forwards. Silence sizzled between them.

She could tell he was sizing her up. The thousand needles of fear pricking her scalp, forced her to take a few steps backwards. She re-emerged back out on to the deck and clutched at the railing for support. Hearing approaching footfalls on the parquetry flooring pushed her even further back across the deck. She lingered at the top of the back stairs leading down to the garden, poised to break into a run.

A thin pale face, hiding beneath a baseball cap and a billy-goat beard, appeared in the doorway. He sauntered out on to the deck, leaned up against the side of the house next to the railing before shoving his hands into the pockets of his low slung jeans.

His aura of menace sizzled across the deck. She glanced at the flimsy paint-brush in her hand and exclaimed 'Who are you? What do you want?'

He swept dull opaque pale blue eyes towards her, sniffed and dragged a finger under his nose. 'So – you're the new bird, huh?'

His assessing eyes sent her hand to involuntarily fly up to her throat. It was a pathetic, act of protection, but she was nevertheless thankful for the jacket, zipped up to her chin.

He cocked his head. 'What's with the hair?'

Delia's left heel hovered in space over the top step. Adrenalin pulsed through her veins. She readied herself to turn and run yet she managed to spit back 'You've got no right to be here!'

He snorted and looked off into the middle distance. 'Got more right than you!' he retorted. 'Yeah, that'd be right. Didn't fuckin' mention me, I guess.'

He bit into a ragged thumbnail and squinted at the river. 'S'pose he didn't tell ya that we're goin' up the coast tomorrow either.'

Delia clutched hold of the balcony railing, mind whirling in confusion, while his eyes turned towards the easel.

'You gotta be kiddin' me'. He sauntered across to the canvas.

Who is this rude arsehole? She winced at the sight of his index finger tracing the outline of her river painting.

With a sniff he turned to walk back into the house. 'You're not gonna last five minutes.'

Bastard! She shook off her muteness. 'You can't just come in here, acting like you own the place! Answer me! Who the hell are you?' she yelled.

He flicked his dead eyes towards her and said 'You'll see' before swaggering back down the passageway.

What the hell? She scurried across the deck just in time to see him smirk back from the entrance to Ronan's bedroom. He tapped on the keypad, the door clicked open. 'See ya at dinner', he said, before closing the door behind him.

Delia stood frozen for a moment before she managed to use her jelly-like legs to scramble down the back stairs. The thought that he might be standing at the window watching, sent her scurrying towards the emerald lawn in the front garden. The sentry row of white roses outside the portico nodded in her direction. From here, everything looked normal, perfect and peaceful. Yet she'd breathed in his menace and now she felt sick.

A cold breeze sent a few parchment leaves skidding up the driveway towards the entrance. A breeze whipped hair across her face. Between the haze of confusion and seething anger, she saw herself packing up her belongings and dragging her heavy case up the leaf-strewn driveway and out of Ronan's life. She could just step through the wrought-iron gates and disappear right now.

She dropped onto her back and for a long time stared at the pendulous clouds above. By the time she ascended the stairs to collect the forsaken easel, dark bloated underbellies loomed low and heavy over the river. The threat of rain washed away thoughts of leaving until to tomorrow.

*   *   *

She looked like a modern-day Medusa, standing on the deck, pink hair streaming around her pale, upturned face. The tempest was closing in now. She stretched out her arms and willed the splats hitting her cheeks to turn into a torrent.

'Come on!' she yelled to the grey sky. She could still see him holding up last night's quail like it was a court exhibit. 'Looks like roadkill.' His opaque eyes appealed to Ronan to join in the mockery, then turned sour with disappointment.

'Now, now, Simon,' Ronan had scolded, 'be nice. Delia is my very special guest. She has many hidden talents.'

'Yeah, well, cookin' ain't one of 'em,' he'd grinned.

She marched down the stairs, eager to stand in the open and meet the rain. How she needed to wash that man's menace away. She passed by the garden shed that backed onto the shore and stared through the wrought-iron speared fencing to the white-capped river beyond.

She spread her arms wide on an imaginary crucifix and willed the fury in her heart to go away. '*He should have warned you,*' came the hiss on the breeze. '*But he apologised,*' she spat back to whatever force was out there, making life more difficult that it already was.

She replayed the way he'd admonished Simon in a softened tone 'see, you have made my Delia unhappy' before turning to her, 'I am so sorry, my Delia. Simon's arrival was a surprise even to me. I was to tell you the news tonight that I was going away. You will have the house to yourself for all of Easter. So no more interruptions, you will be able to paint to your heart's content.'

Simon had flicked a contemptuous look in her direction. His unsaid words blaring across the table 'he love's me, better get used to it bitch.'

How the hell Ronan find this morose, rude man attractive was beyond her. She'd matched his death stare conveying she had a right to be here too.

She watched a yacht bob haphazardly offshore in the ink and green swell, allowing the rain to drive into her upturned face. The cold seeped deeper into her jumper and bones, while her hair formed thick ropes across her shoulders. Yet still she stayed, listening to the sound of nature's orchestra, of rain slicing into the river and waves sloshing up against boulders.

Could she be in the house, with him? What was the alternative? Leave? How many times had she packed up and left in her life? An image of the old farm flashed through her mind, where the ghost of her happy childhood resided. How many times had she shifted from one foster family to another? Her hand fluttered up automatically to hold her throat, feeling the unfairness rage through her. The blotch beneath her hand pulsed, its angry stain threatening to seep upwards to her face.

She stomped her way through the garden and up the back stairs. Breathless, she slid open the door and made her way down the passageway into her bedroom, leaving puddles in her wake. Stripping off, she surveyed herself in the bathroom mirror. The stain around her neck was as bad as ever, maybe even worse. She stepped into the shower and tried to conjure up the image of dragging her old brown case down Larke Avenue. *To where?*

It wasn't until she was on the sofa, under a shawl and sipping coffee that she felt herself relax a little. The rain, streaming sidewards across the plate-glass eased her into a daydream. She sat there for a long time, watching slipstreams of water on glass, thinking about her canvas begging to be completed. Behind her, the house lay silent, a sanctuary of stillness.

CHAPTER 7

Rafting Into The Shadows

Delia felt a surge of energy through her right arm, as she worked to control each brushstroke. Painting on the back deck, infused her with limitless inspiration. She was completely immersed in the moment, painting to the soundtrack of wheeling seabirds. She cast a critical eye at the textural quality of the river, marvelled at how the dramatic dragon-scales of yesterday had been smoothed away to reveal slick bitumen, before adding the final brushstrokes to the canvas.

After moving the easel back into the lounge-room, she paced back and forth before her three completed canvasses incredulous that she still had it in her. *How on earth had she allowed this talent to remain dormant?* She flicked aside the slideshow of foster parents' faces and instead, allowed a little firework lightshow to ignite in her heart.

She smiled at the *Mythical River* sure that it was a piece worthy of any gallery.

The sound of voices made her jerk her head towards the foyer. In an instant she ran barefoot past the triptych into the passageway leading to her room.

'*Bonjour*, Delia – we're home!'

Delia whipped the Indian cotton scarf around her neck, glanced in the mirror before yelling down the passageway 'Hi Ronan. I wasn't expecting you.'

She walked back into the lounge-room and spied Ronan standing in the marble foyer. The prince, returned to his castle. A fleeting movement behind him confirmed that Simon was there, loitering in the background.

Delia held her breath as Ronan strode across the polished concrete towards the canvasses leaning up against the plate-glass in the lounge-room. She tried to read his face but his emotions were impenetrable behind his grey whiskers and regal façade. He gave nothing away, marching between the canvasses before coming to a standstill in front of *Sea of Tranquility*.

'Delia, this is *magnifique!*' His face erupted into a smile. 'The light playing on the water, the way it appears that evil dwells just out of sight, hidden beneath a veil of mist. It reminds me of your early work, the mystery in the shadows.'

The words were like a gift from heaven. Tears welled in her eyes.

'And here,' he pointed to *Mythical River*, 'how the energy of the diving whale and the soaring birds connect with these rolling spirals. I presume these spirals depict energy. Am I right?'

'Yes, yes that's right! I tried to depict spirits of people, of tribes, long gone, transcended there over the skin of the river,' she said, her heart near bursting with pride.

'Well, you're rolling spirit idea is excellent Delia. And here, he moved on to *Golden Grasses of Home*. 'I can feel the wind in the grass like I am standing there. Your interplay of light and dark …', his voice trailed off as he threw his head back and drew in a deep breath. 'You see, this house, is inspirational for an artist. An exceptional artist, like you, my Delia! These are worthy of an exhibition!'

'*An exhibition*!' The word rang in her ears as he went on.

'I purposely left you, Delia. I wanted you to prove you were the person I had been searching for – and you have not disappointed me!'

'Thank you, Ronan. I couldn't have done these without your support.'

At that moment, Simon stepped from the shadow of the foyer and her smile dropped away. She felt the hostility like a wave as he sauntered over to the canvasses.

He stood in front of *Sea of Tranquility*, legs spread, one hand in his jeans pocket, the other stroking his tuft of a beard. 'Vague – nothing compared to *The Hunt*,' he muttered.

For a moment she saw something in his dull eyes. He was lost, floating in a sea of self-pity. It made her wonder what affliction dogged him and maybe what drugs he took to block it all out.

He scuffed a shoe next to *Grasses of Home*, mumbled something before walking towards Ronan's bedroom.

Delia watched the way he moved, slow, deliberate, entitled.

'Is he an artist?' she said, her words tinged with incredulity. Delia thought of her unfinished canvasses, the ones she'd dragged around for years and were in her bedroom right now. They were certainly worthless, futile, painted when only pain and bitterness filled her heart. She decided there and then to burn them, break the bond to those aching years of nothingness.

The sound of Ronan's voice snapped her back to the present.

'Do not worry about Simon, *ma chérie,* he is just a little jealous of my new star.' He waved a dismissive hand in Simon's direction. 'Yes, he has done a painting or two, but they are not of your standard, my Delia. So, tonight we shall celebrate your success and plan your exhibition.'

*   *   *

Ronan poured Cointreau into the pan and smiled. 'Ah, my Delia, tonight we shall have wine and duck á l'orange, my favourite.'

For the first time, his rigid stance, the way he held his head so high, didn't put her off. She could stand here and breathe in the burnt orange aroma, without feeling anxious. The realisation that she was home and that her paintings had worked to strengthen their bond, made her heart swell with joy.

She watched Ronan's hand stirring orange strips, marmalade and cornflour paste to make the jus. 'Can I help you at all', she said. She flicked a dark look towards Simon, leaning up against the island bench. In a show of empowerment, or maybe bravado, she stepped closer to Ronan.

'*Merci*, Delia. If you could take the duck from the oven and bring it into the dining room, I'll bring the jus. And you,' he grinned at Simon, 'can bring in the wine.'

Delia noticed the intensity of Ronan's gaze. His aqua eyes were shining brighter than she'd ever seen them.

Delia placed the roasted duck on a platter and carried it into the dining room. She sat next to Ronan and watched him uncork a bottle of wine while Simon watched on exuding an aura of sullen discontent.

'Tonight we shall celebrate with this Grenache from the Côte-du-Rhône. It is a drier wine, so will offset the sharpness of the oranges and the richness of the duck.' He held the bottle aloft and poured the light red liquid into three glasses. For a moment he looked lost in reverie, then added, 'you know, the grapes from this region, they can be used for the Châteauneuf-du-Pape. Tonight we have this grenache, but when we sell your first painting, Delia, that is what we will be drinking!'

Ronan lifted the glass to his nose and inhaled. Frowning as Simon slammed his plate down, then smiling in her direction.

'*Bon appetite*!'

Simon swigged his wine before shovelling the duck into his mouth.

'Now, now, Simon, where are your manners? The duck, it should be savoured,' Ronan admonished.

Delia jerked her head up at Simon's response, a sharp and high-pitched laugh. She assessed his pallid face, trying to discern what was so funny.

'You must excuse Simon. He is a little annoyed that I have found you, my star. The artist I have been waiting for my whole life.'

Her throat squeezed a little and she fluttered a hand up to her best pink chiffon scarf. 'Well, I don't know what to say, Ronan. That is very, um, generous of you.' She felt herself being reeled into his world. For a moment, she forgot Simon existed. There would be no end to her gratitude; she would cover the walls with her art.

In response, Ronan reached out and placed a comforting hand on her shoulder, never for a moment relinquishing his piercing gaze. Her heart-rate grew rapid and she started to feel a little light-headed. They were connected now, in a bubble, just them. Mesmerised, she let him lightly trace her jaw-line with a fingertip.

In little more than a whisper, he said 'I have a present for you.'

She chose to ignore Simon's muffled giggle and watched Ronan collect a package on the floor, near his feet. He placed his gift on the marble tabletop.

Delia was content for now to just look at the beauty of the rice-paper wrapping and feel the magnitude of his generosity.

'Now, before you open this, Delia, I want to ask: what do you know of art? I think you are an extraordinary artist, but I can tell already, by your face, that I have hit upon a truth.'

His question jolted her a little 'Um, how do you mean?'

'Don't get me wrong, I think your style is captivating, the way you use light and shade. But,' he tilted his head back and breathed in deeply, 'there is scope for improvement, and that can come when you learn about things that touch the soul and the mind. What do you know, for example, about foreboding as death edges its way closer? Human frailty, the clinging and grasping to survive, and then blessed relief as death comes. And what do you know about the tightrope we walk between sanity and madness? How do you depict these aspects of humanity, in art?'

Delia gripped the chair, fingernails digging into polished wood, as his words gathered momentum. She wanted to go back the way there were just moments ago, but now there was fire in his eyes. Her chest felt heavy, lungs moving in and out like a ruptured accordion.

'Humans', he went on 'we are so vulnerable. We live such precarious, tenuous lives. And what of those who enforce their power over the weak? What of the afterlife? You have touched on this a little in your *Mythical River*, but, you can go deeper. True art is about the story of man's need for survival, his aversion to Hell, or his need to befriend the Devil himself!'

He was animated now. Delia felt the blood drain out of her face.

'This book, Delia, will teach you about real art.'

What did he mean – that paintings of nature weren't good enough? She placed her palm over her ratcheting heart and looked down at his gift.

There seemed to be something cold and mean about it now, lying there beneath the rice-paper.

'Ronan, I, um, I'm not feeling well. Do you mind if I open your gift later?'

'It will only take a moment, *ma chérie*. This book, it will be good for your learning. It will lift your creativity to new heights. You can take ideas from here. Your exhibition, it will be full of death, of power and passion!' He stopped to gasp for air.

'Ronan, I can't possibly – I can't paint death!' Her words sounded like an echo, squeezed from the inside of a tomb. She tried to follow the thread of a thought to move, get up, but her legs were like stagnant blobs of skin and bone.

'But you are so talented, Delia. And my star must paint as I wish. Here, let me help you.'

His large hands eased a glossy book from the wrapping and turned it over to reveal the back cover. Delia recoiled in her chair. 'This is one of my favourites, Goya's '*Saturn Devouring His Son*'. Yes, Delia, your reaction. The way you just gasped. That is exactly what I mean.' He pointed to the wiry beast with long matted grey hair and demonic boggle eyes. 'See how the bloody torso captures your eye first, and only then do you realise, that the head is inside the hell-hole mouth. See how the artist has built a story. That's what I call art.'

Delia gripped the chair tighter. A vague thought bubbled up: had he put something in the wine?

His fingers flicked through pages filled with religious scenes and crucifixions before stopping at an image of waxen white bodies, broken and adrift at sea. Ronan pointed at the caption, *The Raft of the Medusa*, 1818–1819, by Théodore Géricault. 'Another favourite – it is in the Musée du Louvre.' He breathed in long, loud rasps, took his hands off the book and gripped the edge of the table instead.

Out of the corner of her eye, she could see his fingers white with effort. Somehow frozen, she watched as a smoky haze floated out of Ronan's mouth. He leaned forward, lips stretched in a silent scream, as the vapours drifted and morphed together in a cloud. She heard herself whimper.

It's the wine, he's done something. But she couldn't think, not when Ronan's face was lost behind a veil of mist. She willed her legs to move but found herself trapped in the chair instead.

'It is time, my Delia.' The massing vapours obscured his face while his husky words filled her with ice.

'Let us see your beautiful throat. Here, let me help you.'

'No, Ronan ...' She struggled to breathe and tried to bat his hand away but his fingers were undoing her scarf undeterred.

'Fuck, look at it!' Simon's face floated into view. He was leering, just like they all used to do. A crowd of kids pointing and scrambling to get a better look, bubbled up from the depths of her consciousness. 'It's like a mouldy stain. I never seen no bright-green birthmark before!'

'You see, this is what you couldn't do for me, my darling Simon. Only she can give me what I need.'

Delia managed to turn her face back towards the sound of Ronan's husky voice and heard her own scream reverberate off the walls. The image hovered between them like a mirage. The eyes were missing but she could make out an old seaman's cap pulled over straggly hair.

'It's no good to fight him Delia,' said Ronan.

She tried to lift her arm up to push at the thumb tracing the bare skin at her throat, but it was useless. Her vision blanked in and out, on threads of light and fog.

'He's been patient, Delia, waiting while I searched for you. Did you not feel me hunting, Delia?'

Ronan's face moved back into her vision, his eyes cracking like Antarctic ice, helter-skelter, full of madness. She tore her eyes away to try to focus on the mirage or whatever it was and blanked out for a second.

Feeling hands shaking her shoulders, she opened her eyes and whimpered. 'Didn't you feel my thirst for your talent,' he yelled. 'It is beyond human. And didn't you feel his need for your energy? How angry do you think I was Delia, that you didn't stay still long enough, you didn't keep your name long enough!' He swept a hand through his salt-and-pepper hair, while the old seaman's image hovered in her peripheral vision.

'So thank you Delia. Changing your name back to Drakos', he grinned 'was so very helpful'.

'Now, you will do as the Captain commands. We are, you will see, both his servants. It is no good to fight him.'

'Simon ... get behind and pull her head back, bare her throat!'

Garbled, protests slid from a mouth that refused to work properly. Her body was numb yet she could still feel Simon's putrid hands, one on her forehead bending her head back, the other unbuttoning her shirt, lingering for a moment to feel the ridged, green skin.

'Check it out – it's all over her chest!'

Waves of dense energy settled around her head like a smothering cloud. She wanted to scream but they'd taken that away somehow. Only the tears falling down her cheeks revealed that she was in there, beneath skin and bone.

Simon slipped from view, replaced by the hazy image of the old seaman, its slit of a mouth hovering close to her head. Delia felt duck fat slide in her stomach and felt hands grip her shoulders from behind while the haze enveloped her head. Unable to see, she felt vaporous tentacles inside her throat. *I can't breathe!* Her internal scream ricocheted against the inside of her skull. Her panic spiked as the feasting spirit invaded. The swarm of bees buzzing in her brain reached their crescendo. Blessed blackness swept her far away.

CHAPTER 8

Master and Commander

Hobart Town, Van Diemen's Land, 1838

He could literally smell the blood. Setting a cracking pace towards New Wharf, he knew what he wanted alright: the coming hunt, the inevitable kill. He was born for this. To see the flailing whale and the thick red slick and the story, front page of *The Hobart Town Courier,* no less, that he, Captain Angus McCracken, was the most notorious whaler there ever was and ever was likely to be.

Distant snow atop Mount Wellington made him pull his battered cap further down over his flying grey locks. *It be a frigid place full of pagans and sinners to make a livin'.* Yet, being a man of ruthless determination himself, he'd made a bounty here in this place at the end of the earth.

He passed by the remains of old Knopwood's Rolling Green Farm and stopped at the brow of the hill, where the view stretched across the wharf to the haphazard conglomeration of Wapping. The memory of the squalor always made him stop and gloat, just for a moment. He was a man of prestige now! No more living next to the stinking Rivulet for him. Aye, his new stone cottage on the waterfront in Battery Point was more in keeping with a man of standing.

A far cry from the child left on a sodden earthen floor by his mother. He knew not whether she was alive or dead, and he cared less. He was a survivor, through and through. He'd made a life for himself through his own sweat, his own will.

He puffed out his chest and took in a deep breath of sharp, icy air before continuing his march towards the port. Out on the deep and hazardous Derwent, he spied the usual mélange of small wooden whaleboats, cutters and schooners. There were a few trading ketches with their sheet topsails flying, and the topsail schooner, *Enterprize,* was in port unloading its precious cargo of livestock and supplies. Yet it was *Le Dauphin,* tied up at the dock next to the immigrant barque, *Jane,* that caused a smile to crack his craggy face. For all his fearlessness on the high seas, this was his reward, his very own three-masted grand barque!

He tapped the prized mahogany spyglass hanging from his belt, checked his gold pocket watch and continued his brisk walk down to the large stone warehouses and ordinance stores of New Wharf. The cacophony of noise pulled him onwards – convict picks chipping at the quarry face, calls of seamen unloading cargo, cows bellowing while being hoisted ship to shore. As always, the Whalers' Return was heaving with mariners, all cheering and cussing. He'd thrash any of his heathen crew if they were in there drinking and merrymaking when there were whales to be harpooned and fortunes to be made!

He strode along the broad section of the wooden port, dodged a horse and carriage and made his way through the throng of sailors, and some old sea dogs like him, bearded with steely eyes looking out for the next prize. Ah, the joys of the colony; so much money to be made off the back of sheep, the fruits of the land, plentiful seals and of course, whale oil. And just the thought of another delivery of whalebone for all those corsets in London sent his blood racing. He marched on with new vigour, passers-by peeling off to allow him through.

He gazed upon the carved figurehead of a dolphin at the prow and the sturdy English oak construction of *Le Dauphin's* hull. It was by far the most beautiful whaling vessel afloat in the harbour, complete with a perfectly rounded Oregon pine bowsprit. This barque was his glory, his stamp of authority. He'd carved out a place for himself in this god-forsaken colony through his own sweat, spit and blood. He was now his own master and commander, and a feared one at that!

'Ahoy, Cap'n!' The youngest apprentice shouted down from the deck to the frenetic port below. 'I'll get the ladder for ye, sir.'

Captain McCracken took one last appreciative look at the bowsprit and concentrated on the task at hand. It was no mean feat to climb the ladder. He had to concentrate on every movement as his ample girth scraped the rungs. Upon setting foot on deck, he noticed the native harpooner following his every move with wise mahogany eyes while the rest of his swarthy bearded crew emerged from below and rushed to their positions.

'I hope none of you motley set are missing!' I need all sixteen of you lousy peasants to be ready, not drinkin' the heathen brew.'

The wild-haired First Mate immediately responded 'we all be here, ready and accounted, Cap'n!'

Captain McCracken felt a familiar rush of adrenalin. The thrill of the hunt always consumed his senses, even before they left the dock. He strode to his position on the quarterdeck and sniffed the light icy breeze.

'We're in for a wild ride! Give the order,' he yelled down to the officer of the charge. He remained at his command post as the crew erupted into life.

The heavily-set, broad-shouldered helmsman appeared on the quarterdeck and took his position at the wheel.

'All hands on deck! Untie the headline rope! You there, pull the breast line, now the stern lines. Climbers, ascend on the windward shroud, unfurl the sails and set!'

The climbers sprang into action, negotiating the gaps in the footropes to scale the rigging and move out over the yards. One climber continued his journey upwards, to the lofty heights of the crow's nest.

They eased their way out from the wharf, edging around the *Enterprize* and between cutters and schooners, and headed in the direction of the far shore. Crewmen busied themselves checking harpoons and lances. The further they moved into the deep, dark waters of the Derwent, the louder the prayers of the apprentice boy.

This was where Captain McCracken felt most powerful, in command

and ready to hunt. With the square canvas sails cracking in the sou'easter, he was as sure as the blood was ripping through his veins that he would harpoon not one but two whales. He could smell it, sense it, see in his mind's eye the carcasses lashed to either side of the vessel, blood trailing in the water as he brought them back to port for flensing.

Captain McCracken looked back at the receding wharf where another vessel was beginning to pull away. 'The race is on, shipmates, but we are fearless and they are mere landlubbers in the chase. They'll not be taking our bounty this day!' Cheers broke out across the deck as the vessel rolled in the whitecaps at the centre of the river.

He looked beyond the horizontal spars and the billowing sails to the sky. It was one of those late spring days, the air thick with the expectancy of a thunderstorm. Bulbous dark grey clouds lay low and heavy yet were etched with a dazzling bright light. An ice-filled breeze blew out the canvas sails as they made good progress across the moody Derwent.

Captain McCracken looked to the barrelman, high up in the crow's nest. He was the keenest of eye and could see a spout from a blowhole a mile away, even in choppy seas. Sure enough, within minutes, the call came.

'There she blows, Cap'n!'

He snatched the spyglass from his belt and scanned the rolling white-caps. Soon the officer of the charge bellowed his instructions across the deck.

'Furl the sails! Square the yards!'

While the climbers clung to the rigging and secured the sails, five crewmen waited on the anchor deck. Upon hearing 'man the capstan', they slotted the heavy bars into position and began their laborious walk clockwise, shouldering the strain and heaving as they went. The grunts of the men and the sound of the two-ton anchor being lowered echoed across the deck.

The tension, the thrill, was nearly too much to bare. The near im-perceptible dark hump was a mere fifty feet away or so. He itched to be off the ship and in the melee, despite only having thrown the harpoon a couple of times. His skills were better suited to being here on deck, shouting orders. 'Lower the whalers as smart as ye can!' he yelled.

He watched as the first of the whaleboats were untied and the native harpooner climbed into position. 'Lower away!' he cried, but a second later he cried out again, unable to resist. 'No – stop, wait! This time, I be in the hunt! I want blood! It will be a hoot!'

He climbed aboard the pine whaleboat and positioned himself at the stern, taking up an oar. The lean native at the bow cast quizzical eyes in his direction but kept his thoughts to himself. Down they were winched, lower and lower, to meet the inky water below. Captain McCracken grinned. This time, that whale would be his! He would let the native throw the harpoon, but he wanted to see the death flurry up close and help haul the massive mammal's body in, feel its blubbery mass under his hands.

They rowed out beyond *Le Dauphin's* hull. They were quite close to the far shore now; they could clearly see the tall grasses and the leaves of the eucalypts and peppermint trees swaying in the breeze. Their prize, however, could not be seen, having disappeared again into the depths.

Captain McCracken set down the oar, raised his spyglass and scanned the rippled, black water. He changed position and at once spied the looming presence of Mount Wellington and the canvas sails of an approaching whaling ship.

'Aargh, where are you?' he cursed. The only sound was the slapping of waves against the small boat. They sat, quiet and idle, bobbing up and down in the swell.

He put the spyglass down in his lap and squinted into the harsh light, scanning the water for tell-tale bubbles or wakes.

The silence was shattered in an instant of roaring, gushing fury. Amidst the screams, the men tried to hold on-to the sides of the boat as it was launched higher and higher, almost in slow-motion. The boat remained in an upright position, before flipping sidewards, smashing down into the Derwent.

Captain McCracken, wide-eyed and thrashing, latched on-to a

crewmate until his death-weight proved useless. He was floundering towards the upturned boat when the hulk rose again from the depths. An eye – wise, purposeful, flashed by before being replaced by a white underbelly, too close. The huge tail rose up and slammed down, sending a wall of water cascading down upon his head. He frantically searched for the surface and clawed his way back up towards the light.

Gasping for air, he glimpsed the indigo monolith of Mount Wellington, the eucalypt and wattle covered foothills and a few plumes of smoke from fires probably lit by the Mouheneene. And there was New Wharf, with its large Georgian sandstone warehouses. Just before his head sank again below the ink, he caught sight of his little stone cottage on the waterfront.

Down, down, he sank into the abyss, his pocket watch streaming after him on its gold chain. With lungs bursting and panicked eyes as big as saucers, he caught a glimpse of the passing hulk in the blue.

It was then, with all hope lost, that he saw a ray of light, like shards of a sunbeam, appearing from the depths below. He thought to repent for his sins and ask for liberation from evil, but those thoughts were interrupted by the strains of a far-off violin drifting to him on the current.

He sank further down towards the light; his mind filled with images of heather, sheer sea cliffs and the shores of a distant loch. He recognised the tune now, and the words filled his very being:

Bonnie Scotland, land of grandeur
Where the sparkling streams meander
Here will I delight to wander,
Bonnie, Bonnie Scotland.

The sunbeam beckoned like a magnet; he could easily have just drifted into that tunnel of light. Yet the song made him think of home, and home was here, across this expanse of river, where he had made his fortune. He thought of that stone cottage up there on the waterfront and his trusty wolfhound, waiting for his return.

He needed to fight! Fight with all his Scottish strength and canny will to reach the surface that lay above him, as high as the sky. It was too late for his mortal body but not his spirit orb.

With all his might he willed his orb free from the carcass of his body. An amorphous light bubbled out of his flesh and commenced its journey up towards the surface. While the Captain's body settled into the silt, his glazed eyes kept watch on the strange glow as it rose upwards, through the gloom.

He cared nought about this body now, it could rot, but his orb must go home, live on. He would approach death as he did life, playing on his terms. There was no convict, soldier, merchant nor mariner who could out-wit this wily old Scot. In death, he would command the next stage of his existence.

The orb broke the surface of the water and ricocheted over the skin of the river.

Drops of rain fell and as the first cracks of thunder was heard across New Wharf, the Captain's spirit orb flew through the cottage window and landed high upon the rafters. The wolfhound, sleeping by the fireplace, jerked his head up and peered with suspicion at the ceiling.

Hobart, 1968

Over the years, the wily Captain's spirit orb stayed in the rafters, feeling the reverberations of change as families moved in and out. It was mostly at home, hovering in the room overlooking the water, but if it at times felt unsettled, it would drift down to slam a door, just to make a point. It felt the vibrations of energy of people unseen, felt arguments across the generations, the love rippling between couples, the rage of others.

One day the orb sensed a different vibration. It was gentle, childlike, innocent, yet its spirit was determined and independent. The orb floated down from the rafters to be closer to the source. Yes, a strong-willed male energy, purposeful, spirited, but with a good heart. It circled a few times, revelling in the vibrations and landed on a small shelf of a shoulder. It clung there, even as the little boy moved next door.

It wasn't until four the next morning that the spirit orb took its smoke-like form and moved from the small boy's shoulder to hover around his mouth for just a moment, before disappearing on the next inhale.

Unseen and unfelt, the smoky tentacles found their way down to the child's compassionate, shiny orb and, by stealth, covered up his luminous glow. The fountain of love, compassion and wonder at the world's beauty that had once poured out, was soon extinguished by the ancient orb's sooty mass. It had taken one hundred and thirty years but now, Captain McCracken was back and the boy would just have to come along for the ride.

CHAPTER 9

The Invasion

Hobart, 1968

Little Ronan's eyes snapped open. He peered over the thick blanket and scanned the room with suspicion. In the dim predawn light he could make out the one glassy eye of his much loved but bedraggled Thomas sitting on the rocking chair, furry snout resting on fat tummy, just where he should be. Ronan looked to the windowsill, where Golly's red and white lips were grinning just as much as yesterday. On the pillow to his left sat his knitted purple and pink Humpty Dumpty. For some reason those big black button-eyes didn't look quite right. Ronan grabbed it and tossed with all his might. The toy sailed across the room and fell forlorn in the corner.

Ronan felt a bit frightened, but he didn't know why. Why did the morning feel so different? Had one of those evil, wart-nosed Wizard of Oz witches flown in on a broomstick and cursed him overnight? He lay there, tense and still, looking to the pressed tin ceiling. Was that a cackling witch, hanging there in the gloom? He stared and stared, then slipped back down under the covers.

The day before had been full of adventures. He retraced the day now, feeling the safety of Mummy's hand wrapped around his and the warmth of the sun on his cheeks. He could see Bronty, his bright-green plastic dinosaur, bouncing along behind them on a string. The three of them had gone past the bakery, and he'd pressed his face up against the glass to get a better look at the creamy, iced buns. He would have been content to stay there drooling over the cakes but he'd been pulled away. On they had walked, past the big sandstone warehouses to the big green train, which hooted and whistled.

He'd stood on the seat, stuck his head out the window, feeling the wind on his face as they rattled their way along the track next to the river. Then there had been the treat of gooey, sweet chocolate at the factory; he'd shoveled so much in, it had left a melted mush around his lips, like he'd sucked on a mud pie.

They'd taken boxes of wrapped up chocolates home on the train. He'd skipped through the park but dragged his feet when they stopped at the house next door. The craggy old man ... maybe he was the problem? Ronan had stayed behind Mummy's bare legs, holding the hem of her red polka-dot skirt while she talked to the yellow-toothed man. His face scared him a bit, all crinkled-up skin and watery eyes under the bushiest brows he'd ever seen.

He'd spotted the old man's grey cat though. It was crouched on the mat in the darkened hallway, and he'd edged past to stroke it. He loved the feel of the cat's deep, soft fur and its perfect white mittened paws. The cat had responded by purring and nuzzling his knee, which had made him giggle.

Yet thinking of the cat now, well, he felt only ... he couldn't find the words. His stomach churned like when Mummy tried to give him brussels sprouts for dinner. Disgust, that was it – but why? He'd always loved it when the cat had padded onto their lawn. He would play on the grass with her, nuzzling his face into her fur. Now, just one day later, he felt repulsed at the thought.

In a fit of anger, he threw off the covers, snatched his dressing-gown and charged down the hallway. He reached on tip toes, pulled at the doorhandle, and ran into the garden. Round and round the lawn he ran, screaming, before he came across a stick. He grabbed at it and felt the pleasure of stabbing the lawn again and again.

'Ronan – you get in here this instant!' cried his Mummy.

Ronan found himself being hauled back inside.

'Don't you scream at me like that!' Ronan watched her open the kitchen drawer and pick up the wooden spoon. He sniffed and bit his bottom lip.

'Right – that's better. No more screaming – okay. Now eat your cornflakes like a good boy.'

Ronan shovelled spoonfuls into his mouth, his fury only giving way to a giggle at the sound of the phone ringing in the lounge-room. He waited until she was out of view and scrambled into action, standing on a chair to pick the biggest knife off the counter. In seconds, he'd pelted into the conservatory and overcome with pure glee, stabbed the white leather ottoman over and over again.

He stood back puffing, surveyed the mutilated ottoman before turning his thoughts to building a fort. Yes that's what he'd do. He'd make a fort from cardboard under the billiard table, so Mummy couldn't see in. It would be just him and Bronty, his camouflage-clad GI Joe, pieces of Lego and his pumper fire truck.

Ronan spent a whole day running the bright-red Tonka fire-engine up and down the parquetry flooring, in and out of the Lego stacks, until his mother stopped screaming and turned to begging instead. But he wasn't going to stop. He drove the pumper truck harder into the flooring.

At the end of the day he heard his father's loud groan and readied himself for war. Looking through the stab marks he'd made in the cardboard, he could see his father's polished leather shoes and suit pants striding closer.

'Ronan, get out from under there, this instant, do you hear?'

The barricade was torn down in a second. Ronan cowered under the billiard table until he felt himself being dragged over the tangle of cardboard. He cried out, twisted himself into position and stabbed at his father's tailored pants.

'Ahhh! You little bastard!'

Ronan felt himself flying through the air before slamming into the wall. The room erupted with screams and howls of agony and the sound of Ronan's laugh.

He felt alive, bursting with glee, as he watched his father clasp bloody fingers around his thigh. The blood dripping onto the parquetry floor, it somehow stirred something like a memory. He couldn't quite grasp hold of the thought, but it felt good. All he knew was that blood was beautiful, thick and red and oozy.

Hobart, 1990

Ronan coughed and threw his head back for a moment before concentrating once again on the landscape sliding past the taxi window. There it was, the silken blue expanse of the Derwent, licking the parched tip of the Tranmere peninsula before flowing out to sea. Ronan could feel his stomach twisting, a cross between anticipation and recognition of the dark urges dwelling deep inside his body, eager for the fight that lay just ahead.

The taxi was at the highest point of the Tasman Bridge now. From here he could make out the upright facade of Wrest Point Casino. There was a familiarity, a sense of home and, finally, of belonging. How he had longed for the deep blue and foaming whitecaps of the Derwent. That much had sustained him while he had seethed half a world away. Yes, he remembered the shoreline, how the water lapped at the rocky beach below the house, how the seabirds swooped. Memories made a lifetime ago.

As for them ... He sneered at the thought of his parents, waiting on the sandstone steps after so long. The prodigal son's return .... *Je suis revenue des morts.* For a moment, he could see the spire and clock tower, etched against the garrison like, rock face of the Cornettes de Bise. His gut twisted with familiar rage at the wasted years.

Now his mind played games, super-imposing the sandstone warehouses of Salamanca with the grand buildings of Boulevard Saint-Michel. The memory of the past few years, where he'd been able to pursue pleasures in thumping dens filled with torsos shining psychedelic bright, made him shift uncomfortably in his seat.

He automatically rubbed his knees, still indented from years of pretending to pray on cold stone as a child, but that only served to remind him of everything that he wanted to eradicate. The scars of that school had forever marked him. They thought it would release the devil, iron out his strong will and make him a man. His mouth curled upwards in a near imperceptible show of triumph. Let us see who has won the battle! He'd learned a thing or two, oh yes.

The taxi rounded the corner into Larke Avenue, passing manicured box hedges and came to a halt outside the wrought-iron gate. From here he could just make out the rust-stained roof of the old man's cottage next door. He straightened his back, sniffed and contemplated why the old coot had left it to him.

Ronan could see himself as a child, there on the pavement, surrounded by a massacre of sunflower heads. He could remember how good it felt, lopping their heads off and how he'd laughed up at the crinkle-cut face of the old man. Yet the old man's watery eyes had reflected something other than anger. He remembered how a giant wave of unfairness had washed over him. Why hadn't the old man screamed like his father did?

Now he knew. It had taken years to figure it out – years of having to live with the devil inside him, of enduring the pain of having its gaseous form clogging his lungs. Relief, that's what he'd seen in the old man's eyes.

'Wait a moment,' he said to the driver, before exiting the taxi and pressing a button on the wall next to the gate.

'Is that you Ronan?' said a wary male voice.

'Let me in,' he replied, his grin incongruous to the coldness of his tone.

The gate slid back against the wall and the taxi edged into the driveway. Beyond the white roses, he could see them clutching hold of each other on the sandstone steps. The taxi pulled up beside them. They were clearly trying to stand united, to look like they were in control, yet beyond his father's perfect pin-striped Italian suit and his mother's bobbed hair, he could tell, their fake smiles were set in drawn and pallid faces.

He stepped out of the taxi and filled his nostrils with their cornered animal fear.

He felt the Captain inside him restless, pushing up against every crevasse of his body, making it hard to breathe. Soon he would strike fear into their hearts and no amount of praying was going to help.

CHAPTER 10

Smoke and Mirrors

Hobart, April 2009

Ronan eased the ruby-red Maserati into his usual port-side lot. He sat for a moment, content to watch cloud vapours sweep the Derwent River's surface. The phenomena known as the Bridgewater Jerry forewarned of a deep chill beyond the Maserati's warm interior. He flicked his eyes across to the long merino scarf and an exquisite, wrapped package lying atop the passenger seat.

He rubbed his clipped to perfection whiskers, incredulous at his good fortune. He'd cornered her at last. As if sensing victory, the Captain flexed his power, pushing up against the inside of Ronan's throat. 'It is soon my Lord', Ronan gasped, tilting his head back against the car seat. 'Just a few', he sucked in air 'more days.'

Ronan stepped out of the vehicle, breathed in the Antarctic air and willed oxygen to find any pockets of space in his lungs. Leaning against the drivers' side door for support, he gasped like a trout caught in a net. 'How can I set you free my Lord if you do not help me', Ronan muttered. 'Give me time.' The Captain obliged, retreating into the dark recesses of Ronan's body.

Able to breathe again, Ronan flung the merino scarf around his neck and began the two-minute walk towards the historic sandstone façade of his office. He passed by a tangle of masts and decks piled high with craypots before turning his back to the port.

As usual, the sight of the black cast iron blubber pot at the entrance to the office caused a quicksilver thrill to rush through his veins. How many of his clients had chosen to ignore it in their haste to sign their lives away?

Ronan clasped hold of the antique wrought-iron doorknob and hauled open the heavy timber door. He took a couple of steps across the original 1800s oak floor to stand beneath the glow of the crystal chandelier. 'Tom – I'm here!' He glared at the black painted door behind the desk and took a seat on the leather chesterfield.

While his foot tapped with impatience, he thought of the hopeful who would shuffle in the door in less than an hour. Like thousands before, they would breathe in the quiet opulence. This was the place to project themselves from their impoverished lives. The trustworthy looking man in the round spectacles told them so. All they had to do was sign up to the good life.

The sound of nervous breathlessness filled the foyer. Ronan jerked his head up to see Tom's hand sweep across the billiard ball smoothness of his scalp before adjusting his glasses.

'Um – I've got the editorials all here,' said Tom, holding up a briefcase. 'Shall we walk across to the pier for coffee?'

'Just make it quick,' huffed Ronan. He could feel the Captain press against the inside of his throat again. *Soon my Lord – Delia would soon prove her worth then you can feed on her power. Be patient.*

'Did you see yesterday's editorial in *The Australian*? Tom's breath billowed into the freezing air, while he tried to keep up with Ronan's stride. 'The world economy, it's all going to collapse.'

They entered the warm cocoon of a café and took a seat next to the plate glass.

'... global downturn in investment.' Ronan stared with disinterest at the view beyond the glass. He scanned the deck of the *Lady Nelson* and the parade of ruddy faces and puffer jackets scurrying by until his eyes rested on a man sitting on the edge of the dock. He felt a prickle of knowing. He narrowed his eyes to focus on the hooded face beneath a billow of chain-smoker haze.

'That's him isn't it?' Tom said, following Ronan's gaze. 'See, he's wearing a ripped jacket, like you said.'

Ronan drove a death-stare through the plate glass. '*Oui*, I think so.'

'What are you going to do? I mean you can't have him following ...'

'Are you in for breakfast or coffee?' interrupted a waitress.

'I'll have a black coffee and Tom here will have a cappuccino.' Ronan wondered why someone with a face so pale would wear black lipstick before turning his attention to Tom's billiard head creased with worry lines.

'Tom, you worry too much. And I can tell by the redness of your nose – you are drinking too much whisky. It is pulsating, a beacon of stress. Whisky and wine, it is your downfall.'

'Well one of us has to worry!' Tom started rifling through papers in his briefcase.

Ronan placed a hand over Tom's 'Let me save you the effort and I'll deal with people like him,' he motioned to the man outside 'in my own time. Now, you are about to tell me of repercussions of the Lehmann Bros collapse, the repeat of the 1997 fall in the Dow Jones industrial average ...'

'Listen,' he sighed. 'Where do the unemployed go? Do they not beat a path to our door? And what does that mean?' he stared into Tom's bloodshot eyes. 'It means that we divert pensions, earn commissions – you know all this. Why worry?' He raised quizzical eyebrows at Tom and added 'just keep doing what you are doing. Make it sound like we care, sign them up for ten years and ...'

'Oh my goodness ... fancy meeting you here!' Ronan jerked his head to see a vision of sapphire blue polyester active wear bearing down upon him.

'Oh it's just so amazing to see you here ... just such a coincidence!' the bottle-blonde gushed.

She stood at the table and unzipped her stretched tight tracksuit top to reveal breasts which were straining to burst from their push-up bra cage.

Ronan swallowed his groan and smiled through gritted teeth. '*Bonjour ma chérie*!' he managed. He noticed the deep heave of breasts, the brightness of her emerald eyes, the way her never-done-a-days-work soft hands fluttered up to her hair. Now he understood. All those mornings she happened to be beside her letterbox, waving good morning with the enthusiasm of a cheerleader. In a moment of brilliance, he exclaimed 'why don't you join us?'

'Oh I couldn't possibly ....'

'*Oui*, come sit. My meeting with Tom is *finis*.' Ronan smirked in the direction of Tom's incredulous eyes.

'Well, if that's okay?'

Ronan patted the empty seat beside him and waited while she crossed her legs and leaned forward to emphasise her cleavage. 'Can I have a cappuccino please?' she called to the black-lipped waitress.

'Now that's settled ... I would like to introduce you to my Director, Tom. Tom, this is my neighbour ....' he hesitated. 'I am so sorry, after all these years, I do not know your name. We met once, it was so long ago, but ... I do know that wave and special smile.' They held eye contact while laughing at his little joke.

'Narelle – my name is Narelle.'

The grating Australian twang assaulted his ears. 'Narelle – ah, such a beautiful name.'

Narelle's face flushed 'and you, I know, are Sir Ronan St James,' she said, all a fluster. 'Yes, when we met, I remember thinking you were in the movie business,' she giggled, 'but I know from the news, that you are quite a celebrity educator.'

She stopped for a moment while the waitress delivered her cappuccino before once again launching into her animated speech. 'My, you were only in *The Mercury* just the other day, pictured with the Premier, talking about how you educate the unemployed – such a kind man.'

Ronan forced himself to look away from the close proximity of tightly harnessed flesh to chocolate covered froth and smirked at Tom. 'Ah yes, kind. That's me, isn't it Tom.'

'Always so welcoming to the unemployed,' Tom said in a dull tone.

'Oh my, look at the time!' Ronan exclaimed. He rose to leave and motioned for Tom to do the same while watching Narelle's brow crease with disappointment. In an effort to seal a future deal, he captured her fluttering hand. She squeaked an almost imperceptible sound at his touch. He made sure that his bulbous thumb pressed long and hard into her flesh, while all the time never breaking eye contact.

'Ah *ma chérie* ... it is time for us to go.' He grazed her hand with his lips, dragging them slow and tantalizing along her sickening rose smelling skin and forced himself to look deep into her yearning eyes. 'Perhaps we can continue our conversation; say this time next week?' Before she could utter a response, he pushed his chair aside, gave her one last appreciative gaze and walked towards the counter.

'What the hell?' Tom's bald head bobbed beside him. 'God it's not like you could possibly be interested. Those breasts ... you'd see them from the moon! Why bother? Wrong age, wrong ....' His words withered and died beneath Ronan's glare.

'I have my reasons!' he hissed as he thrust the bill in Tom's direction. 'I'll see you next week.'

Ronan pressed the long merino scarf close to his neck and marched back into the frigid air. From this side of the pier he could see tourists standing on the *Emmalisa*'s bow, clutching at their jackets, looking in wonder up at the bright orange hull of the icebreaker, the *Aurora Australis*.

He contemplated this new turn of events as he walked back to the Maserati. How had he not thought to commandeer her house before? It made perfect sense.

By the time Ronan arrived at the Maserati, Narelle's house was long demolished. In his mind's eye he could envision a series of pavilions leading across the three- block monolith that would soon become his new home.

He revved the engine with thoughts of Delia's bloody artwork lining the walls of his future palace while he would be free, far from the Captain's clutches.

CHAPTER 11

Divine Nature's Destiny

Hobart, late April 2009

Vague muffled voices and scattered images like macabre puzzle pieces, floated to Delia in broken segments of time. Everything was hazy. The threads of reality had come undone and she was peering through holes into a parallel universe.

Her throbbing cheek and the concrete under it seemed her only reference points.

Turning her eyes upwards, she saw that she was lying on the floor beneath the dining table. Scanning her body, she wished for the blessed blackness again.

The inside of her throat was on fire, like it had been scraped red raw, while her left hip pulsed in pain. She felt splayed out, like a human swastika, her right arm pinned beneath her body. In the strange green light she could make out Ronan's highly polished shoes pacing the floor in front of her.

'You're going to have to swallow it, Simon. We have talked about this. I warned you.'

A dark shape moved to block out the green light. The thought of it, the spectre, or evil spirit or whatever it was made her head buzz. *Don't breathe, don't scream* she told herself as its smoky tentacles licked the underside of the table before moving out of view.

'I can't let it inside me! Don't make me!' Simon's voice sounded frantic, all his bravado gone, replaced by some squeaky replica of his former self.

'Listen ... my dear Simon.' Delia heard Ronan's voice take on an affectionate, softer tone. 'Do this for me, for us. Once the Captain gets what he wants, he will leave us alone. We can be together in peace, just you and me. It is what we have been building up to. Once he has her power ...' he trailed off.

'But look at her! You've seen what happens. I don't want no green mould all over my skin. And that thing you have in you. It makes you gag. I can't do it! I'm not fuckin' doin' it, alright?'

Delia heard Simon gasp and saw his runners scuff the concrete.

'Fuckin' let go of me!'

'We can do this the easy way or the hard way, Simon. Sit there and do as I say!'

From her position on the floor, Delia could see Simon's body squirming on a chair beyond the table.

'There's got to be another way,' he gasped. 'Can't you swallow it?' She watched his leg start to spasm.

They've forgotten you. The thought swept into her mind and shone like a brilliant diamond. She tried to think beyond pain and their voices. What was the best route: through the back door or through the kitchen? The kitchen was closer to where she lay but all the lights were on and what if it was locked? She made a first tentative movement, releasing her arm from beneath her body. Only their yells covered the sound of her agonized moan.

'You expect me to have both of them? I am getting angry now, Simon. How do you expect me to breathe? *Tu es ridicule!*'

She slowly pushed herself up on to her left arm, the movement causing tears to spill down her cheeks. Still she pushed on, adjusting her thudding hip and legs beneath her, to hunch cat-like beneath the table. Tears dripped on-to the concrete and she bit her quivering lip, waiting for another bout of yelling.

'The Captain's getting restless, Simon – *être rapide*!'

The fury and urgency in Ronan's voice made her shake even more. She watched Simon's leg shake uncontrollably. 'Get him away from me!'

'Don't worry about him! He's more interested in licking at her power. Now, bend your neck back Simon!' There was a garbled cry that quickly escalated, giving her an opportunity to shift from beneath the table and crawl towards the living room. *Don't look back, keep your head down, keep going.*

'Hold still, Simon! It will be easier if you just hold still!'

She started to crawl towards the living room, with her mind set on the passageway ahead. It was a longer route but with the lights off, she might just make it.

Yet, the fierceness of Ronan's commands and the agony of Simon's tormented cries, made her steal a look backwards. She blinked, refocused, unable to comprehend what she was looking at. For a moment, the pain in her body ebbed away as she took in the beauty of an alien crystal floating above Simon's face. Green and purple amethyst with bubbles of gold, shining so bright, that it cast an aurora-like light across their faces.

It was wondrous, magical. It conveyed something pure, like the forged light of angels. How could such a thing be shining in this evil house? All the pain flooded back, and in a moment of clarity, she knew this was somehow what they had dragged from her very own body.

How could she have suffered all those years with something so beautiful inside her? Shouldn't she have felt the green glow shining through the cracks of her being, under the weight all that grief and loneliness? Her heart squeezed with loss and desperation to get it back. But getting this light, this orb, or crystal, whatever it was back was impossible.

The flickering rainbow light played on Simon's upturned face. She could see his eyes, wide and panicked, as Ronan held him down. 'Simon, open your mouth! Do as I say!'

The thought of that malevolent spirit, that thing with the cruel slit of a mouth, touching her precious orb filled her with rage. Yet what could her broken body do? She cringed against the wall as Ronan placed one hand on Simon's forehead while the other grabbed hold of his ragged beard.

'Right, I can see I will have to force you!'

The evil and madness in the room pushed Delia onwards. She navigated her painful limbs bit by bit down the step into the living room and started to crawl along the polished concrete. *Keep going* she told herself. *Keep aiming for the deck door.*

The living room floor felt never-ending but finally she reached the parquetry flooring of the passageway. In the gloom, it stretched out before her like a long, dark sea. Her mind started to flicker in and out of consciousness, but in her lucid seconds she recognised the break in the skirting board represented Ronan's bedroom doorway.

Keep going, you're half-way there. Yet the floor tilted into the wall and only the sound of Simon's strange guttural cry jolted her back to the present. She managed to haul the jagged pieces of her body forward again, using the skirting board as a guide, before teetering against her own bedroom door.

'*Magnifique*, Simon! You see, it was not so bad!'

She saw the door to the back deck, floating like a portal to another world while the surety of her bedroom door was right at her side. Escape through the portal seemed impossible now – all she needed to do was curl up and allow the darkness to block everything out. She slumped against the bedroom door, drifting in a fuzzy, far-off place.

'Delia, come here, my little star. Where have you gone?"

The sound of Ronan's maniacal voice was like a slap in the face. *What else was he going to do?* Her primal need to flee ignited her body into action, moving her beyond the wretched pain in her hip.

'Now, now, you cannot hide. There's nowhere to go, my Delia.' He flicked the lounge room and passageway lights on, capturing her body in a freeze-frame beside her door.

The horror of his gaze launched her upwards to grapple with the doorknob.

'Delia!' He was striding down the passageway now.

She used her last ounce of energy to scramble inside the room, slamming the door behind her and sliding the lock into place.

The doorknob turned from the other side. 'Delia! I am not happy, Delia! You will come out and paint for me, you hear?'

But the darkness had already closed in around her.

* * *

Delia awoke on her bedroom floor. A gnawing emptiness was eating at her insides while her shell of a body throbbed from having crashed onto the concrete floor of the dining room.

The knocking sound was back again. Hadn't she heard that noise hours ago? Now it was more insistent, but she ignored it just the same.

A grey void had consumed her for God knows how long. She hadn't minded floating there, beyond the reach of reality. The realm of her dad; she thought she'd seen him, walked with him maybe. But now she was back. She lay there, trying to think, but it was impossible. She felt soulless, lost. They'd done that to her – extracted her very essence.

Unable to cope with the crushing truth any longer, she half rolled, half dragged her body into the ensuite and curled up on the shower floor. The hot water flowed over her throbbing hip and broken heart, but nothing was ever going to make her feel human again.

Finally dragging herself out, she pulled a towel around her torso and looked in the mirror. No wonder her cheek throbbed so much. Her swollen cheek, the bruise that spanned her right eye-socket, the cut on her brow-line, told the story of her smash into the dining room floor. Yet, the damage was nothing compared to her throat. She trailed her fingers along the skin, perplexed. It looked so odd without the green stain. Only yesterday, the blotch had flushed brighter and wider. Now her skin was pure, just like she'd always wanted. She slumped to the floor and sobbed.

Now she understood: painting had brought her alive again and her light or essence whatever it was, had shone even brighter from within. She had been at her happiest, her most creative, free. And they'd ripped it all away.

She jumped as a new knocking started at the door.

'Delia, it's Simon. Please, let me help you. He's not here.'

She bore laser beams of hatred into the door and crawled from the bathroom into bed.

'Delia, come on. You've been in your room for ages now. I'm worried. You haven't eaten. Let me in.'

Well, that wasn't going to happen. The thought of her beautiful, shining orb floating inside his vile body was more that she could stand. She pulled the doona over her head and cried herself to sleep.

Almost at once she was back in the void. She was giggling, skipping behind her dad. He beckoned for her to follow, to keep moving towards a golden light up ahead. As they turned a corner, she took hold of his hand and together they stared up in wonder at the millions of golden balls of light hanging in the sky. Their energy felt good, and she went to smile at her dad, but he was gone.

She tried to hang on-to his memory, to the surety of his hand. She wanted to stay like that forever, but even now the threads of him were drifting away to somewhere in her sub-conscious.

'Delia!' Simon's voice interrupted her thoughts.

'Look, I know you don't trust me or nothin' but you gotta eat. So I'm gunna leave this food at your door, okay? It's just a sandwich and a coffee.'

Coffee. Now that he'd said that she wanted it. The lure of it got her out of bed and dragging her heavy, aching body to the door. She listened. Nothing. Why was he being so nice? It sounded like a trick. Still unsure, she quietly slid the lock back and opened the door a crack. Just as he said, on the floor were the coffee and a sandwich on a tray.

The passageway was empty. Yet she could still see herself huddled on the floor and Ronan striding towards her. She snatched the tray, slammed and locked the door. It might look peaceful out there but she knew evil plied that passageway. The spectre was out there, somewhere.

She looked at the coffee with suspicion, took a tentative sip and waited for a moment. *Why would he be so nice?*

The steam rising from the black liquid made her think about the smoky fingers of the spirit, how its tentacles had filtered under the table then drifted back up to lick at her beautiful, bright orb. She could feel its malignant force crushed inside her mouth, scraping the inside of her throat. She snapped herself back to the present, willed her hand to stop shaking and brought the mug to her lips.

Then it dawned on her. Simon had acted through generosity. She let the dark liquid slide down her aching throat and contemplated this revelation.

Did she really trust her intuition? What was the evidence? *He's lost his bravado* she thought. He's got a newfound compassion and all that's happened since ingesting her orb. She stared and stared at the door, trying to wrangle her scattered thoughts into a plan.

Take a risk, win back your orb, spoke her more courageous self. She thought of fighting off all those schoolyard bullies, the one's that had pointed and jeered at her neck. *I'm weaker now*. She scanned her body and tried to picture herself sliding back the bolt on the door again. If she did that, Ronan would have access too.

She stared at the door, weighing up her options. Should she stay or should she fight? Finally, the thought of leading an empty life, always craving for her essence, forced her to down the last of the coffee, drag her aching body to the door and slide open the bolt.

CHAPTER 12

Full Moon Rising

Delia yearned to stay in the place of her dreams, in the realm of a million golden balls of light, but the sound of Simon's footsteps wrenched her back to reality.

She used all her strength to pull herself up to a sitting position. *Keep nurturing him, just like you've been doing* she told herself.

She beckoned for him to come closer. He put the tray down and like all the other days before, took hold of his own mug and sat on the edge of the bed. She went to reach for the tray but jerked her head towards the sound of footsteps in the passageway. Her heart froze. She cast a panicked look between Simon and the bathroom door, knowing already she was too weak to run. Ronan's rigid, straight-backed form appeared at the door.

'Ah my two favourite people,' he said, stroking his whiskered covered chin. 'So good you are getting along. I trust you are gaining your strength *ma chérie*. Perhaps you have even started to draw?' he nodded towards the sketchpad lying on the bedside table next to her photos. 'Not well enough yet?' he said not waiting for an answer. It is good I am such a patient man, *non*?' He turned on his heel, leaving Delia shaken and breathless.

'You'll feel better if you drink your coffee,' offered Simon. 'Look, all you gotta do is draw for him.' He reached forward and patted her on the shoulder. 'It's not that bad. Livin' here, painting every day,' he shrugged.

Their eyes met and a silent knowing passed between them – both broken, shells of their former selves.

She shook her head, blinked back tears and tried to stick to the plan of getting close enough to him to somehow extract her orb. 'I can tell by your eyes Simon. It's worse today isn't it?'

He squirmed, made an odd, muffled sound and refused to look her in the eye. She took a gulp of coffee and placed the mug on top of the sketchpad. 'Let me look, Simon. I know how it feels. Perhaps I can help?'

'There's nothin' you can do. Nothin'. I can't stop cryin'.' His voice came from the bottom of the well of misery, cracked, torn, forsaken.

'Let me look,' she whispered again.

After a moment he undid the buttons on his flannel chequered shirt and bared his neck. She studied the green track marks, like a network of fine veins creeping towards his jaw. Red welts made the abstract patchwork looked raw and angry. The skin above his collarbone was the worst, where the network had joined together to form a blotch of green, scaly skin.

She knew how it felt to run her fingers over the scaly surface and feel sheer revulsion. Only when she was a small child did she ever feel normal. Her neck was where her mum and dad kissed her goodnight. Didn't every little girl have a lizard neck like hers?

She squeezed her eyes shut to blank out the image of the wreckage just outside the old farm gates. *What a cruel world she'd had to navigate since their deaths* she thought. All those adoptive parents whispering in corners. Their hushed tones always pre-empted her next move. How dare they feign compassion, take her home, make her change her name all the time. Yes, she knew what it was like to be treated like an alien, even in what was supposed to be your own home.

She relegated the images of pious, smug faces to the dark recesses of her sub-conscious and focused her attention back on Simon.

His voice shook with anguish. 'He's a bully, makin' me do this ... thing.' She recognised the way he swept his hand up to his throat. He'd mastered the technique already, the flutter of a frightened butterfly about to be squashed by pointing fingers and unforgiving faces.

She reached out to him. They swayed together for a moment on the edge of the bed, his scrappy beard nestled in her dull pink hair. Her orb was close, shining bright from within his scrawny neck. *Perhaps I can take it somehow by force?* Like a baby bird flying into a window, the absurd thought collapsed in a heap of broken wings. Her body was a mess, weakened, hollow and empty. No, she'd have to find another way.

'Why do you stay then?' she soothed.

He sniffed and dragged the back of his hand over his wet face and moved back on the bed. 'I dunno. At first it was like …,' he trailed off, picking the ragged edges of a thumbnail. 'I impressed him, I really did. I blew him away with my art so much that he tracked me down. Reckoned my art had a 'raw honesty,' that's what he said, an embedded truth that he'd only ever seen once before. My style showed how truth …'

'Can tear at tender hearts,' she said. She met his startled glance but motioned for him to continue.

'Yeah, that's right. But it wasn't just *Ache*. Livin' in this house, close to the Captain, I mean, you've seen it for yourself.' His eyes lit up for just a moment, before adding 'it's inspirational for my style of art.'

'What the hell is it Simon?' she said in just above a whisper. She felt her skin crawl at the thought of its smoky tentacles reaching down her throat.

'Fuckin' scary, eh. Ghost of a sea captain, apparently lived with Ronan since he was a boy. I mean …' His eyes glazed over. He looked out the window, caught in a memory before adding 'I was like you the first time. Fuckin' traumatised, that's what I was. But, I've got used to it, sort of and it's got used to me.' His face brightened, 'And through my paintings, Ronan figured out how to get rid of it.' He tugged at a piece of skin before moving from his bleeding thumbnail to the next finger. 'So I've painted and painted. Ronan reckoned it was the good life havin' me around, paintin' for him, fillin' the walls with my art, scheming about our next move.'

Delia saw a reflection of her ashen face in the gilded mirror. The thought of all that blood-dripping art filling the living room made her stomach churn. Beyond her revulsion, she managed to muster 'so there's a plan to get rid of it?'

'Yeah, he needed to track you down. I mean I was fuckin' annoyed, takin' down all my work like that, but yeah I see now. So, yeah I know he's a bully and all, but I stay cos things'll get better. A few more days and I should be rid of your thing in me, get rid of the Captain and then it'll just be us. He's promised.'

Delia tried to discern the range of emotion that drifted across his face but all she could do was pull the doona up to beneath her chin in a show of self-protection. She felt her heart fill with molten lead. 'What do you mean? What about me?' she managed to stammer.

'Look's like he'll keep you on. For some reason he loves your art even more than mine.' He rolled his eyes then brightened and added 'means more time for us though. And don't worry, being his artistic slave. Best thing that ever happened to me. You'll be able to paint and paint, just like you've always wanted. You better get drawin' though' he nodded towards the sketchpad.

Delia gulped 'and the Captain?'

'Gunna get rid of it by the full moon. Can't wait to get this green shit out of me. Anyway, thanks for the chat. Maybe it'll be good to have you around after all.' He sniffed, dragged his nose along the cuff of his shirt and rose to walk towards the door.

The way he looked at her just then, that glint in his eye, was the old Simon, simmering under the surface. He was in there alright, just waiting for the darkness to deliver him back.

Delia wanted to yell, scream, throw the tray at his back. She loathed every particle of his being. What were they going to do with her pure, shining essence? Were they going to kill it?

She couldn't smother the whimper that escaped from her mouth as he pulled the door closed behind him.

* * *

That afternoon, Delia staggered back from the bathroom, kicked the offensive sketchpad aside and crawled back into bed. She bit her nails and willed her hollow body to stop shaking but the sketchpad lying there on the floor just made her feel sick.

Thoughts swooped like eagle talons. The inane pencil marks scarring the pages of the sketchpad spoke of the awful truth. They'd kill her. She was sure of it.

Her hand fluttered to her throat out of habit, settled there and willed for her orb to be back inside her. She needed it like air. All those years of not wanting her lizard neck and not painting, only to realise that now her orb was gone, so was her skill. How could she have taken it all for granted, thinking her talent was of her own doing?

Now it was clear there was no surviving without it and the thought of her beautiful orb inside that man's neck was more than she could stand. She pictured the orb's luminous form suppressed by arrogance and darkness, crying to get out, smothered by evil and her heart squeezed in agony. There was no hope of taking it back by force. While Simon gained strength she had faded, hovering between worlds, moving like a skeleton in the shadows of reality.

She thought about pushing her body out of bed, pictured herself crossing the deck, moving down the back steps, to where? How could she live without her orb, without ever being capable of painting ever again and feeling like this weakened version of herself?

She closed her eyes and tried to think but was soon lured by the realm of dreams. In her fantasy world, golden balls of light drifted down to hover next to her, like a circle of protective friends. Why leave this beautiful space, where she felt buoyant, calm? *Because you have to fight!* The words flew like javelins, piercing her dream, shaking her back to reality.

Think, god-damn it! Judging by what he'd said, she had maybe two days at best before the full moon to do something. Through a veil of tears, she stared at the tray by her side. What if she could convince him to bring her something more than coffee? Before the thought was even fully formed, she found herself yelling. 'Simon!'

His distinctive steps clomped along the parquetry flooring in the passageway and the door eased open. 'Did you want something, Delia?'

"Um, I've been thinking to get my strength back, I need to stop having nightmares. Do you think you could get me some sleeping pills?'

He hovered in the doorway and pulled at his beard, then shrugged. 'Yeah, s'pose so.' He pulled the door closed again.

The thought of what she'd have to do next, made Delia's stomach churn. But, she'd do whatever it took to get her essence and her energy back.

*   *   *

The familiar steps and sharp knock in the passageway pulled Delia from sleep. She blinked against the sudden brightness of the light being switched on.

'Rise and shine! Oh you look like shit.' Simon stood grinning in the doorway. 'Now, now, no need to get upset. You should see yourself!'

'Yeah, well, more nightmares ...' Her words fell away. *Something's changed – he's more assured.*

He set a tray down and nodded at the packet of pills next to a bowl full of noodles, a bottle of water and a glass of wine. 'Don't take 'em all at once, hey?'

She averted her eyes from his lopsided grin and wild eyes and focused instead on the scene through the window of a full silver moon above the far hills.

'How's the drawin' going?'

As he reached out she snatched the sketchbook away and shoved it under the covers. 'Not yet!' she cried, then added 'I wasn't in the mood. The nightmares, they make me too tired.'

He shrugged, walked to the window as if mesmerized by the rising moon and said 'His highness has run out of patience you know.'

'What do you mean by that?' She watched his waxen reflection in the window and longed to smash him, pin him down and take back what was rightly hers.

'Just sayin', you're gonna have to get 'in the mood' and pretty quick.'

A silent scream squeezed at her throat. Without her orb, her very essence, her talent was non-existent. Panicked, she reached for the wineglass on the tray, wanting to guzzle its contents but her fingertips brushed the packet of pills. Her panicked heart filled with knowing. It was now or never. She slipped the box beneath the doona and coughed to mask the crackle of the packaging.

'Simon, you know I'm too sick!' she cursed how pathetic she sounded. She made sure he was still transfixed upon the moon before dropping a pill into the wine.

'Simon. Can we talk, artist to artist?' she cajoled. 'Come and sit with me,' she held out the glass. 'At least tell me, as an artist, what you would do if you were me.'

When he turned around, she noticed how he seemed caught somewhere between anxiety and commitment to an inevitable, unstoppable force. He accepted the glass pushed into his hand before jerking his head towards the sound of footsteps in the passageway.

'Simon, come! It's time!' Ronan barked. His statuesque, rigid form cast a shadow into the room. 'You'll have a ringside view tonight *ma chérie*,' he cooed in an eerie tone, before retreating down the passageway.

Delia's heart felt like it would split in two. Simon set down the glass and grinned. 'Gotta go – time to get this filth out of me.'

'Simon, wait, I need you're help! What if I can't?' The words escaped from her lips and dangled in the room like a carcass above a crocodile-infested waterhole.

'Look,' he pushed his lank hair back 'I'd be getting' my act together pretty quick. He's not someone you want to disappoint. Anyway, gotta go! Gotta date with the dead!' He wheeled away in hot pursuit of Ronan, leaving his maniacal laughter to echo around the room.

CHAPTER 13

Demons in the Deep

The river looked a vision of peace beneath a large silver moon, high in the night sky. She'd kept vigil at the window for hours now, waiting in the darkness of her room for whatever the witching-hour would bring.

Her old self could have captured the ink and shimmer on canvas. All those wasted years, when she could have channelled her talent into beautiful landscapes, gone. *They'd done this!* She bit her lip in despair and contemplated the weight of her heart, full of lead.

She squinted. Was that torch-light, there, at the shoreline? A flash of light illuminated a man rowing a dinghy just offshore.

Now's my chance! The thought bubbled up, shocking in its abruptness. Her heart jumped a little at the prospect that she might still save herself. She pictured herself staggering up the driveway and going through the gates, yet she made no effort to move from the window. *What was the point?* The sketchbook proved that her great artistic talent was dead. Without that magical power or essence or whatever it was she'd been born with, she was doomed to forever lurch through life like a zombie, weak and unfulfilled.

She clutched at her throat, feeling helpless, watching her very reason for living being rowed to where – to its death? In that moment, she felt the threads of the beauty that had once resided inside her, plead for help across the moonlit water.

Her body responded in an instant. Without thinking, she jumped up, grabbed her old polar fleece jacket and stumbled out to the back deck.

The fierce winter chill and sudden exertion made her chest heave, forcing clouds of stale breath into the bitter night.

Two beams of light flashed between the dinghy and the shore. For an instant torchlight captured the man on shore, tall, straight-backed, rigid.

Delia watched the man she presumed was Simon, stop rowing. *Now what?* The cold air tightened around her while her fate hung in the balance above the infinite black of the Derwent.

She imagined herself running, swimming, catching him off guard, all fleeting, all useless. Look how fragile she was, trembling, a bony, breathless vision of her former self. Instead, she looked to the heavens, the Milky Way and gods. The astounding stillness and beauty of the night sky stared back at her. The stars had never seemed so close and so bright.

'God, please help me!' The words started out a whisper. 'You, or someone deemed from birth that I should carry this power, this essence through my life. As the chosen one, I'm begging for help! Please, I think they're going to kill it and I need it back! I promise to be true to it and never ignore it again ...'

Her words trailed to a whimper. Something was out there. A shadow flashed through the torchlight. There it was again! Whatever it was circled like a buzzard. Suddenly she understood. The enormity of what she was looking at made her stomach feel leaden. The spirit of the old sea captain was out there, willing her pure and precious power to die.

She held a palm against her heart to stop it from splitting in two and gasped. Simon must have fallen forward in the dinghy and dropped the torch. For a split second, she caught sight of a strange green haze surrounding his body. A high-pitched, primordial scream splintered the night air and in an instant, the green haze disappeared from sight.

Panicked, Delia swept her eyes across the pitch-black water and back to the huddled form of the man in the dinghy. Already her mind was filled with images of her luminous orb drifting down to settle in the silt and seaweed of the riverbed. It had taken only a few seconds, but she somehow knew that the death of her sacred orb, her power, her reason for living, would mar her for eternity.

Delia wiped her tear-filled eyes and squinted at the spot where the edge of night and river merged with the silver ripples of moonlight. *Was she seeing things?* Just in that one spot. There, the water seemed to glow with the light of an underwater aurora. She forgot to breathe, as the water shimmered purple and bright green, the colours deepening with intensity with every passing second.

Staggered that her essence had somehow floated, even somehow expanded, forced a wolf-like howl to erupt from her raw throat. As if in answer to her call, the underwater aurora intensified to wide bands of exquisite turquoise and jade. She pleaded with every cell of her body for this majestic, wondrous being of energy and light to burst through the surface of water and somehow make its way back to its rightful place, inside her body.

A yell from the foreshore interrupted her prayers. *What was Ronan doing pacing up and down the beach?* He yelled something, but it was Simon's victorious sounding hoot in reply that smothered her senses in suspicion.

She looked towards where they were both shining torch light. The skin of the river burst open in an explosion of iridescent spray. Delia's mouth dropped open, as the hump of something ancient erupted from the water. *What the ...?* Torchlight captured water cascading off what looked like an ancient body which appeared to groan to life.

She rubbed her face, doubting the optical illusion. Yet before her eyes, a three-headed alien being seemed to shake, teeter sideways and right itself. Beneath the torchlight and the light cast by the silver moon, she caught sight of a dolphin freeze-framed in a mid-air leap. Within moments, the prehistoric being, or whatever it was, floated off beyond the torchlight into the darkness.

She scanned the darkness for any sign of the being or what was left of her essence. Only the distant sound of Ronan and Simon calling to each other filled the night air.

She dragged her eyes to the dinghy floating in the moonlight and groaned at the sight of Simon. He stood with his arms outstretched like Christ the Redeemer. A buzzard-like shadow swooped through the moonlight, circling Simon's heroic stance. The flash, fleeting but deadly, made her shiver. The Captain's evil was still out there. *What evil had they done at his beckoning?*

Simon's deranged words came into her mind, in a sudden electrifying moment of clarity: *'gotta date with the dead!'* What the hell had they raised? Whatever was out there felt depraved and it had taken her essence with it.

A fast-approaching bank of light caught her eye. It approached at an odd angle, sweeping in from the stars. Delia clutched hold of the railing for support. She cocked her head, unable to decide if it was the approach of many helicopters or some sort of optical illusion. Had the evil playing out on the water somehow unhinged her mind?

Then the quiet hit her. She heard Ronan cry from the shore, then nothing. Only the sound of lapping water reached her ears. She had to let go of the railing to shield her eyes from the brightness. It seemed edgeless but in the blink of an eye, it was gone. She jolted backwards in shock and stared and stared at the space where the great luminosity had been only a millisecond before.

A magnetic force started to pull at her body. It made her snatch at the railing again in panic. Instinct told her to look to the sky where a vast cluster of cloud now blocked out the silver moon.

'You are not alone.' The words echoed inside her head.

She felt a sudden strange compulsion to reach out to hold her dad's hand. *Was it her Dad?* For a fraction of a second she remembered the bright golden light of her dreams and the comfort of holding his hand.

'Who are you?' She looked to the cloud formation for answers and looked down, only to see the deck was now a tiny dot, far, far below her feet.

How had she floated up so high? Had she died of shock and simply entered the light? Here, in this place, she felt timeless. She could drift forever in this golden, gaseous tunnel. Shielded from evil, held aloft in levitation by a magnificent source of truth and love, she had never felt such utter peace.

'*We heard your prayer and we are here to help you, your grace.*'

The voice, neither male nor female, resounded inside her head. She tried to ask who they were, but already the answers to that question and others formed in her mind.

'*The Light of Truth, to protect your essence from being used against the laws of nature,*' said the voice.

'They've stolen it from me – I couldn't stop them!'

The sphere flushed pink at the outburst before returning to tranquil gold. '*You cannot fight him alone. This time we have traveled a great distance to help you.*'

'But why now?'

'*We are always with you, your grace, but you closed your heart to us long ago. To connect with you, we had to turn to your parents for help.*'

'My parents?' Delia felt herself falter.

'*Yes, they are with us.*'

Waves of compassion caressed her body. '*There is no time to see them. We must protect your essence, your grace.*' The voice was crystal-clear, empathetic yet commanding.

'But you must let me see them! Mum, Dad, where are you?' The sphere wall pulsed bright red at her screech. They must be behind there somewhere, but no sooner had she thought to try to move to begin searching, an invisible force exerted its pressure on her body. Unable to struggle or break free, she had no choice but to remain still.

The sphere's wall returned to gold. Her body floated on a wave of loving kindness. Suspended in space she witnessed the horror unfolding below. The entity illuminated the scene of a jade mist hanging amidst the ragged edges of an old vessel. *That's what she'd glimpsed?* The mythical beings' multiple heads revealed itself as masts and struts of an ancient ship, streaming with seaweed and broken rigging. There – the static dolphin, just a figurehead. Dark shapes staggered on deck. A humanoid figure lurched towards a section of jade mist and snatched at it as if in a feeding frenzy.

'*See what they are doing,*' boomed the voice.

'But, it can't be?' Ghosts dragged from the riverbed. It was unthinkable, some aberration of reality.

'This is our last chance to save your essence, your grace.'

In an instant she felt the frost-bitten wooden paling of the deck underneath her. She staggered to her feet, strained her eyes in the darkness. Flashes, like fireflies, were her only clue that a supernatural battle was playing out before her.

She felt her heart bursting. She had allies. They'd been with her all along. All those years of loneliness, of feeling abandoned, bullied. Tears rolled down her cheek. Why hadn't she heard them? How did she not feel their existence?

She swept her eyes from the torchlight moving on the edge of the shore, to where shouts emanated from the direction of the dinghy. A beam of light flashed on to a section of deck, extinguished in a second, under impenetrable blackness.

Went the hell was going on out there? A piercing screech, like a witch on the wind, made the hair on the back of her neck stand on end. She heard Simon's yell, a splash, followed by the sound of frantic thrashing in the frigid river.

Had that been a cry of defeat? She strained with all her might to see the firefly flicker of battle but the darkness refused to give up its secrets. How she craved to feel whole again, to hug her parents, be free of this nightmare.

'Did you save it? Is it over?' she called, frowning at the silver moon.

A knife-blade of panic stabbed her in the gut. *Where was the cloud? Why could she see Simon rowing back to shore?*

She felt the back of her neck prickle. A feeling of doom made her turn. There in the distance, high above the hills, was a bank of luminous, edgeless light. In a flash, the light elevated at a rapid pace and vanished. 'No – come back!' she cried.

Delia crumpled to her knees on the deck in shock. *Where was her essence now? Where were her parents?* She'd been on the brink of victory. *Hadn't she?*

A hand, large and possessive, clamped tight on to her shoulder. She unleashed a piercing scream into the freezing night air.

'I see you have powerful allies, Delia, but they have abandoned you.' His speech was controlled fury.

'They'll be back!' she spat.

'I think we both know that's not true, Delia.'

She glared at him, but the feeling of doom in her heart meant the effort only made him sneer.

'Get inside!' His grip tightened around her birdlike shoulders. Beneath his clutches she staggered forward over the threshold of the deck door and braced for impact. Pain ignited through her forehead and right shoulder blade like red hot pokers. Instinct told her to curl into a foetal position yet her body remained motionless, splayed out across the passageway.

'The Captain will make you pay! I will make you pay! He was to resurrect his crew, to sail away, leave me be. Now look what you've done!'

In her peripheral vision she saw pieces of lime-green seaweed attached to a black polished shoe. *Look unconscious. Stay alert.*

She felt the toe of his shoe prod at her body but still she remained a static, misshapen heap. He growled something in French before striding towards his room.

Wait. Be patient. Remain still. Stay alert.

The voice in her mind was neither male nor female. Could she dare to think that her allies, the great light or higher beings, were still with her? Their meteoric elevation to the stars made her think, *why did you abandon me*? Her silent plea would surely be heard across space, if they were listening.

Seconds passed. A heavy, aching loneliness kept her body pinned to the floor before her jarred body, racked with pain, felt the embrace of an ageless, loving entity.

Strange – she felt herself sprawled on the floor but also hovering above her body. Looking down, she could see a symbol being pressed into her forehead, the spiral impression searing her skin like melted wax. She could feel the symbol moving like an energetic force through her skull, making her scalp tingle before settling where her essence once resided. From above her body, she could see energy rippling outward, like heat waves. They encircled her physical body inside a protective cocoon.

In a flash, she realised Ronan was nearly upon her. Without being impeded by the spirit of the Captain, he seemed younger, more agile. She disengaged her mind from the vision and fully re-entered her physical body, still thudding with pain. She had just enough time to clamp her eyes shut and centre herself in her silent charade.

Murderous thoughts smothered her mind, yet even with his breath now on her face, she lay still, unresponsive.

'Now my Delia, you're not going anywhere, are you?' If you are listening, remember this: you are weak and alone. You will stay here while I rescue Simon and yes, when I return, you will pay the price.'

She heard his shoes scuff the passageway, cross the wooden palings of the deck and descend the back stairs. Only then did she scramble to her feet, rub her forehead and aching shoulder blade and slip into the night.

CHAPTER 14

Spectres At Dawn

Orange sparks drifted like fireflies into the pre-dawn light. Delia stood on the back deck, transfixed for a moment by the sight of the bonfire on the shore. *Was that a dark figure there, moving behind the flames?* A shower of sparks obscured her view while thick waves of something mystical swept around her body.

'*Come warm yourself.*' The bonfire hissed and crackled. '*Just follow you heart – come closer.*'

She held a palm over her aching forehead and rubbed at the pain radiating through her shoulder blade while her body descended a couple of stairs, drawn towards warmth and comfort.

Blood pounded behind her ears. *Was that Ronan down there?* Her mind flooded with images of him helping warm a half-awakened river creature or burning evidence of its existence. The vision of its flesh melting like wax made her stomach squeeze in revulsion. Alert to danger, she pushed her pained body down the stairs, shaking with effort at every step.

She staggered across the paved patio and found her way to the convict brick boundary wall. The height of the wall mocked her, looming tall and mighty above her head.

Was there no way out? Should she follow the wall down to the bottom of the garden, to the wrought-iron fence? How could she think straight through panic and this new incessant heaviness?

'*Come quickly, soothe your troubled soul.*' The firelight at the shoreline pulled at her body like a magnet.

Beckoned by an invisible force, her feet crunched with purpose over the gravel path towards the bonfire's brilliance. Another shower of orange sparks beyond the wrought-iron fence welcomed for her to come closer.

Whisperings of an incantation, strange and ancient words that connected the afterlife with the now, reached her ears. She halted at the garden shed next to the fence, feeling the warmth of the blaze on her freezing face. Words from another time wormed their way into her heart and soul. For a moment, her breathing eased, until Ronan's voice drifted to her from the direction of the shore.

'Enough is enough!'

In an instant, the energy that had held her entranced, evaporated. The invisible cloak of magic swept away across the river, leaving her exposed and alone. Incredulous at her own stupidity, exposed and close to Ronan, she cringed against the old wooden palings of the shed and strained to hear beyond the crackle of burning logs.

Footsteps crunched over the pebble-strewn shore and a torch illuminated a section of spearhead fence to her left.

'It is all we can do, my lord. Let me get back to the house. *Sacré bleu!*' From her vantage point she could see the beam of light waving along the fence-line. Every few seconds Ronan yelled expletives. He rattled the wrought-iron fence before moving on to the next section.

He's agitated, losing control.

Ronan staggered forwards, the torch extinguished in an instant. Another burst of French expletives punched through the darkness before a haphazard beam of light waved in her direction. She slammed her body backwards.

Something whooshed past her head in the darkness. The thing flashed, swift, bat-like over the bushes next to the gravel path.

A tidal wave of panic ripped through her body. There it was again – barely discernible, in her peripheral vision, swooping, sniffing out its prey. She gagged at the thought of the spectre, the thing, slithering over her tongue, squeezing out her air, scraping the insides of her throat.

With fingers trembling, she ripped off the polar fleece jacket, smothered the sound of the bolt being slid back and slipped inside the shed. Pitch-black descended the moment she quietly pulled back the old wooden door. Entombed, she strained her senses, beyond the smell of mould and dust and salty air. *Don't move – listen, feel.* Her eyesight adjusted a little, allowing her to discern dark shapes in the cluttered shed. Firelight flickered like a long-lost friend through a gap in the palings. The bonfire, the shore, it was so tantalisingly close from where she sat in the gloom.

The dull clank of a metal gate and crunch of footsteps on the gravel path outside made her eyes bulge with fear. Footsteps stopped somewhere outside. Torchlight flickered under the wooden door.

'Let me go to the house! Enough!'

Agonising seconds crept by as she cringed, waited.

'Let me help you, my darling!'

Delia gulped back bile.

'I nearly fuckin' drowned!' Simon surrendered to a series of hacking coughs.

'I know my brave one. Let me help you.'

Delia heard another staccato coughing fit. Even from inside the shed, she could tell Simon was milking his new martyr role for all it was worth.

The footsteps moved further away, their voices grew distant. The shed returned to its former inky blackness except for the gap in the palings, revealing orange flames beyond. The crackling bonfire, the sound of gentle waves on the shore, worked to slow her breathing.

In a habit of a lifetime, she fluttered a shaking hand up to her throat. The indiscernible evil energy that had clung to the darkness, smashed her backwards in an instant. Already it was cloying, pushing up against her mouth, hunting for any last semblance of essence.

She flailed at the force sweeping around her head and felt her body smash up against what felt like a heavy, steel trunk. The Captain swooped from nowhere, slamming into her windpipe. *Air! I need air!*

In a flash, the spiral symbol erupted in her mind. With her last vestiges of strength, she forced the image of the spiral into her consciousness. If she must die, at least the gift from the Light of Truth, the higher beings whoever they were, would be her last thought. The grip on her neck seemed to release a little. She gulped in a breath and traced the symbol again in her mind.

Was that a growl or the wind? She sucked in another precious gulp of air and traced the symbol again and again. The symbol cast power from her third eye, causing waves of protective energy to surround her physical form.

I am protected – I am not alone.

A deep, guttural growl filled the space, the sound of a devil dog, beaten in a brawl. Its sickening menace retreated under the door. Only the sound of waves splashing on rock and wood burning on the shore remained.

Delia sat shivering in the shed, her back up against what felt like a trunk, hugging her knees. Minutes passed. She scanned her pain-racked body, listening, praying.

What was that? She smothered a scream at the sound of footsteps on the rocks outside. *Had Ronan doubled back?* Pebbles crunched underfoot.

'Miss? You okay?'

Delia quivered, shell-shocked at the sound of another man's voice. It took a few seconds to drag herself back from utter desolation and suspicion. 'Who … who are you?' she called through the gap in the palings. The firelight still flickered out there, beckoning like an old friend.

'There's no time – he's gonna find you missin' any minute. You gotta get out quick! See, I'll push this torch through to you. There must be somethin' in there to use to break a hole in these old palings? If you break through, you'll be out here on the shore – you'll be free.'

Torchlight suddenly illuminated the chaos of the shed, dazzling her senses. The beam of light wavered in the space between them, revealing stacks of pots piled on top of old steel shelving.

Delia eased her battered body off the floor, scrambled past the steel trunk and weaved her hand between the pots to take the torch from a bear-paw of a hand. Their fingers brushed together for an instant causing an electrical charge to surge through her body.

She waved the torch back and forth across the jumbled mess. 'Did you light the bonfire?' The words slipped out, inexplicably.

'I tried to show you the way out, eh.'

It was hard to see through tear-filled eyes. Silhouettes loomed in the torchlight – an upturned wheelbarrow, a forest of chair legs.

'But how did you ...'

'Quick, he's lightin' up the house! He's lookin' for you, for sure.'

His words were laced with fear and urgency, making her swing the torch in a rapid haphazard arc.

'There's a spade here!'

'Good, now clear the stuff away from the wall and smash it against those palings. They're old – they're gonna give way.'

She snatched up the spade and scrambled back to the small opening.

'I can see him marchin' around the living room ... there he is, at the windows. He's got the place lit up like a casino. You're gonna have to be quick!'

Frantic now, she swiped away the clutter. A clay pot careered onto the floor and shattered at her feet but she was beyond caring. *You need to get out – move*! Her brain clanged an alert.

She positioned the torch on the steel shelving, gritted her teeth and swung the spade. A satisfying splintering sound made her bash it again into the weathered wood.

'Stop! I'll try to open the gap this side.'

She saw his large hand snatch at the splintered wood, pulling away large sections. The space widened and the red glow of the fire beyond the shed looked larger, brighter.

'Just give it one last go, then you should be able to crawl through. Both of 'em are in the living room now, they'll be out 'ere any minute ...!'

With one last almighty heave of the spade, the lowest section of palings broke away. She flung the spade aside, got down on all fours and squeezed through the hole. 'I can't get my shoulders through,' she gasped.

Warm breath brushed against her cheek. Large hands tightened beneath her armpits and in one last heave she felt herself being hoisted upwards. Her head fell against a large chest while strong arms worked to support her weight.

The crackling bonfire and a swirl of wood smoke spoke of freedom. Why had she tried to avoid coming to the flames? It felt primal, like a long-lost friend. She blanked out for a moment, caught in the euphoria of relief until a thought spiraled through the fog of her consciousness. You avoided the flames because it's a trick!

Her eyes flew open wide. *Who was this holding her – a half-awakened river creature?* She wriggled out of his grasp and fell with a thud onto the pebbles next to a large burning branch. In a reflex action, she rolled away from the radiant heat and scrambled to get up, slipping on seaweed instead.

Landing on her back, she caught sight of him for the first time. In the flickering light of the fire she saw a colossus hovering above her. She struggled to comprehend and shuffled backwards in panic, ignoring the sharp edges of barnacles and broken shells beneath her palms. What stood before her was an affront to her senses.

The whites of his eyes stared back from a face obscured by a hood. Dark hair frothed, scarecrow-like around where his face should be. Fuzzy-white woolly innards spewed from a puffer jacket and something bulky, hung from his waist. From her position lying on the rocks, he looked like an ominous effigy, some sort of shadow man.

Where's his face? I can't see it! Frantic now, she staggered upwards and turned to flee, but he already had her in his grasp. A large palm stifled her scream and pushed her back down on to the pebbles.

'You crazy woman! I'm tryin' to help you, eh?' he hissed.

She gasped at the sight of his face in the firelight and instinctively recoiled. Still he held on tight, pushing his blackened lips and the shocking, swirling pattern that lined his cheeks close enough to scare her into silence.

'Shhh!'

Delia squirmed in panic but knew it was futile.

'I don't mean to frighten you, eh? You're not going to scream are you?' he whispered.

Delia found the courage to follow the arrowhead lines stretching from his temples to the corners of his eyes. His eyes, she noticed in the flickering light, conveyed a kaleidoscope of emotion. They beseeched her to be quiet. The spectre of some sort of shared grief hovered between them for a second before she nodded in agreement, that yes, she would be quiet. At least she knew now that he was no more river creature than she was. Still, her instinct told her to be careful.

He jerked his head towards the house. 'Quick, the lights are on outside now. We've gotta get further away.'

'But where ...?'

'Dinghy ... up ahead.'

Without giving her a chance to reply, Delia felt her shattered body lift upwards. Once again she found her head resting on his large chest. With the bonfire at their back, the darkness closed in around them. She felt his rasping breath on her face and felt him stumble but still he held her tight.

'Delia!' Ronan's roar punched through the darkness. 'I will find you – you cannot escape!'

'This is it,' he rasped, breathless from the effort. She felt herself gently placed in a patch of long grass and found the side of an upturned dinghy to lean against.

'Here, this will keep you warm.' He unlooped the bulky folds from his waist and placed what felt like a blanket around her bony shoulders. The smell of cut grass, dank earth and something indistinguishable, like a wet dog smell, assaulted her nostrils but already she felt warmer.

A light breeze skimmed the surface of the river, bringing the distant sound of Ronan's fury. 'Delia!'

Delia settled further beneath the blanket. 'Why are you helping me?' she said to the shape sitting next to her in the gloom.

'He's a lying, conning Pākehā that's why. I've been following him for a while now. Trying to work out my next move,' he hissed.

She leaned away from the wall of hostility to her right and wondered if he would lash out. Still, curiosity forced words to tumble over her quivering lips 'You know him?'

'Yeah, I know him,' he snarled. 'Said he'd get me a job and I'd be earning the big bucks. Destined for movie roles eh – that's what he said. But it was all just a big con. He just gets you to sign up, then bam ...' His words hung heavy, cracked and raw in the space between them.

She looked towards the faint yellow glow shrouding the hills to the east. 'But I don't understand. What happens when you sign up?'

'Then he's got you by the balls. My pension got siphoned straight into his account. There's no job. There's nothin' – just cold hard nights livin' out here.'

'But he can't do that! Why don't you go to the police or someone?' Delia felt a wave of pity wash through her.

'Who are you kiddin'? He's schmoozed everyone, conned everyone. Slimy Frenchman.'

'That's only the half of it ...' she said so softly he didn't hear.

'Then I knew. He'd conned you too. The way you screamed at the sky, stood there in the rain. I knew you were in pain then.' He rubbed his forehead, as if to erase the pain of his existence.

'You see', he continued, 'Spirit is teachin' me things. Things like helpin' you and forgiveness.' He stumbled over the words and sighed. 'Helpin' you was easy. Forgiveness though – it's a bitter pill. I'm still learnin', eh.

'How can you possibly forgive all that's he done,' she spat. Surely, they'd marred her for life. Maybe, if she was lucky, the nightmare would seep into the recesses of time. Forgiveness, though; that was impossible. The depth of hatred boiling inside her told her so.

In the first light of dawn, she saw hate flash across his obsidian eyes. He crushed bubbles of seaweed with his shoe before continuing. 'Spirit and my ancestors are my guides. I can feel them stretching their arms across the Pacific, all the way from Rotorua. As long as I feel their presence, as long as nature is my home, I can cope ...'

They sat in silence, allowing a vortex of secrets and grief to swirl around them. 'But how can you possibly cope?'

The furrows in his brow deepened. His shoulders sagged downwards in defeat.

'I'm everywhere – nowhere. I know a few warm places and being close to nature helps.' 'Thinkin' about Rotorua. That helps me cope.' He threw his arms to the heavens, as if appealing for divine intervention.

Delia diverted her eyes to the orange burst of sunlight above the hills in the distance. The glow signaled a new beginning.

For the first time in what seemed like an eternity, the hint of a smile glanced across her face. 'Thank you for getting me out, helping me. I couldn't have done it without you.' She placed her hand on his shoulder for a second. The heavy ink-lines were clear now. She wondered how many people bothered to overcome their prejudice and look beyond the surface of his skin. For there, beyond the stark emptiness, were flecks of wisdom, perhaps even pride, from long ago.

She stood up and pushed the blanket into a blue-black tattooed hand. 'Take care – I hope you can go back to Rotorua – one day,' she said in the barest of whispers.

She pulled her eyes from the intensity of his gaze and started to edge away as fast as her pained body would allow.

'Best go round that way, avoid the house, eh.'

Delia's feet struggled to keep up with the demands of her frantic mind. She felt the black eyes of the tattooed stranger boring into her back, half willing her to stay, half cheering her on to a new life.

CHAPTER 15

Lost Fortune

Delia pushed her aching body to navigate the slime-covered rocks hugging the shoreline. Even beneath a pink-streaked sky, she could feel the tentacles of evil lick at her back. Onwards she staggered, past the dilapidated pier, rounding the corner into a cove she did not know. Pushed beyond her physical limits, her breath came rapid and ragged. Still she aimed for a boat-ramp ahead. *Keep walking.* She repeated the mantra in her head. Where was she going? Only her feet knew the way.

She made it up the ramp, onto the road and passed white picket fences and sculptured hedges. Shapes slipstreamed past her peripheral vision. *Should she rest in someone's garden? Where was Ronan? Was he out looking for her, hunting her down?*

Frantic thoughts pushed her still further on past the whitewashed walls of the *Shipwright's Arms* into a park. Old oaks stretched their naked Autumn branches towards her. She dropped onto the cold earth at the base of a gnarled tree to rest.

You're not in your room. You're not in that house. You're free! Waves of relief washed through her, working to soothe her soul, steady her breathing. Her eyelids fluttered and grew heavy. She drifted in a haze, vaguely aware she'd collapsed at the base of the oak tree.

Dampness creeping into her jeans pushed her to wake up. If only she could stay here. She needed to feel the strength of the oak. She ached for someone to help, but the puffer-jacket parade of distant beings slid by, oblivious to her pain. She yearned for her parents. What would they have told her to do?

In a split second, the harshness of reality, of what she'd done, caused her to clamber back from her half unconscious state.

The weight of loss crashed down upon her. All her treasured photos on the bedside table, her mother's exquisite heirloom necklace left next to the basin in the bathroom. She tried to picture her future without her prized possessions. Never again would she see the only photos in existence of her parents. Never again would she feel the surety of the turquoise stone necklace around her neck.

Her mind raced across the desert of her grief, scavenging some vestiges of hope but losses were at every turn. *'Golden Grasses of Home'* came to life and waved their goodbye. She pictured herself floating in the darkness, at the edge of the *'Sea of Tranquillity'*. There was her battered old brown case stuffed under the bed. Her wallet, ID, the few remaining dollars – all left behind.

What the hell was she to do? Who could she turn to? She scoured the wasteland of her life, hunting for someone, anyone. There was no-one, except ...

She felt her body change, fear subsiding a little. She dragged her aching body upright and took a step towards the City Police Station but memory of the tattooed man's words made her lean against the tree instead. *'He's schmoozed everyone, conned everyone.'* How could she explain that the man pictured with the Premier had held her captive? Who would believe that an evil spirit lived inside him and plied the passageway of his home?

She slumped back down to the earth and tried to think beyond panic and cold. Where was she to go?

He protected you once. He'll protect you again. He's survived cold and being alone. He'll show you the way.

The man with no name was her only answer. With the decision made, Delia began the walk back the way she came, passing a troupe of morning walkers. She reached the boat-ramp, swayed and squinted to focus on the never-ending shore before her. It stretched for eternity. Somewhere around that corner, far, far away was the man with no name. She sat on the concrete ramp, contemplating him. *Who was he?* A shadowman; a lost soul?

Cracked, breathless words landed like an arrow into the centre of her back.

'At last, I've found you!'

Run! Delia tried to obey her instinct but fatigue rendered her body unresponsive. She whipped her head around, to see a strange, robed figure standing behind her. The woman looked part grey nomad, part mad conductor, the way she waved her walking stick in the air.

Delia noticed a long grey braid poking from beneath a bright red beanie. The braid snaked down over the hand-knitted shawl covering her chest. Even from where Delia sat, she could discern a life-force in the woman's eyes that refused the concept of mortality. Her chin, poking above wool, spoke of defiance more than defeat, or perhaps it was a will to walk a life-path on her own terms.

'There you are!' The woman wiped a watery eye with the back of a gnarled hand, a smile crinkling her crepe-like skin. 'My, my, you really are in a bit of a state, aren't you? It is as I thought. My Queen of Cups has been in terrible danger! Every night ...'

Delia staggered to her feet. The woman was obviously caught in some delusion. In frustration, she managed to push words through her strained throat. 'What did you call me?'

The woman's eyes stared deep into Delia's. 'How about you come with me dear? The woman turned and commenced her shuffle back up the road.

An image of Ronan's imperious face flashed through Delia's consciousness. The ground shifted a little, or was it time sliding sideways? She could crumble under the weight of it all right now, just lie her exhausted body down on the ramp.

The woman turned and cast Delia a quizzical look. 'Well, come on dear. I didn't break my meditation for nothing. My Higher Self told me you were here. It's never wrong!' She dipped her chin. 'The Universe is watching, dear. I'm your only choice,' she said in a cracked voice.

Delia sighed with defeat and forced her weak legs to catch-up.

The woman tapped a sun-spotted hand on Delia's shoulder. 'You've been through hell, I know. I've felt your presence, near, crying at night.'

Delia felt as if her heart might lift out of her chest. The words were enough for her heart to know; someone cared. Her eyes pricked with tears as she stepped slowly alongside the woman.

'What's you name dear? I only know you as the Queen of Cups, or the pink-haired goddess of my dreams.' Her eyes flicked over Delia's faded tresses. 'Well, maybe pink once, as you will be again.'

Delia flattened a hand over her scalp. God, she must look a sight. The woman's words, both odd and kind, hung in the air between them. 'Delia,' she near whispered.

'Good to meet you at last, Delia. Your name suits you well.'

Delia found herself being drawn close. Who was holding who, it was hard to tell. They trudged breathlessly up the incline and turned into Larke Avenue.

'I can't ...'

'Don't worry dear. Although I live opposite that awful man,' she pointed towards the golden Buddha sitting atop a letterbox 'I'll protect you.'

'How do you know about ...' Delia tried to find the words but her throat refused to work. How could she ever voice what she had endured?

'I know many things, my dear one. You first appeared as the Queen of Cups months ago. I sensed your deep connection to the earth and the sea. Then there was a shift. You moved through the Five of Pentacles, lost and alone. You thought you'd found kindness, there.' She pointed her stick towards Ronan's wrought-iron fence. 'I have so worried for you. That place ... it makes me shiver. There's something there that's not ... right. Like a rift in energy, where the darkness has forced its way in.'

'I don't even know your name,' Delia managed to croak.

The woman's eyes glowed and the crinkly laugh lines deepened. 'I'm Athena, dear. Now, we both need a good strong coffee.'

CHAPTER 16

Call of a Wild Spirited Place

Hobart, June 2009

Delia studied the fire willing the flaming logs to burn out the sickening slideshow coursing through her mind. In a show of compassion, the cat next to her rumbled deep, comforting purrs. It circled the cushion, nuzzled a grey-felt ear against Delia's hand before slumping back in the same position.

'Perhaps you might put one more log on, dear – that should do us for the night. It's so lovely to have you here to help, you know. My back is not what it used to be and look how much Tarot loves your company.'

Delia swivelled on the floor at Athena's feet. Looking up at the mane of grey hair, Delia felt like a vulnerable cub under the protection of the wisest lioness. What secrets of a life well-lived lay beneath the surface of the time-beaten face? Athena appeared part guardian, part gypsy, part angel-in-waiting, walking a tight-rope between the physical and spirit worlds.

Delia slid over to place another log in the firebox, slamming the door shut on plumes of smoke escaping into the room. She stared at the tentacles of smoke licking the glass and bit her trembling lip.

'Are you okay, dear?'

'I'm fine, just ... a memory.' Delia picked up her wineglass and gulped. The dark cherry and spice slid down her throat, drowning any remnants of the Captain's vaporous fingers. She resumed her position on the floor and focused on the yellow-tipped flames grazing the top of the firebox. Ronan's ice blue eyes stared back at her. She pushed the image down into the volcano-red embers. Burn in hell!

'You're not fine, dear – look at you, you're shaking! I know you're not ready to speak to the police, but you could tell me ...'

Delia maintained her focus on the flames and muttered, 'I need time. I can't ...' She turned to look up at the woman's troubled face and raised her glass. 'Anyway, cheers to you, Athena, for helping me, for feeding me. You've made me feel half human again.'

'Good to see you smiling, dear. It won't be long until you've recovered all your strength.'

Delia averted her watery eyes. She needed to scream into the flames 'No! She'd never regain her full strength!' In silent fury, she touched her bare neck, willing her fingertips to feel traces of green, scaly skin and the smooth surface of the heirloom turquoise stone.

Where was the stone now? Where was the faded photo of her dad, flannel shirt rolled up at the sleeves, his big arms wrapped around her? Was it still next to the bed? Or was it forever lost, like yesterday's garbage, or in Ronan's bedroom, locked away like some despicable trophy?

A new feeling, beyond hatred, shifted in the pit of her stomach, working its way up through her veins and around her heart. She searched the flames for answers and found herself back at the bonfire, looking into the courageous face of the man with no name. The 'shadowman' as she'd come to think of him.

Athena's cracked voice broke through her thoughts. 'Shall we try that guided meditation again, dear. It might calm you. Or shall I just leave you to your thoughts?'

'I think I'll just enjoy the fire tonight, Athena. Thank you anyway. Sorry.'

'Now don't you worry. Tomorrow's a new day, and I think I know just the thing to lift your spirits!'

Delia moved to the high-backed leather chair opposite the fireplace. The peace of the room settled around her like a comforting blanket.

Everything felt so right, so balanced here, a far cry from the starkness of Ronan's mansion.

Thousands of books graced the opposite wall, the centre of Athena's universe. Only yesterday she had scanned the volumes on natural medicine, healing and meditation and by chance had found a book on tribal wisdom. There in the pages were drawings of Māori warriors with thick spiral tattoos lining their noble faces. Sacred '*tā moko*' lines, she'd read.

She gazed again at the flames. She couldn't stay here forever. Where to go to truly feel free? Was 'free' somewhere wild and faraway? She pictured herself high up on the snowline of a distant mountain, the wind tangling her hair. '*Nature is my home*'. The shadowman's words spoke to her heart.

The yellow-tipped flames morphed into the grasses of home, waving in the breeze. Yes, she needed a wild-spirited place, far away, where she could feel the majesty of the earth like she did when she was a child. Yet how could she live and breathe anywhere on earth, knowing that Ronan held everything precious hostage? How could she rise above the ashes of herself to find a new place to be reborn?

Her eyelids grew heavy, her head slumped backwards. For a moment she watched shapes dancing on the ceiling in time with the firelight. A ship mast and hunched figures collided into the shape of daggers and arrowheads as swirling *tā moko* lines lifted off the ceiling. They spiralled towards her, glancing off her forehead and settled around her as her eyes closed.

*   *   *

The taxi eased down Athena's driveway past clumps of verdant bamboo. Bracing for what lay ahead, Delia reached across the back seat to find Athena's hand. Once again she marvelled at Athena's vitality pulsing through paper-thin skin. She closed her eyes to erase the image of Ronan's estate in her mind, but the blackness just turned her thoughts inwards, to the last time she was in a taxi, driving towards the 'good life'.

'Don't you worry, dear – soon you'll be bright and full of smiles.'

Delia glanced down at the sun-spotted hand resting in hers and wondered how that could be possible.

The taxi slowed and came to a halt. 'The hairdresser is just through there,' Athena said, pointing to one of the historic sandstone warehouses. 'I'll be back to pick you up in two hours. It's all paid for – just sit back and enjoy the pamper, dear.'

'You're the grandmother I never had, Athena! I have to say, it will be amazing to get my colour back.'

Delia crossed the wide Salamanca pavement, navigating around a cluster of tourists, and opened the salon door. When the young brunette at reception jerked her head a little in shock, Delia glanced into the opulent mirror on the opposite wall. It reflected a gaunt woman, cheeks flushed pink matching the remnants of the dye that clung to limp hair.

For a second, she thought to retreat. Only Athena's disappointment pushed her forwards towards the front desk. 'Um, I have an appointment … for a colour,' she managed.

The woman patted her Audrey Hepburn do and raised a perfectly plucked eyebrow. 'Of course, come through.'

Delia followed the designer boots and sat as indicated in front of a mirror, staring into her own dull eyes. The hairdresser frowned as she picked up a clump of lifeless hair.

'Um, I've been … out of town,' Delia muttered.

She draped a cape over Delia's shoulders then stopped to scrutinise her in the mirror, cocking her head to one side. 'You're not one of those greenies from the Weld Valley or the Tarkine, are you?' The woman's eyebrows remained arched.

'I didn't want to say…'

'Oh wow!' she gushed. 'I think you're so courageous. All that clear-felling is just a travesty! I wish I had the nerve to do what you do. But it's the thought of living without all those things like, how do you cope without a proper loo? And the leeches, no way could I deal with those. Ew!' She screwed up her nose before adopting a professional stance.

'So, the same watermelon pink again? So feminine, and so radical! You'll look a million dollars when we're finished.'

Delia relaxed into the moment watching in the mirror as she mixed the dye.

'Fun fact,' the stylist said, glancing up. 'Carmine is made from insects that live in cacti!'

Delia raised her eyebrows in surprise.

'I know – amazing, right? You would think that if I can mix insects and lather that in people's hair then I could cope with the leeches, but,' she sighed, 'then I'd miss Friday night drinks with the girls. So, I reckon a hothouse and a bunch of cacti is about as close as I'm gonna get to nature!'

Delia studied her reflection as the thrill of an idea rippled through her body. The hairdresser's words flowed over her while visions of her next move formed in her mind.

Delia departed the salon with hair as vibrant as a champagne cocktail at sunset. She strode towards the waiting taxi, beaming with newfound confidence into strangers' faces. The shattered forsaken soul of just two hours ago had been washed down the basin. She felt like a parakeet spreading its wings, about to launch itself from the canopy and fly high over the jungle of life.

'Oh, my dear, look at you!' Athena called through the taxi window. 'Simply stunning! You wait until my friend Giovanni sees you, dear. You'll make his eyes boggle – especially when you put this on!'

'What have you done, Athena!' Delia climbed into the taxi and looked from Athena's shining eyes to the glossy bag with black satin handles.

'Just a little something, dear. And anyway, my friend is used to sharing the stage with stars, so today, you shall be the one to shine! She chortled to herself for a moment, before addressing the taxi driver. 'To Larke Avenue, please.'

Delia pushed her hand into the bag and pulled out the most exquisite jacket she'd ever seen. She pressed a fold of luxurious fawn-coloured wool against her cheek and turned her face away to study the river slipping past the window. She noticed the white caps pushing south towards the place where her possessions lay. *He thinks he's won.* The quiet fury sitting in her throat, close to where her essence once resided, swelled with indignation. *Tomorrow – I'll fix it tomorrow.*

'So,' she focused back on Athena's eyes, full of warmth and humour, 'now I know what you've been up to while I was getting pampered.'

'Oh, I'm full of surprises, dear,' she replied, her sparkling life-force gleaming with extra vigour.

Within minutes the taxi turned back into Larke Avenue. This time she forced herself to look as the taxi cruised past Ronan's wrought-iron fence, imagining how she could turn her hatred into something useful.

The taxi continued up the street and stopped where the bare branches of elm trees poked above a tall, rendered wall. The taxi driver grinned at the tip Athena left in his palm before driving off, leaving them standing outside a high steel gate. Delia peered through the gate, glimpsing the river, while Athena used her walking stick to punch the intercom button on the wall.

A tinny voice replied, 'Yes?'

'Gio. It's Athena! I have a surprise for you!'

'*Buongiorno*, Thenie! Ah, between you and Musetta, there's no peace!' he chuckled. 'Wait a minute, while I open the gate.'

Athena tapped her walking stick impatiently.

'So, that's the 'famous' Giovanni!' Delia giggled.

'He's very nice dear, you'll like him.' The electronic gate clanked into life. As she pushed through the half-open gate, Delia saw the young girl Athena used to be. The arched back and the walking stick fell away and in her mind she saw Athena running down the crushed gravel driveway towards the charismatic man on the other side of the intercom.

Delia examined the bare-branched elm trees inside the walled garden. They stood like naked sentries, resolute, in the chilly June air. Beyond the driveway stood a historic-looking sandstone home, with an iron roof, wide verandah and intricate wrought-iron balustrades.

An older gentleman appeared from the side, wearing grey overalls and carrying garden shears. 'Thenie – so good to see you!' Then he stopped dead in his tracks, blinked and brushed a floppy white fringe out of his eyes. He had a kind, animated face with crisscross laugh and brow lines, all moving in time to a range of expressions that formed and fell away.

'*Bella*! Athena, you have found her! She exists!' He flicked his eyes to Athena in surprise.

Delia felt her mouth stretching upwards in response. How odd she was still able to smile. His strange reaction was so welcoming, warm and genuine. His thick bushy brows worked up and down in time with his sparkling green-grey eyes. He put the shears down and, before Delia could stop him, hugged her warmly.

'*Buongiorno, bella*. I'm Giovanni,' he cooed. 'Thenie! So, this is the woman of your visions.' He stood back and assessed her. 'My, my, you remind me of a young Mirella Freni,' he said a soft tone. 'Look at the cheekbones, the expressive eyes. Ah, can you imagine? Mirella was there at La Scala with Pavarotti, one of the finest times of my life ...'

Giovanni gazed into the distance until the sound of a revving car brought him back to the present. He jerked his head back towards a car reversing out of a garage beside the house. He motioned for them to step aside for the polished silver Mercedes.

The car idled beside him and Delia caught sight of teased blonde hair, heavy makeup and a fur coat.

'You will never get your jobs done if you just stand around chit-chatting!'

'Yes, yes, my sweet,' replied Giovanni.

The woman humphed, flicked judgmental eyes over Athena and Delia and recommended a rapid reverse up the driveway without a goodbye.

'Apologies, my wife, she is ...' he sighed deeply, 'still in mourning.'

'Oh, I'm sorry,' offered Delia.

'No, no,' he waved expressive hands in her direction, 'she only suffers now that I am no longer conductor at La Scala. The grand opening nights, the magnificence ... it is all gone.' He rolled his eyes. 'Plus, like you, she had an unfortunate run-in with him ...' Giovanni cocked his head and motioned down the street.

Delia felt the blood drain from her face.

'Gio! We don't need to talk about ... that man!' cried Athena. 'Look you've upset her now!'

'I'm sorry *bella*. I'm so glad to hear you are staying with Thenie here, instead of living with ... how shall I say it?'

'The devil,' Delia offered in just above a whisper.

Delia shifted under the weight of Giovanni's stare. 'Yes, I fear that is exactly what he is.' He rubbed his chin and narrowed his eyes.

'Now, now Gio, look how cold she is. Come on, dear, let's go inside. It's no time to gossip out here.'

'Yes, of course. Come, have tea in the atrium *bella*. Now, Thenie tells me how she's been teaching you meditation and that you've been a great help around the house. Wonderful for her to have company, I worry. That is my job, I worry!' He threw his hands up in the air, before linking an arm with Delia. 'For Thenie, the oceans, the planet – you name it, I worry!'

Delia heard a giggle erupt from the depths of her being. How could she hold on to thoughts of Ronan's magnetic aqua eyes and the evil that dwelled within him, when she walked in the glow of this man's energy and warmth.

Athena called over her shoulder 'You're walking too slow, even for me! I'm going inside!'

'Just treat the place like it's your own!' yelled Giovanni, winking in Delia's direction.

'So, Athena said you were conductor for the Tasmanian Symphony Orchestra,' said Delia softly.

'That's right. I left La Scala, came to Tasmania and yes, for a while worked with the Symphony Orchestra. Now ...' he looked at her with eyes shining as excited as a schoolboy, 'I have embarked upon the most important phase of my life. Not that Musetta thinks my venture is worthy,' he rolled his eyes, 'but, conservationists across the world thankfully do.'

'Anything to protect the environment is worthy ... whatever you are doing I'm sure is perfect.'

'Thank you *bella*. You and Thenie can be champions for my cause! Now in you come out of the cold.'

He ushered her up the stone steps, across a wooden verandah and into a long hallway. She passed by an exquisite collection of jade and bronze whale sculptures and tribal faces carved in stone and followed him into a glass-covered atrium.

'I see you're in my chair Thenie!' He swept his arms into the air again, gesturing to the river flowing beyond the glass. 'Spread out like a queen!'

'At last you recognise me for the woman I am!' she retorted.

Delia smiled at their affectionate repartee, took a seat on a cream-coloured leather sofa and became mesmerised by the water; bevelled glass, the colour of night. It sucked at her, tempting her to capture its shades and moods on canvas.

Giovanni came and stood beside her. 'You look suddenly sad *bella*.'

Delia inhaled deeply and dragged her eyes from the view of the river to look at their worried expressions. Her story burst to be told. Yet how could she tell them?

'It's so beautiful here. I feel the water more. Even more than from his place ...'

Silence descended, only the sound of seabirds and the waves on the shore could be heard above her thumping heart.

'What to do you mean, *bella*?'

'Do you want to talk about it, dear? You've said so little, I've been so worried,' said Athena. 'All I know is that you lived with him for a short time, and every time you think of him you tremble. See, like now.'

'Um,' Delia rubbed her face, willing herself to not break down and cry. 'He took so much ... I was an artist and he's taken that ...' She felt her throat tighten and bit into her thumbnail. 'There's no words to describe ...' She slumped, with her head in her hands.

'Oh dear! We didn't mean to upset you. We just want you to know that we're here for you, and as I've said, we could go to the police, whatever you want to do.' Athena tut-tutted, delved into her bag to extract a tissue, and leaned over to Delia. 'Here, use this, dear.'

'Bella,' Giovanni crouched down beside her. 'Listen, to me,' he said softly. 'If you were an artist once, you will be again. You will know in your heart when the time is right to create once again. As a conductor, I know these things,' he said with eyes full of understanding and compassion.

'Thank you. Both of you,' she sniffed. 'Um, that's all I can say for now. I'll find the words, one day. Maybe, Giovanni ...'

'Yes, *bella*, anything.'

'Can you tell me what happened to your wife? You said she had a run-in with him?'

Giovanni's face darkened. 'He's got a lot to answer for,' he huffed.

'Oh please, don't talk about it Gio. Can't we just have tea?' groaned Athena.

'Well, I think she deserves to know!' Giovanni threw his arms up and started to pace in front of the plate glass window. 'My wife only had a small encounter. He ruined her suede trousers in a shop recently. It's the other story that still gets me, here!' he placed a hand on his heart.

Delia felt her insides start to free-fall away from her body. She went to tell Giovanni she didn't want to hear after all, but too late, he was on a roll.

'I met them once – nice people. I can still see them at the gate the day we moved in. She had a kind smile but there was something in her eyes ... I couldn't quite put my finger on it at the time. She hung back a bit anyway, so I spoke to him more. He was quite a dignified type of man.'

'For goodness sake, Gio, nothing was proven!' said Athena in a disapproving tone.

'Sorry, I don't follow, I'm not sure ...' said Delia.

'His parents, *bella*,' he replied. 'That was their home, until,' Giovanni jerked his head towards Ronan's estate, 'he came back from overseas. Turns out he'd been gone for years. He arrived back, then *voila* – they vanished.' His conductor arm waved to the sky to emphasise his point.

The bleakness of the house a few doors away pulled at her psyche. 'But, well, perhaps they went overseas,' Delia offered.

'The police investigated, quite a high profile case at the time, but nothing was ever found. It's still listed as a cold case, as far as I know. And now I know what I saw in that woman's eyes that day.'

The hair on the back of Delia's neck prickled. 'Yes, *bella,* just the same as you – a haunted look that I will never forget.'

'Look at what you've done, Gio! You've made her cry!' Athena stabbed the walking stick into the paved atrium floor. She groaned with effort to stand and started to walk towards the passageway. 'A good cup of tea, that's what we need. And no more talk of that awful man.'

He held his hands together in apology and looked genuine in his concern and regret. 'I obviously don't know what happened to you but what I do know is that you are safe and always welcome here, *bella.* Now, let me tell you about my big venture,' he said with a grand conductor flourish. 'What do you see in this framed photograph here,' he said pointing to the back wall.

Delia scrambled to think straight. 'Um ...' She scanned a photo of a bright orange hull of a vessel, spray flying over its deck. Yet the treacherous dark ocean the vessel was crossing made her bite her trembling lip. Somehow it made her think of those poor people. She imagined them floundering, out of their depth, frightened out of their wits.

'*Bella,* I'm sorry. I shouldn't have told you. Thenie's right, enough about that man now.' He puffed out his chest, 'time to talk about my favourite topic, my pride and joy!' He gestured again towards the framed photograph.

To try to stop her hammering heart, she walked across to the photograph. 'Um, it's a research vessel, called the *Tangaroa.*'

Giovanni flicked his flop of white hair and paced towards her. Delia could see him then, commanding the respect of an orchestra, his passion and charisma capturing the hearts and minds of all who came to watch the master on his grand stage.

'*Tangaroa* was the Māori God of all the living creatures in the ocean, and in Māori culture, whales are viewed as being *Tangaroa's* descendents.' You would have seen the artworks on the way in.' He nodded towards the entrance. 'My little curated collection reflects how whales have been revered for thousands of years by many indigenous cultures. For example, the whale is viewed by one aboriginal culture as being the greatest of all sea totems. Some Māori tribes thought the whale as sacred, supernatural beings. There's deep sacredness and significance of the whale in native Hawaiian culture. I could go on. You see *bella*, the whale is so honoured and respected. So as a conservation vessel, it seemed apt to give it such a revered name.' He swept a hand across the frame, eyes full of pride.

'Is it yours?'

'*Si bella*, well, co-owner. I'm part of a philanthropic group. We pooled our money to fund whale conservation in the Southern Ocean. Have you been to Antarctica, *bella*?' Not waiting for an answer, the words tumbled straight from his heart. 'It is the brightest, windiest, starkest, rawest, most fascinating last frontier on earth. You know ...' He rubbed his chin for a moment, deep in thought, then turned to Delia. 'It's due in port very soon. I'd love to take you onboard, show you around. Perhaps, if you'd like, you might want to join the crew – if you're game?'

'Oh, Gio! What a thrilling idea!' gushed Athena.

Delia's head jerked back in shock. She turned from Giovanni's twinkle-eyes to gaze at the spray-covered deck of the *Tangaroa*. She tried to picture herself standing on the deck, traveling to a wild-spirited place over vast expanses of rolling ocean. 'Antarctica! Me? You can't be serious!'

'Not quite that far, but close. Ah, *si bella*, I am deadly serious,' he grinned. 'Why there's so much you could do! Help launch and retrieve the Niskin water sample bottles, or help with acoustic data collection from the echosounders, hydrophones and sonobuoys.'

He paced the floor, throwing his hands up with glee. 'Imagine recording humpback whale songs. They are so beautiful *bella*. Or, you could help with monitoring their migration patterns, observing, taking photos of their tail flukes. And above all,' he placed a hand on her shoulder and looked at her with intense eyes bright with passion 'it would be an adventure, a new chapter in your life. How about you give it some thought. No rush, it will be in port for months, take your time. Talk it over with Thenie, eh?'

CHAPTER 17

May the Angels Lead Thee

Delia trudged head down, hands deep inside the Mongolian yak-hair jacket, mind consumed with thoughts of him. She pictured their meeting, the shock on his face. Yet with every breath that hung in the air she couldn't help but wonder if the freezing walk would all be in vain.

She crunched across the empty carpark speckled with frost, slid aside the glass door marked 'Open'. A man in overalls behind the counter jerked his head up. 'An early bird,' he grinned. 'Can I help you?'

'No, I'm fine, thanks.' She moved through the shop crammed with birdbaths and stone Buddhas and breathed in the warmth and peace of the indoor garden section. Long tendrils dripped from hanging baskets and show-stopper pink and white orchids waited to be admired, but she strode past without a glance.

She stopped for a moment at a cluster of kentia palms and slid back the thick glass hot-house door, to reveal – nothing. Heat licked her face while she scanned the plant collection, from the spiny cacti with yellow flowers lining the path to a clump of jade green spires beyond. Reality dawned – there was nowhere to hide here.

The dangerous barbs of an '*Opuntia echios*' threatened to snag at her fairy-floss hair. She touched the tip of a lethal spike with a forefinger and thought how satisfying it would be to smash it into Ronan's pompous, lying face.

'Hey, you!'

The nurseryman in overalls was gesticulating in her direction. *What the hell am I doing wrong?*

'Come on, get out from there!'

As she wavered in confusion, a subtle movement caught her eye from behind the palms. A man emerged into the light. Even from a distance and through the hot-house glass doors, she could make out the battered puffer jacket, fuzzy white stuffing sticking out. The black hair, matted and in disarray, stuck out from beneath a beanie.

'I'm just ...'

'Listen mate, we're not a bloody charity. Out you go!'

The shadowman turned his ink-covered face towards the hot-house. The intensity of his stare, those haunted eyes, were a pain she knew only too well. She held his gaze as she walked towards the door. There was something else, something harder in his eyes – judgement.

As she slid the door back, he was already shuffling along the pathway. The nurseryman threw his arms up at her, as if to appeal to her sense of repulsion.

'That's it! Keep going, and don't come back!'

Delia felt a jolt of anger. 'Actually, he's with me.' The words hung in the air.

She ignored the nurseryman's gawping mouth and narrowed eyes and continued. 'I was thinking of getting that prickly pear – in there,' she pointed through the glass doors to the hot-house beyond 'before we get a coffee.'

The shadowman turned his eyes towards her but remained silent. Only his furrowed forehead conveyed his confusion.

She glanced back at the nurseryman and returned his disbelieving stare with her best smile.

'It won't tolerate frost, you know,' he said in a haughty tone.

'Well, it would be for my conservatory.' She smoothed her jacket and flicked back a vibrant tress of hair.

The nurseryman stroked his jaw. 'Fine, I'll place it on the counter for you at the front.' He cast one more look of disdain at the man in the ripped puffer jacket before backing away.

Delia turned to the shadowman, noticing how his shoulders drooped. 'I found you!' She walked towards him and stared into black eyes. 'I'm so glad I did,' she said in little more than a whisper.

'Yeah, well, I don't need no pity.'

A weighty silence hung between them and she wondered where the compassion of the man who'd saved her had gone.

'What? What do you want?' he huffed.

'I need you.' She gulped back her fear but did not waiver, not looking away for an instant.

'What the hell would you need me for? Look at you all dressed up. Someone's lookin' after you!'

He looked wild in that moment, hard black eyes boring into her soul. Still, she stood her ground.

'If you help me, I'll be able to help you. I can get you as far away from … what did you call him?'

'The man who conned me, the Pākehā?'

'Yeah. I'll help get you back to Rotorua.'

She watched the swirling ink pattern on his forehead distort again in confusion. The disjointed lines only made him look even more ferocious.

'Yeah, sure.' A turmoil of emotion flashed across his face.

'Please.' Her voice crumbled. He was her only hope, the only one who understood. She dropped her gaze to the pathway and wracked her brain to find the words that would keep him close.

'What do you need help with, eh?'

'I need you to help me break in.' It was the truth, yet despite her conviction she felt herself back away a little. The way he frowned just then, looking so fierce.

'Break in … to the Pākehā's place? You just said – get as far away as possible, but now you want me to break in?'

She wondered if it had been a mistake after all and backed a little further away. Maybe he wasn't to be trusted – she saw unpredictability, an ancient warrior simmering beneath the surface of his olive skin. Then she remembered the book in Athena's room, how she'd learned that his tattoo lines were sacred, part of his culture.

'Look, I know you are a spiritual man.' She willed herself to not falter and to match the intensity of his stare. 'I know how much you miss home and need to return. But to help you, I need you to help me, and what I need is to take back what is rightfully mine. He has everything, my necklace, my only photos – they're very special ...' her voice cracked. 'He's got them all. I can't stand it!' The fury in the pit of her stomach reared like a fire-breathing serpent.

He rested a hand on her shoulder. 'I'll need to pray for guidance first, okay?'

'You're a good man – thank you.' Blinking back tears of gratitude, she added 'I'm sorry, I don't even know your name, after all you've done for me ...'

He looked startled for a moment before softly saying 'Tāne. Each generation there's a boy named after the god of forests and birds. My father is the sky, my mother is the earth. So says the legend.'

She watched the way he pulled his shoulders back, the gleam of wisdom in his obsidian eyes.

'It's so good to see you again Tāne. Let's go and get that coffee shall we.'

*   *   *

'Thanks for meeting me Tāne,' she said to the man leaning against the old boatshed. 'So spirit showed you the way?'

He glanced at the black hills shrouded in a new dawn, shifted from one foot to the other, weighing up his words. 'Spirit told me you are a good woman, eh – that you are special, and it's right to help you.'

'Perhaps I was special once,' she said, addressing the tumbled stones at her feet.

'You just need to trust, eh. Think about your destiny.'

She raised her eyes to see a column of golden light shimmer across the skin of the river. 'But he's taken my destiny,' she whispered, thinking of the years stretching before her without being able to capture such beauty on canvas.

'I thought he'd taken my destiny too. But it was you – you made me rethink ... gave me courage to dream,' he said, reaching out gently to touch her arm.

'You see, last night I lay on old canvas sails in there,' he pointed to the ramshackle boatshed with a rusted tin roof close to the dilapidated pier. 'I listened to the sound of the waves. And because I'd been thinking of my destiny and praying to my ancestors for guidance, they came in my sleep.'

She watched his black eyes sparkle with the memory.

'I had a spirit dream. I can see it clear as you standin' in front of me right now. The spirits, they say they have been guiding me all along, teachin' me tolerance and patience. And I knew that. But, this time, they let me see my hands – older hands, working in the traditional way. I could see pigments next to me in kauri bowls inset with paua shell. I could see my tools, the chisels, shark teeth and bones. And there was a crowd around me too, watching me work. In that moment, I felt the truth here,' he pressed his hand to his heart, 'that I had become a master craftsman, the finest *tohunga tā moko*.'

In that moment he looked taller, wiser, expanded, beyond his physical body. His battered exterior fell away before her eyes while the power of his words bridged the space between them.

'That's amazing – just like a prophecy.' Delia's voice shook with emotion. Her own destiny felt like the Arctic tundra: bleak, windswept, barren. Her hands went to her throat out of habit, where her essence had once resided. *Where was her essence now – beyond the stars, in another galaxy? Forever out of reach.*

She sighed, willing her courage to drown out her fear.

'And you're definitely sure they've gone?'

'Yeah, saw them leave last night around six. No cars in the driveway, no lights on, since then. Reckon it's clear. Problem is though,' he said, rattling the old iron fixtures on the boatshed doors, 'I can't find the gate in the fencing, and this is rusted solid. So goin' through the way you came out is the only way.'

'But the way I crawled out is boarded up now, look,' Delia said, sighing with frustration.

'No problem, eh,' he said, smashing the plywood patchwork with two sharp kicks.

The sound of splintering wood made her gasp, sending plumes of expelled air into the space between them.

She flicked an image of Simon's bearded face aside and scrambled through the hole in the palings. The smell of her old fear was seeping from the mess, melded with soil and dank, unseen things. Even now, assessing the chaos beneath a shaft of dust-soaked light, she wondered how she had navigated her way out of the shed. Tāne's heavy breathing gave her no time to dwell on it. She contorted her body around the mess, weaving through a tumble of upturned chairs and pushed the door.

'It's bolted,' she hissed.

'Stand back.'

She squeezed next to a shelf full of paint tins and winced as Tāne's shoulder connected with the door.

'One more should do it,' he grunted. With a guttural cry he pushed his full weight into the door, sending it smashing backwards.

High on adrenaline and like a surreal dream, she found herself running beside Tāne up the garden path, over the patio, up the stairs to the back deck. She stood for a moment panting, while he assessed the glass doors.

'I'm goin' to have to smash it. Hang on, I'll go back and get the spade from the shed.'

Delia clutched the deck railing for support. She felt sick here, exposed. She glanced at the spot where her old trusting self had painted and looked to the sky for answers. In all that vastness beyond the weak winter dawn, her essence was out there somewhere. She jerked her head towards the sound of Tāne's footsteps ascending the stairs.

'Okay, once I've broken through, we'll have to be in and out real quick. Ready, one, two ...'

Delia retreated to the top of the deck stairs, watched Tāne heave the spade into the glass. Jagged splinters of glass fell like lopped icicles onto the deck and inside, onto the parquetry flooring of the passageway. They locked eyes for a second, waiting for a shrill alarm system to clang to life. 'Looks like we're in luck!' Tāne grinned, tapping the last segment of hanging glass with the spade edge.

'Let's go!' Tāne called over his shoulder.

Delia gulped back bile as she crunched over glass, following Tāne into the devil's cave.

'This your room?'

'He's cleared it all!' She turned away from the cleared bedside table and moved further down the passageway. 'That's his room there.'

Tāne ran a hand over the keypad and bit his lip.

'Can you smash the door?'

'Why not, eh – come this far.'

The sight of the spade smashing into the buttons infused her with a sense of deep satisfaction. *How he's underestimated me!*

A high-pitched alarm ripped through the passageway. Tāne threw the spade onto the parquetry flooring and burst into the room. Delia pushed past him and froze. Adrenaline melded with disgust.

She looked from the macabre collection to Tāne, then back again, to the long spear hung horizontally above the bedhead. She followed the length of the spear to its jagged arrowhead, trying to comprehend the range of barbs, blades and trident spears that took up the rest of the wall-space.

'We don't have much time, eh.'

Tāne's warning pushed her further into the room. She pulled open a drawer next to the bed with a shaking hand, flicking through papers, before moving on. The piercing alarm bounced off the walls, forcing her to move faster.

'Tō tero! Tō raho!'

Tāne's despairing exclamation from behind made the hairs on her neck prickle. She turned expecting to see Ronan's imperious stance but instead, her eyes rested on the mural painted upon the wall closest to the door. Her horrified gasp melded with the shrill alarm.

They stood in silence, frozen by the sight of the hideous mural of whalers in their schooners rejoicing at the carnage before them. There, amidst white frothing sea-spray and a blood-filled sea, a whale, with torn blubber, thrashed in its fight for survival. The pain-stricken eye reflected knowing that the mid-air spear thrown by the whalers would soon herald its last breath. The turmoil in the water, the blood and gore floating like a slick, all depicted the whaler's sheer ruthlessness and glorification of the whale's demise.

'Delia! Security will be here soon! We've got to keep moving, eh! You look in there' he pointed to the robe 'and I'll look in the bathroom.'

With a thumping heart, Delia entered the walk-in robe and flicked her eyes around the space filled with tie racks, colour-coordinated business shirts and plastic wrapped suits. She dropped to her hands and knees and swept her hand beneath the dryclean plastic covering, her fingertips glancing against shoeboxes and rolls of something.

'Delia, come on! I hear a car outside!'

She swept back a swathe of plastic and cried out at the sight of her canvasses leaning against the wall. She hauled one out and unrolled it a little. The edge of the *Sea of Tranquility* spoke to her like a lost child.

She snatched up the other canvasses lying behind the shoeboxes and in desperation, pulled open a drawer.

'Delia! Someone's here!' Tāne hissed.

She clutched the canvasses like a lifeline and fled after him. Moments later, she pushed the precious cargo into his large hands. She scrambled through the hole in the shed wall out onto the rocky shore. 'I think we got away with it.'

'We need to split up.'

She coughed, sending out plumes of mist. 'But I think we're okay.'

'We still need to split up. Cops'll be here soon. You can bet on it. Place like this.'

'Athena will take you in ...' she trailed off. The inked warrior's impenetrable expression crashed over her heart. She traced the swirls on his cheeks with her eyes, committing them to memory.

'Here, take this,' she said, pressing Ronan's prestigious silver and gold Rolex into his large paw.

He stared at the object like it was a rock from Pluto. 'I can't take this.'

'Be careful, it's Ronan's. Maybe don't try to sell it too quick. It should help you get home though – sometime.' The icy morning air bit into her cheeks making her body tremble.

'I'll think about it,' he said, shoving his hand into the pocket of his ripped jacket. 'At least you got these out.'

Delia held out her arms and took possession of the rolled-up canvasses. The feel of them clasped next to her chest caused a tear to drip down her face.

Mauri ora e hoa,' Tāne said in a voice tinged with sorrow.

Delia gulped back the lump in her throat. 'What does that mean?'

He turned and called over his shoulder, 'good luck my friend.'

* * *

'But these paintings are ...,' Giovanni burst from his seat in the atrium and started to pace. Delia felt herself flush as she studied the chameleon river, crested in whitecaps.

'Aren't they just beautiful,' Athena interrupted.

'Beyond magnificence!' said Giovanni. He strode towards the paintings spread over the coffee table and swept his arms across them looking every part the showman, a matador without a cape.

'Look here, at this *'Sea of Tranquility'*! See the darkness, the foreboding in the corners. I hear the spine-tingling opening notes of Toccata and Fugue in D minor. And there,' he pointed, 'is the building of a thunderstorm, the intense spiral down to the depths. The stream of golden light, it is nearly unbearable in my heart. Rossini's "Qui Radames Verra" is here, there is clashing of cymbals and the triumph of the trumpet, leading the angels to paradise in Faure's Requiem opera. The strings and soprano's melody – the beauty of it all makes my heart burst!'

At last, her art had spoken. She watched his expression, his eyes glistening with joy.

'Oh, Delia – I've never seen him so animated!' cried Athena.

'I'm happy that my painting has moved you.'

'Moved me? That is an understatement! When I look at the light, how it plays on the water, it is exquisite. I feel it like an intense pain here.' He thumped his chest for emphasis. 'In my head, the sound of the Stradivarius plays.' He paced to the window, then to the framed picture of the *Tangaroa*.

He turned and beamed such an intense look that it made her heart stop for a second.

'Delia, I am serious now.' The showman dissolved before her eyes. Here was the force of nature that entranced Italy's elite.

'You must, you absolutely must, become my new artist-in-residence.' The passion pouring from his being shocked her in its ferocity, sweeping her up like a tornado.

'Oh Gio, yes! What a perfect idea!' exclaimed Athena somewhere far off.

'I'm sorry, I don't understand. You mean on board the *Tangaroa*?' She looked into his green-grey eyes, feeling a crescendo of panic building inside her gut.

'Delia, listen.' He walked towards her, placing a gentle hand on her shoulder. 'I can see you standing there,' he pointed to the research vessel 'on the prow, wind sweeping through your vibrant hair. I can see you exhilarated, wild and free. I promise you, as God is my witness,' he appealed to the roof, 'you will never be happier.'

'Happy? Where? I'm not sure I understand.'

'Well, Macquarie Island of course! Your magnificent work will move people in a way photographs cannot. You will help me protect the southern right whales and the humpbacks and you, my dear, will become a very famous artist.'

'But I can't go to Macquarie Island – I mean, I don't even know where it is!'

'It is exactly,' he directed an arm down the river, 'fifty-four degrees south and one thousand five hundred kilometers from here in the Southern

Ocean – next stop, Casey Station, Antarctica.'

She looked from Giovanni to the bottle-green water pushing out relentlessly towards the mouth of the river. Beyond lay the treacherous black swells of the ocean.

'Antarctica. Giovanni, I don't ...'

'Ah, but it is the subantarctic. Imagine the beauty of the landscape translated onto canvas. You will bring the World Heritage site to life!'

'Look!' He wrapped her in his arms. 'Look in the sky at the albatross soaring above you, feel the wind on your face, hear the roars of the seals.'

Delia lost herself in the moment, drinking in his passion for the raw place at the end of the earth.

'I promise you, Delia, the beauty will get into your blood. There's nowhere like it, and it will stay with you forever.'

'But, where would I live, onboard the ship with you?'

'No, *bella*! You will have a cabin. Trust me. I need you, no, I implore you, to move millions more people, across the world, in the name of conservation. I want them to see the island's pristine environment, captured like this,' he gestured to her paintings. 'Macquarie Island is one of the last unique bastions on earth, where the beaches are not full of rubbish. There are threats at every turn – acidic oceans full of plastic, barren oceans depleted of fish, and of course, the constant threat of whaling within the sanctuary. It is all too much for me. It incenses me so much I could burst! But you, you have the power Delia. Your paintings have the power to make people realise there's still time to turn it around, to look after our home, our one and only planet. I have shocked you, but you are also smiling, so I will take that as a yes,' he grinned.

CHAPTER 18

The Truth Shall Set You Free

The rustle of bamboo outside Delia's window turned into whispers from the spirit world: '*You liar ... you fraud.*' The words seeping through the glass caused the bitter bile of defeat to burn the back of her throat. Unable to stand it a moment longer, she launched out of bed, grabbed Athena's spare bathrobe, and looked out at the night sky.

The golden orbs of light were there somewhere, on the other side of the silver moon. She visualised their forms flashing towards her like shooting stars and strained with all of her might to feel their connection but the moon held fast to its secrets.

How the hell did she connect with them before? She squeezed her eyes shut, aching to feel their love hovering close. Nothing – it was useless!

She crawled back into bed and watched the shadows on the ceiling. Bit by bit her breathing slowed. The shadows moved in a rhythmic motion, back and forth, while the bamboo rustled to a different tune. She blinked heavy eyelids and tried to keep watch on the shadows. They danced in the shape of her heirloom necklace, swinging back and forth. She closed her eyes and felt herself drift up towards the ceiling and slip into another dimension. She floated free, part of the Aegean Sea, feeling salt in her mouth, sun on her face. The soft voice of her mother caressed her floating form.

The deep blue beckoned
Down, down to the sea floor
She endured like no other
Enticed onwards
To the sacred below the shore

Delia breathed in the whispered words from her childhood. They lodged like oxygen bubbles in her lungs, allowing her to slipstream down, down through the crystal-clear water of her dream. She snatched her prize off the sea floor, resurfaced and held the necklace aloft in triumph. Touched by the sun, the turquoise stone pulsed with life. The spiral symbol engraved on the back demanded to be caressed, to be painted, to behold its power. She traced the symbol over and over, her finger becoming a paintbrush before her eyes. The soundtrack of seagulls and the whoosh of waves slipped into the distance. The world condensed to just the spiral labyrinth on canvas and the rustle of wind through bamboo.

Delia woke with a start and sat bolt upright. She ran her hand over her forehead and scalp and looked out the window to the tangerine sky, trying to discern what was different. Tāne's words echoed in her heart: '*I had a spirit dream ... I had become a master craftsman, the finest tohunga tā moko.*' '*Just like a prophecy,*' she heard her own voice reply.

The dream had been lucid, real and unreal. She threw on the yak-hair jacket and jeans and scurried to the river's edge. The dark denim water greeted her like a watchful serpent. She crunched along the pebble shore becoming aware of how the blue-black periwinkle shells reflected tinges of turquoise in the early morning light. Her need for her lost heirloom stone necklace dogged her every step.

She passed by the silver-wooden pier, arriving breathless at the weather-beaten boatshed. The sagging wooden doors, wedged tight by a pile of pebbles and bracken-like seaweed, made her frown. 'Are you in there?' she called, pushing through the mesh of long grass to the side of the boatshed. 'Tāne?' Her hot breath hung like question marks in the frigid air.

She swept her eyes over lichen-covered palings left to rot on the rocks and picked her way to the back of the shed. A yawning gap in the rear dilapidated wall confirmed the hidden entry point. She edged inside the gap and slumped atop a mountain of mould-spotted sails in a hollow where something heavy had rested.

She glanced fingers across her throat and yearned to touch the missing stone. The spiral symbol etched into the back of the stone – that was the key. Her spirit dream told her it was true. Her heart knew. Her higher self knew. *How had she forgotten the spiral, the way she used to trace the marking on the stone with a finger?* Similar to her protection symbol, as gifted by the Light of Truth, the spiral held power. She felt her body vibrate, fill with hope. That was the key to reconnecting with her true nature, to getting back her artistic powers.

Light streamed through holes in the roof, capturing her in a haze of weak sunbeams, salty air and dust. She could hear Athena's words, *'You must go to the police, dear. It's the only way to get your possessions back.'* No, Ronan was too clever and anyway, they'd probably arrest her for the break-in.

She thought of Giovanni's eyes, once so twinkly now dark with disappointment upon discovering her complete lack of talent. 'Oh, *bella*, your paintings would have made the difference ...'

Where was Tāne? *'Far away,'* said her heart. How could she take back her destiny? *'Courage,'* came the reply.

That's it then. The smell of decay and sea-salt closed in around her. She pushed back out onto the shore and for a moment watched clouds glide above the river. Her body buzzed in anticipation yet looking at that condensed space between river and sky was making her feel like she had trespassed onto a different planet.

She pulled the yak-hair jacket close, picked her way over tumbled rock and broken shell, passed by the forgotten upturned dinghy, trudging slowly towards her fate.

* * *

Delia stood on the rocky shore next to Ronan's shed and frowned at the gaping hole. Evidence of their recent break-in lay on the rocks at her feet. She kicked at the pieces of plywood and leaned down to peer through the jumble of chair legs inside the shed. Beyond the mess of the shed, she could see the door swinging in the light breeze.

They're not home. That thought sent her scurrying in the direction of Larke Avenue. Sure enough, there was no sign of the Maserati in the driveway. Once again she returned to inspect the gap. Looking up at the grey sky for guidance and with blood pounding behind her ears, she crawled inside.

She climbed over the chest, squeezed around tins of paint and stepped over the broken catch from the shed door, lying on the garden path, just where they'd left it. The last time she was here she'd fed off Tāne's courage and muscular strength. This time she was heading into the abyss alone.

She gulped and ran through the garden and up the back steps. Standing on the deck, she could see everything was as they'd left it. She crunched over shattered glass and slipped into the insides of the sleeping dragon.

Each step felt like torture. She stepped over the discarded spade and forced herself further towards the still splintered door of Ronan's bedroom. It creaked open, revealing the sinister array of weaponry lining the walls. She looked away and moved into the walk-in robe.

One by one she flicked open each drawer, rifled through frantically and moved on to the next. She tossed out socks, hunted for hidden edges. Nothing! As she slid open the bottom drawer, the hair on the back of her neck prickled.

'So, the little thief has returned.'

Delia's heart seized. She snapped around to find Ronan standing straight-backed in the doorway. His ruby-red tie hung like a devil's tongue.

'Did you not consider the depth of my patience? It is a bold, but stupid move, my Delia.'

His aqua eyes shone with triumph then narrowed to slits. 'It took years to hunt you down, years of enduring the Captain burning his need into me. And do you think he has forgotten the failure of that night?' He craned his neck towards the ceiling, sniffed the air and growled to the evil force within him. '*Sacré bleu!* Not yet – you will get your chance!'

She felt herself wither, like a rose in the desert sun such was the vengeance in his eyes.

'Tell me, Delia, do you think I like to see all this damage? To be forced to wait here, to live like a street urchin in my own home, until you decide to pay another visit?'

'I just needed my things. You took them – I need them back!' Her anger hung in the space between them.

His nostrils flared and he looked taller, more grotesque. 'Is that right? Well, my needs are greater than yours, Delia.'

She tried to dodge his sudden lunge but his large hand closed around her wrist. 'Ow! You're hurting me!' She staggered after him into the bedroom, coming face to face with the tormented eye in the mural on the wall. She tried to squirm away but he held firm around her throat with the other hand.

'Listen carefully, Delia. Both the Captain and I need you. He needs to suck at your energy and I need you to satisfy my hunger. My appetite for your art is stronger than ever. Now that you understand about survival, it will reflect the rawness of humanity even more. Your painting, as I always knew it, is beyond human. You are the only one in the world who can satisfy my lust. So you will paint for me, you hear! Then, I need my Rolex – it is worth a great deal to me!'

'But I can't!' She forced the words out before he crushed her windpipe even more.

'Ah, but you will! My patience has run out! You will paint for your life, Delia! Then,' he leaned his head back to gasp in air 'the Captain can feast!'

He pulled her down the passageway and into the light of the lounge. Beyond the plate glass, giant spaceship clouds hovered like an alien jury, gathered to decide her fate. The incessant river turned a blind eye, surging ever onwards out to sea.

He shoved her forward towards an easel. 'There is your canvas and your paints. See how much I knew you would return, my Delia? And here,' he swept his hand in a grand, mad flourish, 'is your muse, the river. I want to see something epic. Think of a flood, I want destruction, Delia, I want a river of blood! Here I will help you.' He held her tight with one hand and with the other, squeezed tubes of paint on-to a palette.

'I can't!' she squealed.

'You will!'

In her peripheral vision Delia saw the vindicated commander of darkness stand back and assess the way she took hold of a brush. Tears blurred her vision. She looked towards the silver-wood pier and willed for someone, anyone, to walk by, look up and take notice. Her mind created shadows and movement near the ramshackle boatshed. The illusive bubble, that a miracle would save her, drifted on the tide.

'I can't do it!' She flung the offensive brush at the window causing blood-red paint to drip down the glass.

'*Merde*! You're a fool Delia!' he screamed, nostrils flaring with rage and disgust.

'How do you expect me to paint when you stole my talent! It's your fault!' she screamed. Fueled with adrenaline and rage, she swung the easel in his direction, sidestepped the couch and made a run for the door.

'It's no good Delia! Don't think you're getting away!'

His fire breath was upon her, searing her cheek. Fingers dug into her collarbone, murderous thumbs hovered near her throat. A band of metal clamped around her wrists. She heard a click and tried to flail, but the handcuffs held tight.

'You are a great disappointment to me Delia,' he hissed in an ominously quiet voice. 'It seems all you are good for is to tell me where my Rolex is and then the Captain can do as he pleases!'

'But do you understand! It's your fault!' she sobbed, frantic now that the handcuffs were biting into her wrists.

'I don't believe you Delia. You are capable of infinite power. You choose to disobey. As I said – you're a fool.'

Hauled up the step, across into the kitchen and out the back door, into the gloom of oncoming night, it was all she could do to scream like a banshee. He tried to smother her cries, but she managed to squirm away, kicking him with every ounce of her might into the rose bushes. *Run!*

Frantic, she took her chance to run towards the wrought-iron gate before he struck from behind. A large hand covered her mouth, while the other latched on to her shoulder. Dazed, she felt herself dragged back down the driveway, past the kitchen to the waiting Maserati, tucked out of view at the side of the house. His hands released enough to push her inside the passenger seat. She turned her head away as he leaned in close to secure the seatbelt.

In seconds, the car reversed backwards then jolted forwards in a crescendo of spinning tyres. At the wrought-iron gates, she screamed in the direction of Athena's serene golden Buddha.

'Stop that!' he snapped, the green lights of the dashboard illuminating a gashed cheek from his fall in the rose bushes.

She longed to jump as the Maserati edged through the gates onto the road but, with her arms clasped together in front of her body, it was impossible. Her body pushed back in the seat as he planted his foot on the accelerator.

'Let me go!' she yelled at the bloodied barbarian at the wheel.

He braked and swerved into an empty carpark. 'Silence – or I will put you in the boot!'

Delia nodded compliance. He pressed a palm against the blood oozing from the wound in his cheek and gripped the driving wheel once again.

To the drivers they overtook, they were just two people taking a sports car for a spin. They passed the airport, crossed causeways. He drove on, grim-faced, leaving the city behind.

Delia thought of Tāne huddled somewhere in the cold and Athena, getting ready for the evening. She imagined Athena consulting her tarot cards, calling Giovanni. '*Gio, I don't know where she is!*' The images seared pain into her heart. The distance between them stretched taunt like a rubber band. Night was coming. Where were they heading? The car sped onwards, sucking her into a black hole.

When she could bear the silence no more, she croaked out a plea. 'Why don't you just let me go, Ronan?'

'Silence!' he hissed, taking a hairpin bend like a section of the grand prix.

'Where are you taking me?' she demanded, her voice pitching un-naturally high.

'Not another word, Delia, I'm warning you!'

He pushed his foot down on the accelerator, and she clamped her eyes shut, blocking out the ghost gums flashing past. Eventually he slowed and turned the vehicle on-to a gravel road.

'Where are we?' she said, unable to hide the fear in her voice.

'You will see soon enough, my Delia.'

Cortisol flooded her body as she strained to see in the darkness, beyond the headlights and a ramshackle post-and-rail fence.

They turned a corner and drove towards a light glowing from the shape of a house. In the distance she heard the deep baying of dogs.

She watched Ronan cut the engine and noticed an odd emotion cross his face. She scowled at him and looked at the silhouette standing in the porchlight. The figure pushed two dogs back inside the house and slipped from view, appearing a moment later in the headlights. She knew that arrogant walk, those skinny hips.

'Well, this is a surprise!' The hateful goatee beard appeared through the open driver's side window. Simon touched Ronan's cheek gently.

'I need your help Si,' said Ronan in a matter-of-fact tone.

'Simon to the rescue again!' he snorted, casting Delia a look of pure loathing.

'Get your stuff,' Ronan said gruffly. 'Let's get out of here.'

Simon hovered for a moment longer, as if breathing in Ronan's energy like an elixir, before running back to the house.

A scream welled up from the deepest recesses of her soul and filled the confines of the car.

'No-one can hear you out here, Delia. There is no-one to help you!' He launched himself out of the driver's seat, strode around to the passenger side and flung open the door. Delia felt herself hauled from her seat. No sooner had she thought to kick out and run she found herself shovelled into the backseat and secured beneath the seatbelt.

Ronan climbed into the passenger seat while Simon flung a bag in the boot. 'You never let me drive before!'

Delia watched him run a fingertip along the dashboard, smoothing his hands over the sports steering wheel and mounted gearshift. The engine revved and they lurched forward violently.

Delia's stomach cramped with fear as they turned back on-to the highway. She gritted her teeth at every bend, looking from the road ahead to the portion of Simon's face visible in the rear-vision mirror.

'Where are you taking me? Look I just wanted my stuff!'

'Shut up!' Simon pressed his foot down and the car surged forward, hugging the highway as fast and precise as a rollercoaster cart.

'The Captain pushes even now to suck your other-wordly energy Delia. And still, you have not told me where my Rolex is. But, you will tell me soon enough,' Ronan growled.

'You've got bigger things to worry about than your stuff,' sniffed Simon. 'Ain't that right?'

'*C'est vrai.* Anyway,' he snorted, 'your precious photos and necklace are at the bottom of the sea.'

'Just like something else is gunna be!' Simon thumped the steering wheel with glee and the car swerved left a little.

Their taunts filled her spine with ice. She saw herself floating, hanging in the depths like seaweed, before drifting to the ocean floor to join her beloved necklace in the silt. Then she pictured herself on the bow of the *Tangaroa,* hair flying in the wind, before her future self became just a microscopic pink bubble floating in the vast depths of an inhospitable ocean.

The sudden sound of Ronan's mobile jolted her from her deathly imaginings.

'*Merde!* It is that Narelle from next door.' Ronan pushed the phone back into his pocket but seconds later the insistent tone echoed through the car.

'*Sacré bleu!*' Ronan snatched the mobile out again, composed himself then answered, 'My dear Narelle! How are you?' Delia heard a sharp, high-pitched voice talking quickly while Ronan made the necessary noises.

'Ah, I cannot help you, my beauty, I am on the East Coast as we speak.'

Delia knew her time was now and belted out an almighty scream, worth every second of the stinging backhand that followed.

'No, no, my sweetness ... I am with friends. They are, how do you say, quite inebriated. What's that, my darling? The line is so faint, I cannot.' Ronan ended the call and pocketed the phone, sneering at Delia. 'Nice try, but not good enough.'

Simon snickered. 'What'd she want?'

'Something about her car.' Ronan sighed. 'She thinks I would care, that we have a future.'

'Stupid bitch,' sneered Simon.

'Ah, don't forget, *mon cher*, where there is pain, there is glory. Her *maison* next door, it will be mine. It will take just a little more persuasion.'

The car took a hairpin bend, diverting off the highway. She saw an oasis of streetlights, a community up ahead. Simon slowed the vehicle. They passed by seaside shacks, weatherboard cottages. The headlights flashed onto a pier and boats. They passed a shed with a sign that heralded 'Gulch Fresh Fish' before turning into a driveway.

Delia readied herself to run and scream but there was no chance. As her door opened, Simon's hand clamped down over her mouth, his skinny body belying his strength as he man-handled her with ease out of the car and up a flight of steps, into a dark house.

She writhed in Simon's grasp while Ronan switched on a lamp. 'Get her downstairs, into the wine cellar.' Ronan's caterpillar-thin lips flattened in a half snarl, half grimace. She cringed as he took hold of her wrists. '*Bonsoir*, Delia. Enjoy your last night.'

She felt the handcuffs release and shook her hands to get the blood circulating, while Simon pushed her forwards into the next room. She caught a glimpse of a kitchen bench, before being hauled down a flight of steps.

She staggered through a doorway, blinked in the sudden bright light and heard the dull thunk of a lock clicking into place behind her.

Hundreds of wine bottles lined the walls, all encased within clay tubes, stared back.

She started to pace the slate floor to ward off spikes of panic and the cold. Five steps in, turn, five steps back. She tried to think beyond the taiko beat of her heart. *What to do?* Turn. *Think.* Turn. She stopped, rubbed her arms and stooped to pull out a bottle of wine. With the bottle held aloft in one hand, a fragment of a plan started to form in her mind. She cocked her head, considering the empty clay tube for a moment longer then launched into action.

Quiet as a mouse, she started to pull out each bottle of wine, placing the bottles to one side and the empty clay tubes to the other. She then reassembled the clay pipes in an arc formation and placed the wine bottles back inside.

She crawled inside the arc of piping, twisted the top of one bottle, *Thank God for screw-tops.* The red velvet liquid slid into her gullet.

She held the bottle up to the light and watched the liquid ebb like a mini tide inside the glass.

'At the bottom of the sea ... just like something else is gunna be.'

She thought of herself out there in a raging sea, flailing and gulping water and sinking below the surface. She thought of her turquoise stone lying on the seabed, little fish swimming past, the shapes of whales gliding above. Then she thought of the tortured, impaled whale mural on Ronan's wall.

Then something shifted in her heart, some sort of knowing. She took another swig of wine and tried to latch on-to the thought that moved like shadows in her psyche.

A realisation hit her like a bolt of lightening. *'Down at the bottom of the sea.'* She repeated the words like a mantra. That's where her things were, in a safe, down there at the bottom of the whale mural in Ronan's room, down at the bottom of the sea. She felt a deep knowing in her body, like a rediscovered truth.

The truth was beautiful and ironic and cursed. Now she was stuck here and they would grab her without warning. *How to distract them, overcome them*? She put the bottle down and stared at it. *Think! Yes, that might work.*

She clumsily wrapped the bottle inside her jacket and dropped it onto the flagstones. Wine oozed from beneath yak-hair.

Through the interminable cold night she willed herself to remain vigilant. Finally, muffled footsteps filtered through the wall. Delia slapped her cheeks lightly, took a deep breath and dragged her aching body up to standing. She heard the thunk of the lock and saw the door edge open a little. From her position behind the door, she could make out Simon's low-slung jeans and his torso.

'Wakey, wakey. Time for your swimming lesson, Delia.' He edged further into the room and cocked his head. 'Whaddya know she's made a cave!'

Delia swung the broken bottle as hard as she could, the jagged edge of glass slicing into his cheek.

'Ah fu …!' Simon clutched his head and slumped to the floor, moaning in agony. She sidestepped his body, pulled the door behind her, and slid the bolt into place.

Wild-eyed and frantic, Delia stumbled up the steps, collided with the kitchen bench then careered forwards towards picture windows. There was the harbour beyond, bathed in the light of a new dawn. *Move! Get out!*

She lurched to the front door, grappled with the handle, and burst out into the freezing air.

CHAPTER 19

Elixir

Bicheno, Tasmania, June 2009

The vastness of an ochre sky filled Delia's heart with hope. With eyes helter-skelter she glimpsed a cluster of masts and vessels ahead. She clambered down wooden steps and stumbled at the bottom, flying forward on-to the Maserati's bonnet.

A piercing sound like a gunshot ricocheted across the Gulch. In a surreal, doom-filled second, she realised it was her own scream. She felt a hunter's ragged breath on her face, saw the concrete driveway loom in front of her eyes. Her brain exploded in a cascade of silver stars.

In the distance, through a drum, she heard muffled voices and heavy footsteps on wood. She squirmed against fingers gripping her shoulder and waist, raised her neck and glimpsed a seal, or was it bull kelp, rolling in black water beside her.

'You're gunna pay for that! Think you're clever, eh!' Simon's gaunt face, blood dripping into his goatee, came into view.

'How stupid Delia to try to escape!' Ronan grunted.

An unwitting star in her own horror movie, she felt Ronan's body move against hers. Trapped in his arms, all she could do was squirm, forcing him to re-adjust his grip on her body.

'Merde!' he hissed, billowing sickening breath over her face.

She squirmed again, enough to see a snapshot of a plank over black water, a wooden hull. Her view flicked towards the heavens and down to scuffed planks of a deck moments before her body thudded on-to the wood.

'I have given up on you Delia, but my Rolex, you will tell me where it is.'

'I don't know,' she croaked, aware of the roll of the boat beneath her body.

Ronan snorted with disgust. 'I think by the time we are done, you will tell me what I need to know.'

She gasped like a landed fish the moment he walked out of view. A motor rumbled beneath her and the acrid smell of diesel fuel wafted past her nostrils. She heard Simon shout 'Okay, good to go!' A thick rope landed on the deck beside her head.

Was there any strength left in her sprawled-out body? What was that rhythmic pounding sound? Blood gushing behind her ears, or the throb of the engine?

The deck vibrated under the sudden impact of a heavy weight. She heard a high-pitched squeal followed by hoots and cries that turned her spine to ice. She lifted her head and caught sight of Simon teetering on the top of a huge esky then fall backwards overboard. His shout smothered by a large splash.

A freezing wind skimmed the deck and funneled her hair upwards in a pink streaming mass. She twisted to face the direction of hellish cries, while the thump-thump of the engine continued to vibrate up through the deck into her body.

From her position on the deck she saw a smoky cloud gather force and spin like a tornado around the wheelhouse. The maelstrom blasted the deck, sending plastic buckets flying in the air. Shouts were heard moments before the sound of metal scraped barnacle and rock.

The vessel jolted, sliding in a sickening, sideways dance. She felt herself flung across the deck like tumbleweed and slip over the metal surrounds of the vessel. Managing to snatch hold of a railing just in time, she hung like a ragdoll in space, dangling above rolling black water while lifejackets and fishing rods cascaded over her head. The vessel teetered on a precarious slant forcing the railing to slip from her hand.

The plunge came harsh and sudden. Bull kelp slithered around her body like giant hungry eels as the crush of ice water, pain and panic forced her to thrash upwards.

She sank below the surface again like a stone before renewed panic made her kick and claw her way back to the surface, lungs screaming for air.

'Breathe! Breathe!' A voice boomed from somewhere close.

She sucked in precious air as the hand of God reached from the heavens. Strong arms pulled at her body yet she felt detached, somewhere outside of herself. Peace descended. She floated on a strange wave of knowing that her time had come. There was her ghost-white form lying down there, next to a warrior on top of a large esky. She watched his forearms paddle with the fury of a madman.

'Delia! Stay with me, Delia! Breathe!'

She watched his frantic attempt to save her. All the effort he'd put into paddling now redirected into pressing his blue-black lips on-to hers, pushing life-saving air down her throat. She descended from the ether to get a closer look. Why was he bothering when the thread of her human form was ready to snap? Her time on earth was done.

He cares so much! The thought made her linger. *I'll watch a little more then move to that light beam, just over there.*

'That's it, Delia! That's it, cough it all up, breathe!'

A distant consciousness stirred. She felt the light plop of her soul sliding back under skin and bone. His urgent breath pushed inside her mouth. She opened her eyes and looked in wonder at his sacred *tā moko* lines, drinking in their power and beauty like an elixir.

'Oi, mate, are you okay?'

She felt Tāne's strong arms propel her upwards while other arms grasped and hauled her awkwardly. Delia caught sight of white fisherman's gumboots and felt the surety of solid wood beneath her. A bright yellow jacket made for a giant appeared from somewhere and swamped her shivering body. She met Tāne's black almond-shaped eyes for a second above her and felt large hands smooth sodden hair from her face.

A man's voice spoke at a frenetic pace. 'I've called the ambulance, they'll be here soon, and the marine police, anyone else on board?'

'Two men – they went overboard, didn't see 'em again,' replied Tāne.

The torment – it was over. Even in her fragile state she could feel a wave of pure relief wash like a bursting dam through her freezing form.

'God, better get out there! They might be caught underneath in the wheelhouse or something. I've never seen anything like that! Twenty-five years I've been fishin' here. That whirlwind, or whatever it was, it came out of nowhere!'

'Be careful, eh? It's still windy out there.'

Delia saw white gumboots walk by her face. The boots stopped near the edge of the pier and disappeared from view.

'We've got to go,' Tāne said in a hushed tone. Delia felt herself being hoisted into the air and pushed against his barrel chest.

The man's voice called from below the pier, 'Hey! You can't leave – the ambulance will be here in a sec!'

'I need to get her warm, eh!' Tāne replied.

Unable to keep her eyes open any longer, Delia let her head rest on his chest, hearing his rhythmic steps on the pier, the sound of a car door opening. She opened her eyes a fraction and noticed a dashboard, a glovebox and heard the car rev.

'Heater'll take a few minutes to warm up, eh,' Tāne said beside her.

The sound of an ambulance siren screeched past. For a while, all she could do was shiver and gasp in loud, ragged spurts. Slowly the heater began belting out warmth, lulling her to sleep. Every now and again, she'd open her eyes a crack to watch rolling button grass plains and coves of curling aqua slide past the glass.

Her teeth stopped chattering around the time they entered the township of Swansea. Every now and again she glanced at Tāne. He'd draped a blanket around his body but his tattooed chest was still visible.

'How on earth did you find me?' she asked in just above a whisper. She tried to inject her gratitude and incredulity into the words, but somehow he looked different, inaccessible.

He flashed black eyes at her and turned his attention back to the road.

'I mean, I don't understand how you knew where I was?'

'We'll talk about it later.' His words sounded blunt, detached.

'I thought you'd,' her words trailed away at the ferocity of his gaze.

'Look, I'd rather talk about it later, eh, but it's simple. I saw you inside his place, at the window. I could see you were in trouble. I said a karakia over and over in my head. Then you were screamin' like a stuck pig. So I had no choice – stole the neighbour's car, followed you as far as the bach out in the middle of nowhere. Then he drove like a bat out of hell and I lost you. So I prayed to the spirit of Rongo and the other spirits, and they guided me to you. Don't know why – you shouldn't have gone back in.' He pushed the last words through his teeth and glanced at her with fury in his obsidian eyes.

She sank further into the fisherman's jacket, glad of its warmth and the emotional safety of its cocoon. She needed to tell him so much and to ask where they were going, yet his hard-edged tone left her mute.

They drove on in strained silence. Down a chicane built in the side of a cliff wall, past the pristine expanse of Raspins Beach which gave her a clue they were traveling back to Hobart.

Only when the road was surrounded by tall eucalypts, when the tension in the car was unbearable, did she dare speak. 'I mean, you saved my life. I'd died, you know, and you brought me back.' She sighed, noting his rigid jawline.

'If you hadn't come and risked your own life, they would have ...' Her voice cracked.

Tāne kept his eyes on the road. They drove through a tunnel of green, the road dwarfed by towering eucalypts, the strained silence melded with her fizzing emotions. She couldn't hold back much longer.

'I really need to ...' Tāne's death stare forced her mouth shut. His black eyes blazed with anger, or perhaps disgust. She shrank further inside the jacket.

'You! You don't *need* to do anything, eh!' he yelled. He slammed on the brakes and pulled off the road into a quiet picnic area. Without another word, he flung open the door and stormed down a pathway leading into the forest.

What the hell? She frowned at his back before scrambling out of the car and yelling, 'Wait! Where are you going?'

He half-turned to her, tattooed chest rising and falling with each furious breath. With the forest as a backdrop, he looked like some sort of warrior apparition, half man, half ancient being.

'I need to make peace with spirit, leave me be! You've done enough damage. Take the car, I don't care anymore!'

'But you said the spirit guided you ... I don't understand?'

'Yeah, spirit guided me to you and pushed me to save you, eh.' His staccato words spilled out like a lethal scatter-gun. 'But now, because of your obsessive need to find material things, two people drowned at my hands. Yeah, I hated him, but he drowned. Do you get it? I risked my life for you, I saved your skinny pink hide, but it was your need that created all of this. You couldn't leave it, eh? You had to go back. All this time I've been livin' rough, followin' him. Yeah, I thought about makin' him pay, but I never did!' He turned and started walking down the track again.

'But they stole ...'

He turned once more and yelled 'You're obsessed!'

Delia watched him disappear into the forest, her heart exploding in resentment and confusion. Of all people, he should know the depths of her despair! It was right that they died – she was the victim! She paced beside the silver Volvo like a panther, dragging her fingers through her matted hair. 'What the hell!' she yelled at the trees.

The car beckoned like a warm friend, the keys in the ignition begged to be turned. She climbed inside, settled into the passenger seat and squeezed her eyes shut. Soon her thoughts drifted to the bottom of the Gulch where their bodies lay tangled in bull kelp. She scanned her mind for any semblance of regret yet all she felt was pure release.

CHAPTER 20

Rebirth

A car flashed by, the first for hours. What the hell was she doing out here on this lonely road? She looked to the long shadows cast across the picnic area. She wasn't going to sit here all night! Jolted into action, she exited the car, locked the door, and placed the keys in the pocket of the immense yellow jacket. Pulling it close, she strode with purpose into the forest.

She flicked aside ferns and stormed ahead until the vegetation closed in over the track. She breathed in the peat, eucalyptus and damp earth and heard the raspy predator call of a bird from up high, beyond the shrouding mass of tree-fern and broken mossy boughs. She stopped for a moment and tried to settle her nerves and called out, 'Tāne!'

She walked on beside thickets of native cherries bathed in weak winter light and came to a fork, selecting the wider path to the right. The canopy above acted like a projector screen reflecting images forefront in her mind, the wheelhouse, the spinning malevolent force on the deck, Tāne's *tā moko* lines.

Was that a voice? She remained still, scanned the boughs and ferns overhanging the muddy path. 'Hello?' she called.

She strained to hear beyond the twittering birds. 'Hello?' She squinted up at moss-covered ancient trunks, elongated by time. Way, way above, the canopy shimmered in the last vestiges of light.

'Delia.' A voice echoed from somewhere distant. She whirled around on the eerie path as the forest erupted in a cacophony of frantic bird calls.

She strained to see his tattooed face amidst the ferns. Was she jumping at shadows, out here alone? 'Stop playing with me! Show yourself!' she yelled at the boughs overhead.

'Your grace,' said the voice from somewhere high above.

The words echoed across the silent forest. Her heart leaped. She knew that voice – neither male nor female! The commanding voice addressed her with supreme compassion.

'We have protected your goddess essence, your grace.'

'You heard my prayers!' she cried. A golden beam of light descended through the canopy, forcing her to fall backwards on-to the path. She squeezed her eyes tight and turned her face sideways towards the mud, such was the brightness. Stillness enveloped her body, and a great peace made her sigh with relief. Tentative, she opened one eye then the other, finding herself surrounded in a gentle, golden sphere of light. It made her feel like she was floating on a wave of pure joy.

'The time is right for us to return it to you, but you must use it well, to heal the planet, to stop humankind's destruction.'

'But I can't do ...'

Alien words swirled around her head. She cared not for their meaning once the bright green drops of rain began to fall upon her upturned face.

Overcome by an urge to see the rain soak into her skin, she ripped off the fisherman's jacket and pulled at the wine-stained yak-hair. Precious beads of green rain seeped into her skin, making her arms and throat tingle. She lay down in the mud, closed her eyes, absorbed in wonder and bliss, and awoke to the loud chatter of birds.

She tried to remain drifting in a state of divine rapture but the cold seeping into her back forced her to sit up. Reaching for the warmth of yak-hair and the fisherman's jacket, she glimpsed tinges of emerald goose-bumped skin above her chest. Her fingertips glanced across rippled lizard skin at her throat. She smiled and tossed back her hair, breathing in her own luminosity, feeling part forest, part exotic bird and filled to the brim with the love of divine nature.

She meandered along the path, lost in reverie. Pushing aside the fronds of tree-ferns, she jolted to a stand-still. The wreckage of burned stumps before her looked like a scene from a dystopian movie. She sank to her knees and scanned the scraped ground and piles of twisted roots. How could such destruction be allowed to happen? Seething, she looked up to the large cumulous clouds for answers. The Light of Truth were up there somewhere, watching her reaction. 'How the hell am I supposed to stop this?' she yelled across the barren earth. 'It's impossible!'

She pressed her hands into the dry crust, a token effort to heal the planet as she had been commanded. She was just one person, an artist, that's all. She could no sooner stop humankind's destruction than fly to the moon.

Delia ran back into the life-giving forest, where the moss and the bird calls could calm her shell-shocked body. Finding the fork in the path, she took the alternate route, which soon opened on to a gentle button grass plain, overseen by an immense tree of exquisite beauty. Only a short distance away, giants like this had been mowed to the ground but this one had stood the test of man and time. Here the mighty mountain ash towered with such a regal presence, like it was maintaining the balance between earth and sky.

She staggered towards the tree which beckoned like a lifeline in the dim light of dusk. Its trunk pulsed with an aura, an energy that welcomed her to breathe in its strength and beauty. She pressed her muddy hands against its trunk leaving palm prints and curled up at the tree's base.

A tsunami of emotion crashed into the cliffs of her heart. She thought of the scorched stumps close by and the destruction of nature across the world. In her mind, giant eucalypts and redwoods crashed to the earth and putrid oceans lay dying under plastic debris. A sea of crowds and spinning faces, presidents, prime ministers, destroyers, condensed to schoolyard bullies. They pointed, jeered and jostled, craning to get a look at her throat. There were the solemn faces of foster carers returning her into the care of the State. She pulled the fisherman's jacket close and sobbed into the earth.

When there were no more tears to cry, she sat up, feeling somehow different. She looked across the button grass plain, trying to discern this new, strange, emboldened feeling. Then she realised, she was no longer Delia the orphan or Delia the survivor. She was free to live her destiny on her terms. With her essence once again coursing through her veins, she could truly embrace nature's beauty and paint to her heart's content. All the grief and turmoil of her past, everything that weighed her down, stopping her painting – it was all behind her now.

She breathed in the sense of renewal, flushed with love for the planet, for the rippling earth and the pulsing trees. The forest embraced her like an old friend, and she would be forever grateful for its sanctuary.

CHAPTER 21

Destiny Calls

A spine-tingling sound like ghouls emerging from beneath the earth shattered the night air. Delia sat up abruptly and with a thumping heart, tried to shake off sleep and peer into the darkness.

A great swathe of stars told her that she'd slept too long. The ghouls erupted again, squabbling between themselves. Their demonic growls cried for her to hurry, hurry through the night, before we find you.

Unseen wings flapped overhead. She jumped up in panic, collided with a large mass and unleashed a scream into the night.

'Eh, you're all right. It's only me!'

She felt a strong arm around her shoulder, being guided to sit back at the base of the mighty tree. 'Oh god, you gave me a fright!' she gushed.

'Devils have got a kill, that's all. They make a hell of a noise.'

She felt on edge, alert to something loud but unspoken. 'Should we try to get back to the car?' Her words sounded odd, breathless.

'Best stay here, eh. We might lose our way now that it's dark. This mighty tree can be our home for the night.'

Here heart raced, but she shuffled forward, giving him room to settle between her back and the tree.

'Here, this'll keep us warm.' He unfurled the blanket from around his shoulders and draped it over her body, smothering her senses with the smell of cut grass and earth.

'But you'll be cold.'

'Not if we sit together like this,' he said softly.

Her body fizzed with the intimacy of being pressed close, the softness of his words, his breath on the back of her neck. Each second felt elongated, extraordinary. The world condensed down to their island, huddled below the tattered blanket. She melded into his powerful chest, felt his arms wrap around her body and became encased between his legs. Inside the warm cocoon, pressed against his warrior body and protected by the might of the tree, she felt utter peace. For what seemed a long time they said nothing, just breathing in unison.

The forest erupted again in a series of vicious, ghoulish squabbles. He rubbed her arms and swayed a little to the rhythm of an unsung melody. Her back arched and fell in imperceptible but intimate waves in time with his heartbeat.

'You understood today, he whispered.

Was he speaking another language? She clawed her way back from sleep to listen.

'I watched you – I heard you. Felt your reaction to the earth, to this tree. I saw your true spirit. Before you slept, you looked like you had found home. Here, turn around, put your legs either side of mine, so I can look at you.'

Electricity buzzed on the cold night air. She swivelled around and straddled his body as he'd asked, aware of the arch in her back, the uplift of her breasts, the brush of her nipples against the fisherman's jacket. She breathed in his breath, alert, waiting.

'You've changed. I witnessed it, eh. You shed your old skin, you felt the earth like a spirit being.'

A warning clanged in her brain. How long had he been watching? Had he seen her throat before she'd put her clothes back on? Did it matter? Her body responded by pressing closer.

'You're right … I'm different.' The realisation, the exquisite beauty of the moment, made her voice crack.

She struggled to find the words to express all that she'd seen and felt and done. 'It's like all the poison of the past doesn't matter anymore. Because you saved me, I feel like this.' She pressed her palm over a tattooed cheek.

'What do you feel?'

He placed his hand over hers. 'Pulsing, like rhythmic waves.'

'I can feel the earth now, like I'm one with it. And I can paint and bring my landscapes to life.'

She hesitated, mulling over the shadow of an epiphany that lurked just beyond her reach.

Only when she pressed her hand on his chest did the revelation move from the shadows. There it was in his heartbeat beneath her palm. This was how she was to heal the earth, to stop the destruction of humankind. To make her landscapes pulse with so much life, so much purity, that they would speak to people's hearts and minds. Just like Giovanni said '*Your paintings have the power to make people look after our home, our one and only planet.*'

'I have so much living to do. Thank you for saving me.' Her mouth brushed over his blue-black lips and pressed against his temple. His chest was home, where she could breathe in each tattoo. The lines spun their sacred stories around her head. The rhythm of his heartbeat beneath her ear told her that all was well, that their hearts would forever be connected. After all those years of searching for love and protection, she'd found it here, deep in a dark forest.

* * *

Delia lifted her head from Tāne's chest. For a moment she was lost in his black almond-shaped eyes, shining with spiritual intelligence like a portal to other worlds and ancient times. A burst of kookaburras cackling through the forest made her smile.

They eased themselves up stiffly from their position at the base of the tree and stared at the dawn light which stretched across the dewy clearing. Part of her wanted to stay and expand the moment, to ensure that it was carved into her memory forever. She watched him walking over the button grass with a light grace that belied his weight and build. He stopped and craned his neck back, closing his eyes as the sunlight warmed his lined cheeks. Whispered Māori words, a prayer perhaps, caressed the gentle morning air. She imagined his people doing just that for centuries.

She etched every precious moment into her memory. The smattering of frost on the ground, the way the button grass gleamed like a million diamonds. His tattooed chest reflecting the golden light of a new dawn, the way he walked towards her, oozing peace, wisdom and the equanimity of a man living in harmony with nature. She felt her body lean towards him like a magnet, allowing him to caress her face.

'Were you praying?'

He breathed in her soft words. 'Yeah, a karakia. It's a simple message of gratitude.'

She lost herself for a second in the intensity of his gaze, feeling her cheeks redden as she waited for the press of his lips. Instead, he took her freezing hand and led her back to the crystallised mud of the path.

Delia looked back one last time to the place where her future began, back where her muddy palm prints marked the trunk of the magnificent ash.

They walked back in silence, each lost in their own thoughts and the possibilities that lay ahead. Delia broke the intimate silence when the car came into view.

'What will you do when we get back to Hobart?' she asked.

He dropped her hand and backed away a little. 'We must do what we must do, eh,' he replied.

'What does that mean?' She frowned and cocked her head to the side a little. There was something about his demeanour that made her heart squeeze tight. She tried to search his beautiful sacred lines to find the answer. Something subtle had happened, yet his face reflected pure gentleness and compassion.

'Let me ask you. What do you want to do?'

Maybe he wanted her to take the lead? Was that it? 'Well, I want to retrieve my things. I figured out where they hid them. Then I'm ready to start my life ...' She couldn't quite say it, but her eyes conveyed 'with you.'

His silence sent a bolt of electricity through her body.

'Um, I have an offer to go to Macquarie Island or I could ...'

Her words trailed away. She moved towards him but already, deep in her heart, she knew. In an imperceptible instant it had all changed. Through tear-filled eyes she saw him step backwards again. She tried to read his lined face and noticed his eyes had dulled with something akin to regret.

'You're not ready. Maybe one day, eh?'

She stood bolted to the spot, felt the ache of his gentle caress, and in a blink, he was gone, lost to the forest.

Delia doubled over, gasping at the ferocity of the pain squeezing her heart. His departure was so breath-taking, so final. The thought forced her to scramble breathless back along the track. 'Come back!' she yelled through sobs.

She stumbled and fell onto the muddy ground. How could he do this to her? She'd only just found him! How could he just leave her like that! All the times she'd been left in her life collided in an almighty crash of unfairness. She strained to hear footsteps, a crack of a twig, but there was nothing. The forest had either swallowed him or he was quiet, watching, camouflaged against the green.

In slow, deliberate movements, she trudged back to the car and settled behind the wheel. She took one last look at the path and pressed her foot down on the accelerator, leaving shards of splintered heart on the highway.

It was late morning when she crested the brow of a hill and saw the indigo mountain in the distance, etched against an ominous slate grey sky. The gun-metal grey Derwent snaking through the landscape reminded her of his beautiful *tā moko* lines. *Stop it!*

A vision of Athena's face creased with worry pushed her onwards, over the Tasman Bridge, around the grounds of the Botanical Gardens. In her mind she saw herself knocking on the door and falling into Athena's arms. Yet how could she explain the horror, the madness, the love – the pain?

She drove past the old sandstone warehouses of Salamanca Place and something akin to panic made her veer into the carpark up ahead. She recognised the spot where Ronan had swerved into, next to the water's edge. *'Silence – or I will put you in the boot!'*

She flicked the memory and the images of their rotting bodies from her mind and exited the car. From here she could see the shoreline and the house that had harboured her nightmare. Her eyes moved from the little rocky beach and Ronan's shed, over the wrought-iron speared fencing to the large plate-glass window of the living room.

Bitterness gnawed at her belly. Would she ever be able to erase their hateful faces from her mind? 'They're gone,' she reminded herself. Lost to the bottom of the Gulch where they belonged.

She slammed the car door and followed the pavement through the carpark down to the pebbled shoreline. She crunched over broken shells, passed by the long-ago remnants of a bonfire, moving closer to Ronan's shed. From here, she could still see crimson paint smeared down the plate-glass. She forced herself to think what lay beyond the window and tried to imagine entering his room, moving towards the mural. Somewhere, below the whale's tortured eye, down there at the bottom of the sea, was a safe, she just knew it.

Just break in! She batted the thought away. Even in death, his residual energy had the capacity to drip like poison down the walls. Even now Ronan's ghost-white bloated face, his eyeballs staring beyond the bull kelp, watched her every move.

Sickened by the thought, she walked further on past the gaping hole in Ronan's shed and stopped to lean on the upturned old dinghy with its peeling paint. The cold salt air filling her lungs spoke of freedom and a distant land across the ocean.

She frowned at a flurry of movement back at the carpark. The sight of reflective vests made her scurry on towards the ramshackle shed near the silver-wood pier. She waded through the long grass to the back and lay down on the mould-spotted sails.

She nestled in the same hollow where he must have laid and, somewhere in the twilight of sleep, thought of all the hopes and dreams of people who had lived right here on this shore. No matter their trials, and grief, the waves still crested and fell against the rocks, the seabirds still wheeled in the sky.

Beneath the fisherman's jacket, she drifted in dreams of Tāne. His *tā moko* lines scrolled into the fronds of tree-ferns, his chest morphed into earth's most enormous trees, where the birds sung timeless songs in the canopy. She heard the boom of his heartbeat and saw her muddy hand-print peel off the mountain ash and transplant itself on-to his heart. She heard his gentle songs of love and prayers for the earth and his gods.

Delia clawed her way back from sleep. Something profound had entered her mind. Like a soaring eagle, the thought glided above the clouds of her consciousness. She strained to remember and then the answer came to her in a startling moment of clarity. He had ascended beyond the trappings of humanity, beyond the need for possessions. He was walking the path of enlightenment. Yet what did she do! She talked like a crazy woman about breaking in, taking back what was rightfully hers!

'You're not ready. Maybe one day, eh?' The echo of his words forever tattooed on her heart made her rock back and forth. She ached for him, to feel his breath on her face, to feel his strong, protective arms around her. Yet she ached for her precious photos and her turquoise necklace too. Even now, in her darkest hour, she still wanted them.

She cupped her face in her hands and tried to think beyond this universe of yearning. Her one true godsend was the feel of her essence rippling through her veins, stronger than ever. Then the irony struck her. She wiped the back of her hand against her wet cheeks. She didn't need the symbol etched in stone to touch her skin at all. She'd regained her capacity to live out her destiny, paint for the planet, stop humankind's destruction.

And her photos – could she cope without ever seeing them again? *'Their faces are etched in your heart, eh.'* The arrow of logic, fired from Tāne's bow, launched through time and space and landed with a thunderbolt in the centre of her chest.

Should she return to the mountain ash and wait for him? But could she even find that exact spot again? Even if she did, Tāne would be elusive, a shadowman, lost to the forest. The truth pushed her out of the boatshed into the dim light of dusk.

No, her future lay out there, beyond the mouth of the river. Somewhere, beyond the infinite rolling ink and green of the Southern Ocean a new home waited. As she picked her way along the shore, she hoped the ocean and the Antarctic air would blast away the pain in her heart.

CHAPTER 22

Jewel of the Witches Cauldron

Macquarie Island, Southern Ocean, December 2015

Once there was a reverence
To the land, to the sea
How to set in motion
A return to peace
Mankind's destiny

Delia gulped back bile, tightened her grip on the stern railing and forced herself to withstand the self-imposed rite of passage. Out here, immersed in spray and the squeal of the wind, she felt every particle of her being drink in the savage wildness.

In contrast, the forest always exuded calm. Maybe somewhere in the shadows, beneath ferns and tangled roots, there were places to hide her longing.

Out here she was buffeted, exposed. The charcoal vastness beyond the ship forced her to contemplate her spec of existence while every emotion smacked her in the face and swirled away on the wind.

She averted her gaze from the vessel's frothing wake to the giant wingspan and pure white plumage of a wandering albatross. It swooped down past the vessel before accelerating upwards past a squadron of screeching southern giant petrels. 'We're both on a mission,' she thought. 'Both far from land, doing all we can to survive.'

An unwanted thought barrelled into her as harsh as the subantarctic wind. 'And how much longer do you keep on 'surviving', working like a woman possessed?'

But look what has erupted from those frenzied moments.

She stared at the vertical spray that whipped across the vast bleakness beyond the ship and thought of the star of her greatest work, *Reaching for the Sky*. In her mind's eye she could see the regal silver-barked *Eucalyptus regnans* rising from an ancient fern glen. The painting spoke just as loudly as the catalyst which worked to stop the damming of the Franklin – Peter Dombrovski's famed Franklin River photograph of Rock Island Bend.

Even beyond the howling wind, she could hear protesters condemning the most recent destruction of old growth forest and Sir David Attenborough's recognition of her work. 'You are a catalyst for change, a true conservation queen.' Those words would forever be tattooed on her heart.

Delia looked to the tracks across the skin of the ocean and up to the smouldering sky. 'But it's not enough, is it?' The wild trough-filled ocean howled at her in response, to do more, far more.

She staggered back to the warmth of her bunk, slammed her eyelids shut and tried to block out the sickening roll of the ship. Why was it that she must shoulder the burden of humanity? Why couldn't the wind just snatch her yearning for what couldn't be and fling that useless part of her into oblivion?

Somewhere between a fitful sleep, in the place were imagination and higher consciousness meets, she felt the weight of the treasured turquoise stone against the ridged skin at her neck. The symbol engraved on the back weaved like magic, moving like slippery lines out into the cosmos. The lines spiralled through the dark vastness of space before circling back through her third eye into her heart.

'*I had a spirit dream*,' Tāne's words echoed in her heart.

Delia's eyes flew open. Why had she just heard Tāne's voice?

She lay in her bunk staring into the dark. Had she just had a spirit dream herself? Already his words were drifting from her consciousness.

She strained to remember but pixel images of logged old growth forest lay like giant obstacles across her mind.

The slam of water against the hull morphed into the sound of chainsaws and riots. She'd painted for the forest, for all the living creatures, painted until her heart near bled onto the canvas. Yet still they savaged the land. Why weren't her paintings enough to stop the carnage?

A thought swooped through the darkness and landed with a sizzle of rightness in her heart. What if she hid the engraved symbol on her missing stone into her paintings? And what if she added her own protection symbol as gifted by the Light of Truth? Each symbol had power. She closed her eyes to digest this new revelation.

Just like a prophecy, she heard her own voice from long ago.

* * *

The witches' cauldron of the Furious Fifties had made Delia's stomach feel like oily fish slithering in a bucket. She leaned over the steel railing of the *Tangaroa,* thanking God that they'd anchored, and felt the intense pull of the island across the bay.

It was always like this. The island's rugged rawness carved by pounding ocean and gale-force winds had always made her spirits soar. The rare subantarctic jewel of Macquarie Island, affectionately known as 'Macca', spoke to her heart like nowhere else on earth. She peered through the sea mist at the familiar ridges and snow-spattered plateau, rising like a fortress up from the grey pebble beach.

She pictured herself climbing the two hundred steps to the lookout at Razorback Ridge to her left, where the golden tussock grasses waved their welcome. On her right was the small isthmus of land where the satellite communications radome dominated the landscape like a bevelled diamond ring fit for a giant. Somewhere between the comms sheds and the sharp rise of Wireless Hill, right near the blubbery seals sprawled across the black sand, was a warm cabin.

'I'm home!' The prevailing wind, tinged with rain, snatched the words and flung them across the choppy emerald water of Buckles Bay.

Already a light amphibious re-supply vessel was edging closer to the ship. A green-billed petrel swooped overhead crying an aggressive warning but swung away to avoid the bully of the Southern Ocean, a dusty brown subantarctic skua. She closed her eyes and allowed the shrill screech of kelp gulls and guttural bellows of elephant seals to wrap around her.

'Hey, Floss!'

Delia snapped out of her reverie and giggled at Cy's attempt to batten down his wild hair as he stood on the deck below.

'We'll be the first in if you get your skates on!'

She watched him jump down onto the platform of the amphibious craft and immerse himself in a flurry of back slaps and cheers.

She hoisted her backpack on her shoulders and made her way through the antiseptic smelling corridors.

'Heh!' she snapped at the body pushing past. *'Ola!'* José called.

Within a couple of strides, he'd made it to the ramp and sprang down on-to the platform with the agility of a mountain lion. Delia watched him shake hands with some of the crew before striding towards a redhead. In seconds, he'd crushed the woman against his surfer body and buried her in a curtain of knotted, Rastafarian blond ringlets.

Delia grunted. Only three days earlier he'd tried channeling all that charisma in her direction.

'Not fast enough Floss! I'll catch up with you tonight,' called Cy.

'No way – I can still beat you!' she cried back. Challenge on, she scurried up to the fly-deck where the Zodiac was hooked up to the crane, ready for deployment. She nodded to Emosi, the burly Samoan first mate, and scrambled into the craft. In just minutes, the Zodiac roared past the crawling amphibious vehicle, leaving Cy and his priceless expression, in their wake.

Soon the stink of languishing southern elephant seals became more pronounced as they came into the landing beach. It was unmistakable, that earthy, stagnant seaweed smell.

As they edged closer to the beach, Emosi pointed to a massive torpedo shape cutting through the swell. He slowed the Zodiac, giving the bull elephant seal a wide berth. Delia watched in awe as the goliath tossed them a disdainful look, proboscis in the air, maintaining his course towards another male further down the beach. Soon the two beachmasters would be roaring at each other, battling for supremacy.

They puttered closer to a welcoming party standing on the rocky shore. Delia grinned and waved to the yellow-jacketed brigade of bearded men and one woman with a white beanie. Behind them, hundreds of golden and grey female elephant seals clustered along the stretch of beach, rotund weaners attached to their fatty girths. Predator skuas swooped from the ever-darkening sky to pillage placentas while black velvet pups looked on, vulnerable and ripe for the picking.

Emosi cut the engine and threw the anchor overboard while members of the welcoming party waded towards them. 'Good to see you!' a bearded man called. Delia shook his hand and handed him her heavy backpack.

'Welcome to Macca!' the woman yelled from the shore. 'You got quite the welcome.' She pointed to where two bull elephants crashed against each other in vicious battle.

Delia swung herself over the side of the Zodiac, allowing her waders to slide into knee-deep frigid water. Pebbles shifted beneath her weight, making her stumble awkwardly towards the woman's beaming smile. 'Hi, I'm Delia, artist-in-residence and all-round Macca addict!'

Delia found herself swamped in the woman's welcoming embrace. 'So happy to finally meet you – been waiting all winter for this. You're a real hit in these parts. I'm Dr Anna Turner, by the way – station team leader, until February, anyway.'

'Long stint – must mean you're a Macca addict too then.'

'Sure am. Who wouldn't love these westerlies?' she yelled, bracing herself against the wind's onslaught. 'Skies full of birds, beaches full of ellies ... there's no place like it on earth!' Anna's sea-green eyes sparkled with happiness. 'Gotta say, though, it's great to see another face – winter's a bit of a tough gig down here!'

'Yeah, sorry I couldn't make it earlier. As you know, I planned to. I just got caught up with all the rallies and stuff going on in Hobart.'

'No worries. I mean look at what you achieved and if you'd come in winter you'd be leaving now, not arriving!'

Delia glanced at Emosi unloading bags from the Zodiac then turned to a man who had been hovering at her periphery. 'Hi, I'm Todd, station supply officer, at your service!' he grinned, shaking her hand vigorously.

Delia recognised the likely comedian of the group; the ginger fuzz-covered face, laugh lines and slight Kiwi accent said it all. He looked early twentys, maybe five or so years younger than herself.

She allowed him to guide her further up the beach as Anna called back 'Watch him. He will try to convince you he is the most important person on this island!'

'Ah, but I am,' came his quick reply.

'No me, no food!' chorused other station members who were waiting to welcome the approaching amphibious vehicle.

'Resident black belt and gourmet cook at your service,' he said. 'And chick magnet!'

'I heard that Todd. Yeah, to the penguins!' called back Anna. 'You'll have to excuse him, Delia, a winterer and starved of female company. He will be showing you kicks and blocks before you know it and pestering you at every opportunity!'

'You'll only have to put up with me until next week,' came the retort.

Delia noticed his face drop. 'I know what it's like,' she said, patting him on the shoulder. 'This is my sixth stint down here. Leaving gets you here,' she placed a hand on her heart.

'Yep, back on the *Aurora Australis* next week. When it's back from d'Urville, me and a fair few of these fine folk are going home.' He dipped into quiet contemplation for a moment then brightened up. 'But not without a party! We've got a fancy-dress do at the end of the week for all the returning winterers and to celebrate the arrival of the summer expeditioners and you lot!'

He was interrupted by an almighty clash and roar down the beach. They watched the grand finale of the fight, cringing in awe as the three-thousand-kilogram elephant seal reared its mighty carcass upwards and smashed one last time into the younger seal, which edged bloodied and defeated into the surf.

Delia felt euphoric. She was surrounded by good-natured people in a wild and remote paradise where sea and earth nurtured the masses and nature was at its most supreme. She sighed with satisfaction at the thought of her paintings to come, one day hanging with her other subantarctic works in the Wild Island Gallery in Hobart.

A westerly gust pushed Delia forward a little. Glancing towards the *Tangaroa,* she noticed a bank of ominous clouds rolling over the ship. White caps reared over rippled water while the kelp gulls soared and dipped. Even now the ship looked stranded, isolated out there in an ink-coloured bay.

Anna sidled up to her and nodded towards the amphibious vehicle rolling slowly up the beach. 'Good thing we unloaded when we did, weather's turning. Wind must be getting over twenty-five knots now.' She still had to yell a bit to be heard above the wind and the constant cacophony of grunts from the nearby elephant seal harem.

'Probably got five minutes before it pelts,' interjected a broad-shouldered man in a yellow all-weather jacket. 'I'll take you up to the station. Aaron by the way,' he said, stretching out a gloved hand. 'Volunteer wildlife ranger.'

Delia noticed a section of bull neck beneath a salt-and-pepper beard and felt his bear paw squeeze around her hand.

'Or did you want to go up with them?' Anna said, nodding in the direction of the amphibious craft.

There was something in Anna's eyes, a hint of annoyance perhaps? 'Um, thanks anyway, but I'll wait for my friend.' Delia said, easing her hand from Aaron's grip.

Delia turned towards the vehicle rolling towards them and called 'Hey Cy! You took your time!'

'Funny, Floss. Come on up there's room next to this pallet.' He leaned down and helped Delia to crawl over the tyres onto the platform beside him.

'Cy, this is Anna, the station team leader. Anna, meet Cy, best voyage manager in the south.'

Anna reached up to shake his hand. 'Good to meet you. Funny, I can't remember a Simon on the manifest?'

'No, Cy is short for Cyclopes.' He pushed back his mop of blond hair and grinned at her startled reaction. 'Nickname,' he explained. 'Always keep one eye on the ocean, that's my motto.'

'Gotta love a man with a sense of humour,' Anna replied, casting a distracted frown at the red-headed woman and the man with chaotic hair.

Delia pulled at the hood of her jacket and huddled next to Cy for warmth. The amphibious vehicle jerked into motion, passing by the UNESCO World Heritage sign on its way to the station. Her eyes moved from the ship in the white-capped bay to the huddle of yellow jackets on the beach to the separated loner standing hunched, bowed against the wind. Even across the distance, his stare slammed into her gut. She squirmed next to Cy, feeling a strange flush of hotness rising beneath her jacket.

The vehicle continued across the bleak isthmus, rolling past sheds, the bulbous radome, and another harem full of dreamy-eyed fat weaner pups.

'Check him out – enormous!'

Delia looked to the gigantic bull elephant seal wallowing in a putrid smelling hole amidst tussock grass. The vigilant beachmaster stared back with eyes full of suspicion, as if forewarning that she too would need to keep her wits about her.

CHAPTER 23

Razorback

Delia lay saucer-eyed in her sleeping bag, listening to the slam of wind against wood and the grunts of seals. The squealing wind wormed its way into her ear, morphing into the sound of Aaron's guitar in the mess tent the night before. She'd watched his strong tattooed arms caressing the instrument, her body flushing hot at the thought of him stroking her that way.

She tossed the image aside and rolled over, but her body raged back, agitated, demanding to know just how much longer she was going to hold on to Tāne. *'He saved your life, remember?'* A corner of her heart squeezed in memory of his beautiful *tā moko* lines.

At last, a chink of daylight squeezed under the door. It was probably only 4.00 am but the thought of Razorback Ridge at dawn pushed her up and out of her sleeping bag.

'Don't forget to attach your SPOT,' croaked Anna, still sounding worse for wear after last night's swapping of stories in the mess.

Delia threw the satellite messenger device into her pack, called 'Got it – just off to Razorback!' and opened the door to the subantarctic air.

'Far out!' she gasped. She pulled her beanie down over her ears, sidestepped two listless mounds of grunting blubber near the door and headed out across the isthmus. Seaweed-filled waves crashed on the shore to her right, sending sea spray flying up over the bog known as the 'feather bed'. To her right, early morning sea mist drifted across the tussock grass, enshrining ellies in an other-worldly aura. Out there in the bay to her left, the orange hull of the *Tangaroa* merged with the rippled bay, streaked tangerine and pink by the dawn sky.

She stopped in her tracks, mesmerised by the giant wingspan of a lone albatross before continuing past the sapphire blue radome.

A bull elephant seal raised its proboscis and released a deep, guttural growl. She scooted around its bright pink mouth full of teeth, moving closer to a harem of females nursing their liquid-eyed pups. The scene before her near screamed to be sketched and captured on canvas. Delia watched a languid mother flick an apathetic flipper, oblivious that her milk was being siphoned by a hostile-eyed skua. Above, petrels circled, ever hopeful of the easy pickings of a squashed pup.

She started the climb upwards towards the viewing platform, stopping for a few breathless seconds to take some photos. As always, the *Tangaroa's* satellite dishes looked alien against the rugged beauty of the bay and in this light, the radome looked like a precious jewel dropped from outer space. She took one more look at the bay before pushing up the last incline.

She heaved herself on-to the viewing platform, gasping for breath. It felt liberating up here, with the wind at her back, high above the station. There before her was the ocean, vast, wild and unpredictable, while the ridge behind embraced her like an old friend.

After taking a few photos to record the scene, she lifted a sketch pad from her backpack and got to work. Her hand moved rapid and purposeful across the page as if channelled by an unknown force. Already she knew that the spiral symbol from her necklace would hide in the waves crashing on Cosray Rocks, and there in the ripples of the bay near the *Tangaroa* she'd insert her protection symbol.

She squinted at the source of a distraction. There, something moving in the shadow of the sheds. Someone in station issue yellow appeared, heading fast towards the ridge. This was no dawn meander but a serious run. She watched the figure run around the hulks of elephant seals, giving the boulder-sized bull a wide berth. In little time, the figure started the ascent towards the viewing platform.

The wooden staircase vibrated beneath the force of a weight. She sighed with annoyance before turning back to her drawing. At least at that pace, they wouldn't bother her for long.

Heavy breathing filled the air. She gulped and willed for the runner to be black-belt Todd. With hand poised mid-air above her sketch, she watched the broad-shouldered runner pass by, face obscured beneath a hood.

She watched him double over, sucking in precious air and caught sight of a section of flyaway salt-and-pepper beard.

'Sorry – to – disturb,' he gasped.

'It's okay; I've only just started anyway.'

Why did he have to do that? Push back his hood, expose his neck, prowl the platform like he owned it.

She looked down to the sketch and willed her hand to draw something. 'That was a serious run,' she said, trying her best to sound indifferent.

'Shows how fast I can run towards a beautiful woman.'

Delia jerked her head up in shock and met his piercing gaze. The sound of gulls and the distant whoosh of waves on the pebble shore far below drowned out the sound of her thumping heart.

She heard a strange high-pitched giggle escape her lips. 'You've just been down here too long.'

He smiled and stroked his beard, edging forwards. *Oh God, don't come any closer.* In her mind she'd already crossed the platform, pushed her body up against his and tasted the flesh at his neck.

'Sorry, what did you say?' she stammered.

'I said are you going to the fancy-dress party?'

'Oh, of course, you're leaving, with the other winterers.'

'Yep. I'd prefer to stay longer but our esteemed station team leader declined my request, so ...,' He studied the platform for a second then shone a wicked grin in her direction. 'But – that still gives us a few days to get to know each other.'

'Afraid not,' her voice cracked. 'I'm off to Brothers Point tomorrow. But yes, I'm back in time for the party.' Delia bit her lip and turned away.

How many times had she seen that hungry look, common amongst winterers confined for too long?

'Do you want me to come too? It can get lonely down there?'

Delia inhaled sharply. For a second the wind seemed to encircle their bodies, pushing them closer.

'Um, I want to say yes, I really do, but I'm working.' She tried her best to convey the sane, logical part of herself which held firm to the image of a waiting canvas.

'You're right, of course. I would be a ... distraction. Until the party then ...'

CHAPTER 24

Spectrum

Delia held tight to the side of the rigid inflatable boat as it bashed through the dark swell. Leaving the station behind always made her feel like this, exhilarated, rewired. They hugged the shoreline, following steep ancient cliffs of oceanic crust. She looked through the sea-mist, to the mounds of blubber lying on the grey stone beach to the snow-spattered plateau high above and tried to commit every ecstatic spray-filled moment to memory. It was like she'd been tipped upside down and all the suffocating darkness of her past had just fallen away.

In tune with her mood, the blare of a thousand party horns assaulted her ears. Anna slowed the outboard, allowing them to view the royal penguin colony. Delia grinned at the crush of hipsters with their moulting chicks.

'Those yellow slick hair-dos crack me up!' she yelled across to Anna, her words already lost amidst the ruckus.

The outboard revved into life. Soon the familiar tussock-covered outcrop, looking more ancient landing site for aliens than field base, came into view.

Anna putted gently into the shallows and cut the engine. 'Here we go, your taxi has arrived. You gonna be okay down here on your own?'

'Absolutely – Googie and I,' she nodded towards the egg-shaped orange fibreglass hut, 'are old mates. Lost track how many paintings I've done down here.'

Delia shouldered her sleeping bag and backpack, flung her legs over the side of the Zodiac and plunged her waders into waist-high water.

'Whew – takes your breath away, even with these on!' She sloshed to the shoreline, deposited her bags on the rocks and waded back towards Anna.

'Can't wait to see what paintings you conjure up this time. Well ... as long as it's all about the scenery.'

'Of course; what else?' said Delia.

'You know,' said Anna in a no-nonsense tone. 'Don't forget I know everything that goes on around here. I know when trouble's just around the bend. Those smitten eyes of yours, the way you flicked your hair when he was playing guitar. I know. Not that it's you I'm worried about so much.'

'Don't know what you mean,' said Delia, making a show of struggling with her collapsible easel to mask the annoyance in her voice.

'Mmm ... well, just saying, be careful of that one. There're people here who can't wait to see the back of him. Not the team player we need down here. I mean, why the hell didn't he entertain us like that through our darkest days?'

'Well, what can I say? Nothing to do with me,' yelled back Delia. She dropped the easel on the rocks and looked up at the hut's elliptical windows. Soon she'd be huddled inside, and Anna's judgment and Aaron's hungry eyes would be a world away.

'Ok then. Don't forget to use the satellite device to check-in every now and again,' called Anna.

'Sure will – thanks again for bringing me down!' Glad of the roar of the outboard, she gave one last wave and hoisted the sleeping bag on her back. *Maybe Anna was right?* Two nearby basking seals flicked their flippers in lazy agreement. 'What would you know,' she said out loud.

Indeed, what did she know? She crunched past the seals and puffed up the incline, all the while straining to answer even basic questions. Volunteer Wildlife Ranger, looks fit, capable, plays a guitar. For goodness' sake, is that all she knew? What had she seen in his eyes, beyond the dullness and sensory deprivation of a long dark winter? What was it that made her want to gravitate towards him like a water diviner's rod?

Judging from Anna's comments, maybe he's a bit of a loner? She thought of the way he'd stood apart from the crowd on the landing beach. *He was watching you, wanting you.* She sighed and stormed back down the incline to retrieve her other supplies.

Did she want him? Did his tattoos just remind of her Tāne? Was that it? She sat next to the pack and easel and looked for answers in the gentle waves lapping the shore. Bracken seaweed caught in the swell reminded her of Aaron's tattoos. She imagined trailing her fingertips over his forearms tracing each line, leaning in to nibble his bull neck. 'Stop it!' she berated herself. It would end in disaster, it always did.

Look at dear sweet Caleb. Rallying next to her, cheering her on, she'd let her guard down. *'But I want to see you naked babe!'* The dreaded words, the fumbling in the dark, tugging at her scarf, it was all too much. There was just no point. *It was best to be remote, just like here, just like now.*

In the distance the vague buzz of an outboard motor could still be heard. Soon it would just be her and the sounds of solitude. *Just breathe in nature. Don't think of him. Don't think of anyone.*

How she loved it here, the rugged remoteness of Brothers Point. The grunts of seals, the whoosh of waves on the shore, the way the wind brushed through the tussock grass and whistled around the Googie Hut. Not a soul in sight. Resolved to be true to her purpose and push everyone and everything from her mind, she collected her supplies and trudged back up the incline.

She shoved open the wooden door of the Googie Hut and hauled her packs into the orange fibreglass chamber. The circular interior beckoned for her to come in. The three empty bunk beds and a stack of stored provisions atop the semi-circular cabinet stared back. A sense of calm descended around her. She grinned at the view through the boggle eyed windows, watching Anna's silhouette grow ever more distant.

She skirted the central table, turned on the oven and poured fresh water into the kettle. Within minutes, heat emanating from the oven working to warm the hut and the kettle whistled its home-coming tune. Placing a tin of banana bread mixture in the oven and with coffee in hand, she gazed around the hut, feeling content.

The hut was just as she'd left it last year. The upper shelf held stacked crockery, tins of Milo and jars of coffee, various sauces and the all-important jar of Vegemite. Mugs and utensils hung from hooks. Pots and pans and more stacked provisions including Savoy crackers and tins of soup were all neatly packed in the lower section of the cabinet.

'Come on – get cracking woman!' she said out loud. She placed the easel outside on the wooden landing and spread out the first sepia-tinted canvas. With the smell of freshly cooked banana bread filling her nostrils she mixed the palette of colours and readied herself for the frenzy of painting to come. Already her palms prickled with acute awareness, her breathing slowed, her eyes narrowed. The bay before her morphed into a sea of royal blue crushed velvet.

'I can hear your instrument tuning, waiting for the magical moment when your hands begin!' The memory of Giovanni's outburst made her giggle even now.

In her mind she could see him perched on a camp chair, wedged between an ancient moss-covered myrtle and the fronds of a tree-fern.

'You would think nothing would surpass my time at La Scala,' he had motioned upwards to the shards of light filtering through the canopy. 'Watching you, being here in takayna, one of the oldest forests on earth – I am complete.' His words had stopped her laughing at the time, pushing her to channel his awe and her pride into *Reaching for the Sky*.

Delia studied the waves frothing at the shoreline for a few seconds longer before committing to the first slashes of Prussian Blue and India Red paint on canvas. With her essence pelting through her palms like the gush from a firehose, she worked in energetic bursts. Only when the first layer of paint reflected the scene, did she stop for a break. Taking the canvas inside to dry, she wondered if the triptych she had in mind would bewitch the viewer.

She sank her teeth into hot banana bread, sipped another coffee and narrowed her critical eyes to assess the image. Were the hidden symbols enough? Was it too early to tell? She cupped her aching, frozen hands against the mug of coffee and tried to think beyond herself.

Would it force a viewer to have an indelible emotional experience?

She let out a loud sigh and massaged her scalp, trying to clear the debris from her mind – maybe. Perhaps the painting showed she was on the cusp of something monumental. If only she could grasp the answer that wafted like leaves on a summer breeze, dancing just beyond her psyche. She sighed again, knowing full well she could stare and stare at the canvas and still not find the key to the never-ending puzzle. When would her painting ever be enough to stop mankind's destruction of nature?

One canvas down, two to go. She returned to the easel, set her jaw in steely determination to paint for the planet regardless of the crushing cold. Every now and again she'd treat herself to a dash inside the Googie, make a tea and warm her hands.

Finally, with stars bedazzling the sky, she retreated inside the Googie Hut and pegged the final canvas on the clothesline. She hovered around the oven top waiting for soup to heat before returning to brave the cold just a little longer.

Huddled over the mug of soup, it occurred to her how the waves and grunting ellies were her orchestra, the vast star-studded sky her mental canvas, the freezing air her companion. She sipped the soup, thankful for its warmth and contemplated the strange expectant hush which had settled over the ocean's surface. It was if the earth was breathing in, breathing out, relieved to be far from the mass of humanity.

She looked from the strange elliptical eyes of the Googie Hut, shining bright red from the internal light, across the vastness of the ocean to the horizon. Here she was, alone with her alien spacecraft, a speck on the universe's grand stage. And somewhere way out there, beyond the stars, she felt the Light of Truth watching, waiting. *Why? Why had they entrusted her with such a unique gift?* She thought back to that fateful day in the forest, felt her skin drink in bright green pieces of essence and heard the echo of a commanding voice reverberate through the trees.

She squinted in the direction of a sudden bright light above Mount Tulloch to the north-west and put the soup down in shock.

'Oh my God!' she cried. In those few seconds the night sky had revealed a bright purple and neon green veil of unimaginable beauty, shimmering from Mount Tulloch in the west, out across the surface of the ocean. Her heart strained full to the brim with indescribable joy.

'Looking north at the great Southern Aurora,' she whispered to herself. She stood transfixed staring at the pulsating curtain of light, feeling like a part of the grand design of the cosmos.

'What am I doing just standing here!' she muttered under her breath. She burst into action, once again dragging the easel out onto the wooden platform outside the hut. With a fresh canvas attached, a new palette mixed, and with the torch clumsily wedged between her body and the easel ledge, she moved her hand in time with her rush of emotion. Her palms hurt with the force of her essence, and it was hard to see through tears. Fuelled with adrenaline, she urged herself to paint quicker, harder.

The cold had settled deep into her bones when she brushed a last bold streak of Medium Magenta paint across the canvas and watched the last shimmer of light vanish over the horizon. Dragging her easel back inside, she had just enough energy left to crawl inside her sleeping bag, atop the lower bunk.

Within seconds she saw her own silhouette watching through windows of the Googie Hut. The spacecraft of her dreams blasted off the tussock-covered hillside, passed through the pure energy of the aurora, into pink and red nebula cloud. At once she felt simultaneously part of another galaxy yet part of herself.

The gaseous colours beyond the spaceship window cleared to reveal a broad-shouldered Māori warrior standing in a lush green forest. His smile radiated eternal love, his obsidian almond-eyes conveyed tribal wisdom, his beautiful *tā moko* lines expressed strength and courage. She floated in suspense amidst the hush of swirling nebula cloud and watched him turn and point towards the edge of the clearing. She felt herself squint at the dark shape prowling there, just out of view.

Sunlight filtered upon Delia's face. She blinked while trying to hold on to shadows that were already drifting far over her mind's horizon. *She'd seen Tāne's face hadn't she?* Still in a stupor, she clambered out of her sleeping bag, struck her head on the base of the upper bunkbed and fell forward into the ledge of the easel.

'Aagh! God-damn it!' she yelled.

She pressed a palm against a cheek, scowled at a nail protruding from the ledge of the easel and reached for the first aid kit. After washing the deep cut, applying a sterile gauze bandage and securing it with tape, she muttered 'How attractive.'

She hesitated for a moment, hand hovering over the satellite communication device before typing '*Cut face with nail – need stitches. Please pick up later today.*'

Pulling her exhausted body onto the bunk, Delia looked at her watch. It was only 3.50am. She could cut herself some slack. Cocooned in her sleeping bag in the mist-filled space before sleep, she caught a fleeting glimpse of her muddy handprint on a bleached tree trunk and the tribal lines that etched Tāne's face. His presence danced at the edge of her psyche and she felt herself fall into his arms, the peace of eternal love wrapping around her form.

'Delia? Wake up!' Anna's voice, the sound of boots on the wooden floor, filtered down through the sleeping bag.

'Oh my God, Delia – look at all your work! How could you have done so much in such a short time?'

Delia clambered up from the depths of her cocoon and watched Anna assess the aurora canvas.

'Delia, this is magnificent. The light just here, it's like vertical bioluminescence. I just want to dive into it.'

'Thanks Anna. I painted it in record time.' She rubbed her face unconsciously and winced.

'Oh, look at you! What the hell did you do?'

'Oh, fell into that,' she nodded towards the easel.

'Are you okay?'

'Sore. Grumpy,' Delia said dully.

'I can help with the soreness but sorry, I didn't pack my anti-grump serum. Best get you back then.'

Delia rubbed her arms to get the blood circulating.

'I'll take care of this,' Anna said, holding up the saucepan and pouring water from the kettle into the sink. 'Just get your stuff together.'

Delia released the precious canvases from the washing line and gently placed them in large cylinders. Shouldering her backpack and sleeping bag, armed with precious artwork, she made her way slowly down to the beach.

It felt strange standing on the rocky shore, leaving already. She looked wistfully up at the Googie Hut.

'Got your easel, grabbed the bread and remains of the loaf – delicious by the way,' called Anna. 'Ok, let's go. At least you're not leaving empty-handed.'

They clambered aboard the rigid inflatable boat and within minutes, the alien spaceship on the hill receded from view. If she listened to the tug of her heart, she could see Tāne waving goodbye.

CHAPTER 25

Blackbeard

Delia crunched along the path. The blare of music and laughter from inside the mess reverberated in her ears. She took a deep breath at the door, adjusted her lion's mane, and willed the outfit to transmit some jungle king courage.

'About time you got here!' Anna yelled over the din. 'Been prowling the perimeter or something? I got you a wine already,' she nodded at a glass of white wine on the bar.

'Thanks,' said Delia, smiling at Anna's plastic angel wings. 'Been trying to cover up this,' she motioned to the gauze and taped strips across her cheek.

Anna adjusted Delia's mane a little. 'There, that's better.'

Delia peeled off her red *Tangaroa* jacket and clinked glasses. The wine soothed her senses like an elixir. She leaned against the bar and surveyed the sea of unfamiliar faces and wild costumes. There was the redhead in a French maid's outfit sidled up to José who was dressed as a bikie in leathers.

She nodded at an astronaut with an aluminium foil helmet and swept her eyes across the crowd of dancers. A hairy Chewbacca leaning against a far wall stared back, forcing her to gulp the wine. With her heart racing, she dragged her eyes back across the room.

'Look at Todd, what a character!' she pointed at a ginger fuzz covered chin protruding from a gladiator helmet.

'Check out your mate in the corner!' cried Anna.

The pound of blood inside her ears boomed in time with the music. A bullfighter strode towards them with a flourish of dramatic cape manoeuvres. The cape swished back and forth in front of a black mask and heavy mop of blonde hair.

'Dynamo the Great! ... Master trickster ... at your service!' he declared.

Delia tipped the last of the wine down her throat and grinned at his black texta-drawn beard. 'Mmm – you look more like a bullfighter without his bull!'

'I can prove my magnificence!' he boomed. He snatched her hand, pulled her into the throng of dancers and started to twirl his cape like a demented ringmaster. 'See, I have you under my spell now, don't I!' he yelled.

Delia erupted into fits of giggles and joined in with the crowd, belting out 'Happy' by Pharrell Williams. A wave of euphoria suddenly washed over her. Cy's caped routine, the crowd's energy, it was infectious. She looked back towards the bar and called 'Anna come and join us!'

'You guys are hilarious. Shove over then, give my angel wings some room!' yelled back Anna over the din.

Soon Delia felt every beat pulsating through her body, stomping and gyrating to song after song. She felt herself riding on a high, dashed to the bar, gulped another wine and burst back into the crowd. She booed along with everyone else when a slow song came on and cheered when someone put on 'Cosmic Girl' by Jamiroquai. Somewhere between the bar and tickling Cy's face with the tuft of her lion's tail, she danced with an Elvis. The room spun ever faster. Strange faces and echoes of laughter swirled around her. There was Elvis' slicked black hair and dark glasses, a witchs pointy hat, a cowboy's chequered shirt, the astronaut's foil helmet.

Large hands dragged her backwards against a hard, athletic body. Delia caught sight of Anna's scowl before being smothered in a blanket of hair and a pungent armpit. Hands glided over the plush fabric of her lion suit while a mouth pushed close to her ear: '*Te deseo ... ven con migo.*'

Delia heard Anna's cry over the music, 'José, stop that!'

Instinctively Delia slapped at the wandering hands and dragged her eyes past the sea of shocked faces to a scowling French maid.

'Should have known you good for nothing loser!' cried the redhead, shoving José backwards into the crowd.

'Right, that's it. You two, come with me!' cried Anna.

Delia watched them retreat, the redhead sniffing, the dreadlocked bikie looking unrepentant.

'Well, that was entertaining,' said a husky voice. 'Looks like that lion's suit of yours caused quite a ruckus.'

Delia turned to glimpse a pirate's hat, a salt-and-pepper beard. 'Not my fault ... I mean I was just,' she stammered.

'How was Brothers Point, lonely?' he interjected.

Delia gulped aware that her body felt like butter under the desert sun. She took a step backwards, swayed a little and tried to regain some composure. 'What? Oh no, I got a ... I did a lot,' she said, addressing his beard.

'Hey, what's that?' He traced a fingertip across her cheek, touching the edge of the first aid tape. 'How did you hurt yourself?'

Delia pulled at her mane. 'I accidentally fell into my easel, a nail caught ....'

Someone cranked up the music, drunken voices chorused along to Cheap Trick's 'I Want You to Want Me.'

'Sorry, what was that?' he yelled.

She felt herself sway a little.

His beard grazed her face, hot breath gushed in her ear. 'Come with me, I've got something for you.'

His hoarse voice made her legs turn to jelly, yet somehow, she managed to manoeuvre through a tunnel of drunken faces.

Static and white noise inside her wine-addled brain melded with falling snow. She gasped as he opened the door, pulled the lion's mane closer around her face and cried 'Hang on, I need my jacket!'

His grip tightened around her wrist, pulling her onwards over the snow-spattered ground.

'It's freezing!'

'Don't worry, I've got you!' Aaron yelled.

They passed by the surgery and headed towards Garden Cove at the foot of Hut hill.

Nearly there!' Aaron pulled her into his long pirate's waistcoat.

She stumbled forward beneath a strong arm, her breath coming short and sharp.

What was she doing? She couldn't think straight and shielded her face from a snow flurry. They reached the door. Fleetingly she thought to run but instead swan-dived into his whisky mouth. She felt him grapple with the door handle. They pulled away from each other for a second as he ushered her inside.

'Keep the light off,' she panted.

'Just the way I like it,' he said, his voice cracking with desire.

In the dark, Delia heard a bolt slide into place and felt a hand pull her forward. In moments they were slithering across the surface of a sleeping bag, a tangle of arms and legs. Hot hands slithered over her torso while she grappled with the side zip of her costume.

Large hands hunted for skin, tearing at her costume, rough and eager. She felt her mane peel away, replaced by a muzzle of whiskers and a searing tongue. Somewhere in the distance she heard her groan meld with the wind bashing at the walls. She felt pieces of her being lift from her body and escape the shell that kept her encased in reality. A kaleidoscope of colour exploded behind her eyes. *Why had she denied herself this pleasure?* She drifted towards the ceiling, floated above voices from her past and succumbed to the feel of his weight, his smell, his urgent mouth.

'Delia? I know you're in there! Delia, Aaron – open the door, its urgent!'

Aaron's tongue stopped flicking inside her ear. She felt her consciousness drop down from the rafters.

Muffled voices drifted under the door. 'Delia, answer me. It's Cy!' The door rattled against the bolt.

'Ignore them – come back to me.' Delia arched her back, the suck of a nipple causing her to groan even louder.

'Delia! Giovanni called on the satellite phone – it's urgent!'

'Piss off will you!' Aaron roared in the direction of the door.

The denseness of reality bore back down upon her body. *Giovanni? What?* She felt herself push against the one force of ecstasy that she'd ever known. The seismic well of energy, rippling from within her core, demanded to be fed, to be stroked. Her body raged against sudden denial.

Guttural words poured into her ear. 'Delia – no, don't go! You don't know how much I've wanted you! Just the thought of you nearly sent me crazy.'

'Let me ... um ... hang on!' Delia staggered to her feet, avoiding the snatch of a hand, left flailing in the darkness.

Delia thrust her way forward towards the sound of voices, while her frantic fingers tried to rearrange the lion suit. She flicked the mane back over her head and zipped up the side before colliding with the door.

'No Delia – don't go. We were just getting started,' Aaron cooed.

She felt his whisky breath on her right cheek, his arms encase her body.

Her shaking fingers found the sliver of metal bolt. It clanged into position somehow allowing the door to pull inward. Delia gasped at the ferocity of the cold and shuddered while snow fell on her flushed upturned cheeks. She blinked at the strange sight before her, all the while aware of Aaron's arms encircling her waist.

'Bout bloody time – you ok?' Delia caught sight of the gladiator's helmet.

A caped bullfighter pushed forward with outstretched arms, his face lined with concern. 'Quick – Giovanni's gunna call back from Hobart any minute.'

Delia tried to pry away Aaron's fingers. 'Let me go,' she said softly. Looking back now, into a face set in stone, it dawned on her how little she knew of this man.

His black eyes smouldered with fury. With lips stretched tight he snarled 'Couldn't you have waited, eh? I reckon, yeah, I reckon you're making this all up.'

Delia tried to edge forwards towards Cy but Aaron's tattooed arms were too strong.

'Out the way Cy,' said Todd in a commanding tone. 'I'd be letting her go if I was you mate.' He stepped one foot backwards and adopted a 'ready to pounce' stance.

'What – you reckon you're gunna fight me now? I'm naked here mate!' Aaron hissed.

'Delia – go with Cy – you'll be right,' said Todd, all the while fixing Aaron with a laser-like stare.

Delia peeled herself away from Aaron and fell into Cy's arms. In her periphery she caught a glimpse of Todd looking more killer raptor than human. She heard the dull thud of a body-blow behind her but their fight was lost back there, in the wind gusts and swirling snow.

They staggered the short distance to Cumpston's Cottage. 'Hang on, let me get my breath.' She doubled over, breathless, shuddering.

'Here, put my jacket on. That's it. Now keep moving, nearly there,' he yelled back.

'But what's happened to Giovanni? What did he say?' They staggered on to the porch of the station leader's room and burst inside.

'God you'll both catch pneumonia! What the hell are you doing out there without the right gear? Get her into a sleeping bag, quick!' Anna's sea-green eyes flickered with contempt. She snatched at the satellite phone buzzing on the desk. 'Giovanni? Yes, she's here – yes, right, I'll put her on.'

'My *bella* – I'm sorry – it's Thenie,' he said, his voice thick with emotion.

'What's happened?' Delia found she could barely speak. Her teeth chattered and the lump in her throat felt like the size of a boulder.

'She's had – a stroke,' he battled to get the words out. 'She's alive, but only just. You might just have time – if you board the *Aurora Australis* tomorrow. Come home my *bella*, she needs you, I need you.'

CHAPTER 26

Spirit Hunters

South Bruny Island, December 2015

Jagged-edged mountains topped with flumes of white foam attacked the ship from all sides. Delia watched the stormy conditions for a few more minutes then retreated to her cabin. There she clung to her bunk and groaned with every torturous creak and roll of the ship.

Had the Light of Truth sent this storm? Was she being punished? Could she feel their vibration from beyond the stars, their wrath in the mountainous seas? Was Athena's approaching death a sign? Her mind rolled like tumbleweed searching for answers. Why had she failed herself, let her guard down?

'Good though, wasn't it,' taunted a voice from deep within her psyche. 'That mouth sucking ...' *Stop it! How could she take another two days of this mental torment?* She felt her insides slosh in violent protest and swallowed another sleeping pill, willing herself not to vomit.

* * *

Delia's sandpaper mouth forced her back to consciousness. She rubbed her bleary eyes and strained to return to reality. Where was the thumping press of the Southern Ocean against the ship's iron shell? She guzzled from her water bottle, rocking in time with the motion of the ship and contemplated how close they were to land. Perhaps they were even close to disembarking, judging by the sound of muffled voices in the corridor.

She frowned at the sound of knocking, a high-pitched man's voice. The voices in the corridor became louder. The sudden whoop-whoop of the fire alarm launched her out of her bunk. *What the hell?*

The Captain's voice came over the loud-speaker, 'Attention all passengers and crew – there is a fire in the engine room. Please report for muster on the helideck.' The alarm continued to whoop-whoop accompanied by insistent knocking on her cabin door. 'Everyone report to the helideck – this is not a drill!' cried a member of the crew.

Delia threw on her red *Tangaroa* jacket and beanie, grabbed the lifejacket, flung open the door and became immersed in a sea of grim faces. The vessel shuddered beneath her feet while the alarm blared through the corridor. *Should she run?*

An arm looped around her waist, husky words gushed in her ear 'Don't worry, I've got you.' She felt a prick at the side of her neck. *That voice ... she knew ... that voice ... didn't ... she?* Her peripheral vision narrowed to a tiny funnel of light. The life-jacketed passenger she had been following walked ahead into a haze. Her brain felt like it had been dipped in tar. She felt herself tip forward into oblivion.

*   *   *

At the furthest edges her consciousness, the incessant fire alarm siren wailed. Beneath her the ground jolted unnaturally, sending pain ricocheting through her body.

She struggled to sit up and gasped at the icy air ripping into her cheekbones. The roar of an outboard pushed to its limits made her hold on tight and brace for the next jolt. Through the gloom, beyond the sea spray, she caught sight of his dark silhouette sitting near the throttle.

'Where are you taking me – this is madness!' she yelled, her words snatched away by the wind. A seismic wave of panic surged through her body. She gulped in air, looked beyond the lip of the boat across jet black nothingness and spied the lights of the *Aurora Australis* slipping from view.

'Where are we going?' she screamed at the dark shape commanding the Zodiac. She heard a snatch of laughter on the wind and felt the Zodiac slam hard into the inky chop.

Delia held on tight, squinting through the pre-dawn gloom. *Think!* She looked towards a chink of orange light creeping over a jagged, silhouetted horizon and prayed for a miracle.

The rev of the outboard slowed then putted to a halt. She could make out his features now, his beard flying in the wind, a lop-sided smile, glint of victory in his eyes.

'What do you want from me, Aaron!' She forced out courageous words to mask her white-knuckled fear.

'Well, it's simple Delia. I want you. I've waited for you all this time.'

His ominous words drove icicles into her chest. She held on tight to a rope-hold affixed to the side of the Zodiac.

'You want me, out here?' She motioned to the charcoal expanse. The whistle of the wind, the way the boat wallowed in the swell, made her feel so alone, adrift.

A merciless grin crossed his face. 'No, but we're close.'

A quick glance behind revealed the dark edges of land, plumes of spray, a towering cliff.

'South Bruny. Cabin's not far. Not as good as the other house, mind, but it'll do.'

'You can't just take me!'

'Well, it's obvious that I can, and I have,' he said in a matter-of-fact tone. 'By the way, you're not very grateful.'

'Grateful!' Her eyes boggled.

'Well, I have saved your life twice.' The water slapped a madman's tune against the boat. 'Granted,' he shrugged, 'you missed the fire on board the *Aurora* just now, all hell breaking loose, but surely you remember the other time?'

Delia tried to think beyond his piercing, helter-skelter eyes. She stole another look behind her and tried to gauge the distance to the rocks.

'Wouldn't jump if that's what you're thinking. The water's even colder here than the Gulch.'

'What?' She whipped back around to face him, memories crowding her brain.

'Don't you remember me hauling you onto the pier, and my jacket?'

The only word she could muster was, 'You?'

'A 'thank you' would be nice,' he said facetiously. They thanked me, at least. You and your mate just disappeared.'

Delia's head was spinning. The first rays of dawn lit up his demented face.

'But ... Ronan and Simon,' she forced their toxic names over her lips, 'they drowned.'

'Ah, that's where you're wrong,' he said. 'And that's why Ronan counted me as a true hero.'

'So, they're ... alive?' The very thought of their presence on this earth ... how could she bear it?

'Well, Ronan died after a bit. Such a generous man,' he grinned. 'Simon. No, there was no-one else, well – except if you mean the ghost they call the Captain?'

The boat seemed to rock in time with her sharp, hyperventilating breathes.

'But how – I, I don't understand how that could be? The boat sank, I saw ...' *What had she seen?*

'I went out there remember. I was the one that dived down into the wheel-house – fuckin' freezing it was too.'

He snorted like a bull, flicked a contemptuous look in her direction and swept his gaze out across the vast ocean.

Water smacked a drumbeat into the side of the boat. *The Captain was alive.*

Delia held on tight to the rope-hold and prayed for a rogue wave to smash Aaron into oblivion.

'Found him in an air pocket I did. Dragged him back up, got him breathing again. Then that wind, it just came out of nowhere. One second I was just me, the next I inhaled and felt ... bigger, stronger. Felt bullet-proof, invincible ever since! Ronan said he hated it, you know, but I think he was just weaker than me.'

He sneered, turned his attention back towards her and pulled at his beard. 'Gotta say though Delia – you've tested me – making me wait all fuckin' winter on that island. Thought I'd have you corralled down there. Just as well I had another plan to fall back on.'

'You're obsessed!'

'Hah! Maybe – obsessed with the good life, a better life than what I had. Yeah. Why not? I get you.' He cocked his head and raked fingers through his beard. 'You've already shown we get on in the sack.' He jerked his head back and laughed. 'And soon, all that money's gunna flow in from all your paintings. So you gotta admit; it's a sweet deal.'

He staggered in the swell.

Delia watched the way he snatched at the throttle and envisioned pushing him over the side. *Keep thinking, keep him talking.*

'Not much of a deal for the Captain then,' she spat.

'Oh he'll be doing fine, don't you worry. He'll be feeding on your power Delia to raise his crew from the dead. So, you see – you're a package deal! Just think, because of you, I'll be rich and the most notorious whalers that ever lived will be back to living – and doing what they do best – back to killing! I've just gotta take you back to Ronan's old place. You know it. And just like the other night, you'll be lying back letting us suck ... '

She tried to release her horror into a scream but the buzz in her brain, the bile in her mouth, was all too much. She retched over the side of the boat and watched the swell carry the contents of her stomach towards the rocks. Maybe she could just lean over the side, just a little more? She wiped her mouth, trying to summon the courage.

'It's beautiful, isn't it,' he taunted.

Delia whipped her head around and stared at the gold chain swinging in his hand. Back and forth, back and forth it swung, looking magical and mystical in the early morning light.

It must be a trick of the light. Bewitched, she kept her eyes fixated on the pendulum.

'See how easy it is to command you, Delia?'

As he looped the long chain around his neck, Delia tore her eyes away and dry retched over the side again. Her brain screamed for her to jump. Jump now!

'You look pale, Delia. Best get you home.' He laughed like the devil's court jester and turned to start the outboard.

In a moment of desperation, Delia flung herself forward, snatched the fire extinguisher, and with all her might, smashed it straight into Aaron's temple. His arm flew up reflexively but too late, his body slumped to the bottom of the rigid-hulled boat.

Delia snatched at the rope-hold to stop herself from tumbling over the side. 'That's mine!' she screamed at his comatose body. She dragged the cherished turquoise necklace over his head. With no time to thank the universe for this miracle, she grabbed hold of the throttle and started to navigate her way towards the rocks.

She took it slow, idling alongside the dangerous rock-face being careful of the swell, until she spied a likely gap between boulders.

Easy does it, she nestled the Zodiac into the gap and sidled up to what looked like tessellated rock, worn by time and wind. *I need to get closer.* She edged the boat next to the flat, ocean worn rock-ledge, biting her lip in concentration. The Zodiac pushed dangerously up against the rock-face before sliding back towards the ocean. For a second she looked back out across the stretch of endless ocean and wondered if this was truly the only way. Fleetingly, she glanced at Aaron lying motionless in the bottom of the boat.

Jump! There was only a second or so in it. She willed herself to put every effort into the leap. '*One, two ...*'

'Aargh!' she yelped, landing spread-eagled against barnacle-strewn rocks. One leg plunged into icy water, causing her to snatch and grasp at the rock-face. She hauled herself up over the ledge and lay gasping from the effort. Sudden pain seared through her body. Her hands felt on fire, her thigh throbbed, while blades of ice worked into her bones.

Get up! Move!

She dragged herself to a standstill and looked dismally at her bloodied hands, shredded jeans and oozing thigh. Part of her wanted to just lie down again, let the will of the wind take her.

The wind! She jerked her head towards the boat, drifting just offshore, where Aaron's body still lay lifeless. If she'd killed him, where was the Captain?

CHAPTER 27

Watcher of Gods

Delia stumbled in a blind panic across the flat surface of tessellated rock, all the while feeling the eyes of the Captain upon her. She felt him laughing from somewhere close, watching her pathetic attempt at escape, to where? Everywhere she turned the land and the jet-black swell and ocean beyond looked hostile, freezing. The rock ledge she scrambled across looked like it had been broken down by wind and ocean for millennia. To the left, the rock ledge met the base of an impassable dolerite cliff. To the right, plumes of spray heralded the edge of terra firma.

She skirted rock-pools and crunched over broken shells and seaweed that popped like bubble wrap. *What was that?* An odd sound, beyond the smash of water against rock and the whistle of the wind, made her stop, listen.

In a heart-crushing moment, she looked back to see Aaron in the distance bringing the Zodiac alongside the rock-face. The sickening sight pushed her into a run. Her thigh throbbed mercilessly yet still she leaped across gaps in the rocks and pressed towards what appeared to be a cavern in the cliff face ahead.

She slid down a section of tessellated rock on to a small, pebbled cove, littered with kelp and abalone shells.

'Delia ... there's no point ...'

The sound of his voice forced ice into her heart. She willed her body to keep moving, ignore the pain, keep going. She aimed for the barnacle-covered boulders ahead and the yawning gap beyond. The looming entrance to a cave was her only chance.

'Delia stop … there's nowhere …' His words lost to the whoosh of swell and spray.

She squeezed through a tight gap between boulders which led nowhere. As if by instinct, knowing that the only way out was up, she placed her fingertips inside ledges and striations in the rock face before her, found footholds, and scrambled upwards with the prowess of an injured crab. Reaching the top, she hauled herself on to a ledge and rolled to the side, coming face to face with the carcass of a rotting seabird.

Gasping for breath, her brain screamed at her pained body to get moving, hide! Panic-stricken, she scanned the boulder-strewn entrance of what looked like a large cave and noticed how waves rushed through an internal channel; an unstoppable, treacherous force.

'Delia! Don't make me have to climb up there!'

She jumped at the sound of his voice so close and stumbled forwards inside the cave's entrance. *Now what? Was there a hiding place?*

She watched another set of waves roll into the cavern and then suck back out to sea. In a moment of brilliance, or madness, she tore open the zip of her bright red jacket, flung it into the surging channel and released a blood-curdling scream.

Deed done, she picked her way into the dripping chamber, stepping across a ledge piled high with topaz and emerald seaweed. *Be careful.* One wrong step would send her plummeting into the internal channel for real. She shuffled precariously around a boulder and stepped into the atmosphere of the inner chamber. It felt peaceful here, different, like people had prayed here, long ago.

'Aargh!' Aaron's strangled cry from back near the cave entrance, made her instantly fall to her knees. She flattened herself into a low hollowed space against the cavern wall. From here she could just make out Aaron's silhouette, pacing back and forth like a stalking animal. There was her red jacket tossing like flotsam in a giant's washing machine. She watched him look out towards the ocean and heard him howl at the elements.

That's it. Go back. Leave me for dead! She willed him to walk back towards the entrance, hunched and broken yet he began leaning over the ledge instead. 'Delia!' he screeched.

The rolling waves masked her movements, crabs scuttled, keen to hide within crevasses and beneath folds of kelp. While he hunted for signs of her body, she edged around a section of cavern wall with the greatest of care, coming face to face with a treasure-trove of petroglyphs. *So people had been here.* The hand stencils showed shapes of whales and what looked like a meteor shower or stars. Just in time she whipped her hand away from a scuttling scorpion and moved further into the gloom.

Before her, plumes of sea spray whooshed through a blowhole, drenching a ledge, while the impenetrable rear wall of the cave loomed just beyond. She crept into the mist-filled space, felt the curvature of the cavern walls wrap around her and prayed for a miracle.

'*Delia.*' The commanding voice resounding through her body made her drop to her knees. '*I've been watching, waiting.*'

Instinct told her to stay low, protect her head with her hands, slam her mouth shut. Hunkered down, heart hammering in her chest, she felt like a captured mouse at the mercy of a killer cat.

'*Nature always wins,*' said the voice. '*Come, there is no need to fear me – but there is no time.*'

Delia wavered for a few seconds aware that the voice had a calming tone that resonated through her heart. Surely the Captain couldn't sound so warm, so wise?

'*Come.*'

Her heart swelled with knowing that this was not the source of danger, whoever or whatever it was. She got to her feet and gravitated forwards, where the atmosphere felt strangely warmer and willed herself to speak. Before words passed over her lips, the amorphous body beyond the mist answered her unspoken question.

'*Keeper of the Cave. Guardian of the Southern Gateway. Watcher of Gods. Come, I will guide you.*'

CHAPTER 28

Soul's Journey

In trance-like steps she edged towards the blowhole crevasse, feeling spray splatter her skin.

'But I can't, there has to be another way ...'

'This is the only way – the way of the warrior. Listen to the blowhole's heartbeat, its rhythm.'

A sudden swirl of warm air pushed at both her front and back, forcing her to remain still. Another flume of spray exploded into the air before her, freezing water dripped down her face. The force behind the warmth pushed down upon her shoulders. She dropped and dangled her feet over the blowhole edge.

'Aargh! Fucking scorpion!' Aaron's pained scream filtered from behind.

'Do it now!' The force pushed her down into the abyss. She landed on rock below, immediately becoming surrounded by a dank, dripping hell space. Terror gripped her heart so much she instinctively tried to scramble back towards the dim outline of the blowhole rim above her head. In panic she snatched at the slimy, drenched walls, the voice again rippled through her heart. *'I'll be with you, guiding you.'*

Crying now, screaming in her head she'd surely be sucked out to sea, she felt her unseen guide push her down and forward. In total blackness, she inched ahead. Keeping her head low, she moved across hollowed out rock, smoothed by the ocean since the dawn of time. A rumble erupted from deep in the earth's crust. Time was up. A ferocious surge of fear bit into every particle of her being. *Had she deluded herself?*

It's too late.

A sound like an oncoming aircraft carrier tore through the rocks, the approaching energy of the surge near ripping out her heart.

'*Hold your breath*!' demanded her guide.

Ice water burst from the earth's core. In a split second she felt her torso tumbling across slime-covered rock, down into a black nothingness.

In the distance the water could be heard whooshing back into ancient rock crevasses. *Was she breathing?* It was hard to tell. She felt herself drifting somewhere beyond the pain and denseness of her body. *Was this the afterlife or destiny? Perhaps she would forever be floating here in this space?*

Slowly, she spied her discarded body atop saturated rock. The sea-mist cleared to reveal a gentle rippled rock pool beyond. Hovering above, she watched her flesh shudder and drifted downwards for a closer look.

'*Only true warriors have seen this sanctuary. You are hidden, safe from enemies.*'

She felt the guide's presence, warm, loving, close.

'*But I'm detached! Look, my body – it's down there ...*'

'*I will warm and heal your body while your soul stays here.*'

Delia felt her guide's warm caress and floated back towards the cavern ceiling, where she felt safe.

'*Yes, you must re-enter, you must go back,*' the voice in her heart called.

Minute threads still connected her physical body yet here she was, way out, expanded, light, weightless, floating above the hidden rock-pool. She felt liquid, atmospheric. She had no pain, no feelings, no anger, no need. She was a being, hanging in the moment, in space and time, invisible, free – the ultimate escape.

It was a strange sensation: still aware of her human condition yet floating free of it. She could exist in this space, at peace, feeling the rhythm of the cave. Now she understood what Tāne had told her long ago, how his ancestors had developed the ability to rise above themselves.

Echoes pierced her sense of peace. 'Delia!' The anguish in the voice from afar felt incongruous with the nature of the waves, the breeze, the rock.

He can't get me here. I am timeless, floating.

Tortured cries continued unabated. 'Six years I've lived with the Captain. I've turned myself inside out for you, Delia!' He seemed to scream to the universe, to the heavens, to the rolling waves, to himself.

She faltered, allowing Aaron's cries to interrupt her equilibrium and, losing buoyancy, sagged back down towards her earthly body. The coldness of water and rock, the first pain of re-entry pierced her consciousness. *Where was the Keeper of the Cave?*

The roar of water blasted through the blowhole as she emerged back inside her aching, shivering body and cried out through her heart for help. She begged to go back to the way she was, to cut the threads of her mortal being and float away for eternity.

Within her pained dense body, every breath, every movement felt so hard. She shuffled into a seated position, opened her eyes, and peered through salt-laden air, where the awful face of the Captain hovered. Through a thick vaporous cloud she could make out his old seaman's cap pulled over straggly hair. She squeezed her eyes shut to block out the evil bloodhound that had scented her position and heard her scream reverberate through the cavern.

'Delia!'

Aaron's elated yell came from somewhere close, above where she lay.

'You're alive! See, there was no point in running. Your destiny is with me, with us!'

The cavern echoed with his mad words, spearing into her like poisoned javelins while she remained shaking, silent.

'Delia let me help you. There's no escape. And you must be so cold. Are you injured? Come to me Delia, let me get you warm.'

Delia cursed every hyperventilating breath and tried to keep her mouth shut and her head bowed against the will of the Captain. Even with her eyes shut, she sensed its evil presence hovering closer. Ice seeped into every cell. *Please take me from this hell. Save me,* she prayed.

'Go to the place beyond pain. Call true love – think with your heart. It's the only way ...' The Keeper of the Cave's urgent message trailed off.

How was she to transcend the unbearable pain that penetrated her body? It was so cold. She shuddered, aware that her human light was near extinction.

The Keeper's far-off voice vibrated within her heart. *'Let go!' Think of true love.*

She closed her hand around the turquoise stone at her neck, feeling the only thing that felt right and true. *'Mum, Dad – help me!'* she implored silently.

A cold breeze whistled past her ear, alerting that the Captain was readying to strike.

What was her protection symbol? Think! In desperation, with cold slicing into her bones, she clutched hold of the stone even tighter. The symbol carved into the back embedded itself in her palm. Its lines moved in and out of her psyche, morphing into the tribal lines on Tāne's face. Light and dark shadows moved in time with her fading energy.

She could see his beautiful *tā moko* lines in the dawn light. *Was this her last vision before she died?* She felt her heart yearn to see him. Could he lift her away from this pained existence? How she longed to feel his arms once again wrap around her, shelter her from evil.

The more she ached to be with him, the more she felt herself elevate towards the roof of the cavern. *Was this her soul transcending her limp and forsaken body?* Like before, she wondered if she needed flesh and blood at all, not now, when she felt so expansive and loved. She followed Tāne's face, the vibration of his love, into a space somewhere in the heavens, beyond the cave, beyond now.

Her soul passed through mist, arriving at the edges of a pine forest. She stood for a moment surveying the tranquil scene of a pebble shore and an emerald lake beyond. *Where was this exquisite place?* It felt simultaneously real and unreal. She stepped forward, the pebbles shifted beneath her feet. A falcon screeched from above and swooped over two figures standing on the shore. One figure shimmered strangely yet the other looked familiar. A man with blue-black lips and the face of an ancient warrior turned and beckoned her in greeting.

Delia ran towards him, heart bursting with pure love.

'I've missed you so much!'

The surety of tree-trunk arms enveloped her thin frame.

'Delia, I greet you with all my love and respect.' He pressed his nose and forehead to hers. '*Kia ora.*'

'I've looked for you Tāne. I've searched for you in crowds all these years! And you've been here. Where is this place?'

The being of light at their side shimmered as bright as sunshine glancing off a silken sea. 'This is the realm of the shaman, where only peace resides.'

She tucked herself beneath Tāne's arm feeling safe.

'But there is no time. Your mortal body must be saved,' said the voice within the brightness.

'But I don't need my body, not when I can stay here,' she said, clutching Tāne even tighter.

'The Keeper is right. The Captain must not be allowed to feed on the rest of your essence. You must be saved, my dear one.'

The incandescent form hovered closer. 'I called the wind to trap the evil spirit against the cave wall, but the wind will grow impatient. We must move to save you and your precious essence, Delia.'

Delia felt something crack inside her heart. 'But I will lose you again. Please, let me stay. I'm safe here, with you.'

The voice beyond the light hardened. 'You must live on, to fulfill your destiny, to paint for the planet, to help turn the tide of humankind's destruction. There is only one way. It is full of risk. You will need to be courageous once again, Delia, but remember, we are with you.'

The luminous being encircled his light around their forms. Huddled on the edge of the lake, in the stillness above time, The Keeper laid out his plan. 'To trap a demon, we must use another demon as bait. It's the only way.'

Delia swayed beneath the intensity of The Keeper's powerful light. 'But you said this was the realm of the shamans, where only peace resides. Surely there's no demons here?'

'That's right, there are no demons here.' There was something about his tone, bordering on pity.

'Well, how do we find a demon? Is there one in the cave?' she said, feeling an inexplicable wave of dread flood her being.

'When you go back, yes,' replied the grave voice from within the light.

'But what are you saying? That you'd use me for bait? But you helped me, brought me here ... I don't understand!' She felt herself quiver beneath Tāne's protective arm.

'Delia's not a demon, she's special! Spirit guided me to help her, you've helped her! I've witnessed her purity, her love of nature ...!' Tāne's words tumbled over his blue-black lips. In frustration, he raked a tattooed hand through his shoulder-length black hair.

The voice from within the light said solemnly, 'Yes, I see Delia is more in touch with nature than anyone on this earth. I see before me only light and love and a true yearning to keep all the wild, verdant places on this earth safe from humankind's destruction. But, residing within her is a shadow, a darker self. Yes, I see her inherited power, the essence of Goddess Artemis running through her veins. Yet still, in Delia's human form, she is vulnerable like all humans to darkness. So, it is the darkness we use for bait.'

'But how is that even possible!' Delia turned impassioned eyes towards Tāne. 'Don't make me go back ... .,' her voice trailed off. She watched him stroke the spiral lines on his chin as if appealing to all the revered *tohunga tā moko* in his ancestry for guidance.

'There has to be another way!' Tāne exclaimed.

'I will be with you every step of the way. Once the shadow is teased out from beneath your light, you will forever feel completely pure, enlightened, free,' said the voice, full of compassion.

Delia caught a glimpse of something akin to surrender in Tāne's obsidian eyes. She took an instinctive step backwards but found The Keeper held her within the confines of his luminous force-field. Delia gripped Tāne with all her might, holding on to the one force of truth and love that she'd ever known.

Even before Tāne appealed one last time to The Keeper, the deep furrows across his tattooed brow conveyed his sense of foreboding. 'But what if the Captain doesn't take the bait? What if he goes after Delia instead? How will it even know the difference?'

'You will see. Her shadow self will be bold, enticing, and irresistible and I will do all I can to protect Delia.'

'But what if your protection isn't enough!' cried Tāne.

CHAPTER 29

Birth of a Shadow

The pebbled shore beneath Delia's feet gave way. Tāne's waist slipped from her grip and she felt herself fall backwards into the ether. Down, down through time, back to the denseness of earth. She landed with a thud back inside her flesh and groaned as pain sheared through her psyche. *The cold – how could she stand the cold even a second longer?*

'Delia! I can't see you – can you crawl towards my voice?'

'Aaron, I'm so cold.'

'Crawl to me Delia,' Aaron yelled.

Her body shuddered. She took a moment to hold tight to her turquoise stone, feeling the power of the engraved symbol. She called on the courage of her legendary ancestor Zana, the warrior might of Tāne and wisdom of The Keeper.

Bit by bit, she dragged herself across the ledge towards the dark opening from where she had tumbled. She envisioned their huddled forms next to the lake and prayed one last time. *'Stay with me ... I can't do this without you.'*

In answer, she felt the pulse of the cavern change. The roar of the waves that caused the earth's mantle to tremble and the blowhole to explode with spray, suddenly subsided. The cave became eerily quiet as if within the eye of a storm.

Now! The Keeper's urgent command vibrated in her heart. She took a deep breath and pushed her tortured body onwards into the black hole, into what looked like the place of no return.

I will guide you, I'm here. Blinded inside the dank, dripping space, only the surety of the warm presence kept her crawling forwards.

'Delia! I can see you – keep crawling towards me! That's it.'

A strong hand clasped her wrist and pulled her from one nightmare to another. She scrambled up, cleared the edge of the blowhole, and emerged into the cavern's gloom, feeling the sickness of Aaron's embrace.

'I've got you! Here's my jacket. There you go,' Aaron soothed.

A shrill bat-like squeal echoed through the cavern. Delia caught sight of the demon swirling towards her. Her knees buckled. 'Save me Aaron,' she implored. 'Save me from him, please! I'll do anything.'

Aaron pulled her back up at the same time as nature's cavalry answered her plea. An Antarctic squall pushed through the cavern entrance, sending the Captain's face careering backwards. It screeched its displeasure at being blown from its source of sustenance.

Aaron yelled above the roar of the tempest. 'I'll get you to the boat!'

'Hurry, Aaron ... I can't take much more.'

She felt the brush of his beard against her face and the strength of his arm around her waist as they shuffled forward towards the cave entrance.

Gentle warrior words echoed in her mind. *You're close, trust the plan. Breathe in, feel me with you, breathe out and know I'm there. Feel your goddess nature ... Be bold, my dear one!*

Infused with Tāne's words and The Keeper's warm presence swirling at her back, she pushed on, beyond the pain, knowing that the end, one way or another, was near.

She edged her way around the boulder, home of the scorpion, and eased back along ledges lined with barnacles, slime, and seaweed. A part of her screamed to turn, hurl Aaron into the surging channel but she ignored it and leaned into him for support. She pushed her frozen limbs onwards to the cavern entrance where the sky melded with a battleship grey ocean.

She pulled Aaron's jacket tighter, a mere handkerchief against the elements, and stepped outside the cave.

'Can you climb back down the boulder?' called Aaron, yelling into the wind spearing in from Antarctica.

'I have to – there's no other way.' She crouched, found a ledge to grip and commenced a shaky descent sliding back to the seaweed littered shore.

'You'll be back in the boat soon. The cabin's not far from here!' he yelled, pulling her close.

She tucked her head beneath an armpit and staggered alongside him. Waves boomed into the rock ledge beside them as thunder rolled above the wilderness of jagged wave and foam.

'Wait. I can't ...' she pleaded.

'It's too exposed out here, keep going!'

The Zodiac up ahead looked like a child's toy, bucking wildly at its mooring. It was madness to go out in these treacherous waves – madness to stay.

Breathless, she let him haul her dead-weight body towards their destiny.

'I'll pull the boat towards you. Get ready. One, two ...,' yelled Aaron.

She scrambled into the Zodiac, huddled low and watched Aaron rummage through the supply boxes. He handed her a spray jacket and donned a jacket himself, securing the hood as rain started to stream into his beard.

Delia pulled on the spray jacket, muttered a prayer under her breath and prepared herself for battle. She watched Aaron rev the outboard and turn the boat out towards the black ocean.

The Zodiac was soon crunching over wave after wave, heading out into nature's blast from hell. Fear and loneliness taunted. In reply, a whisper of warmth encircled her body for a moment, reassuring her that The Keeper had not forsaken her.

She looked back through the sea spray and rain towards the cavern entrance. Already the wind had swept a dark mass out of the cave, shepherding a sheet of malevolence towards the boat. She held on tight to the rope-hold, knowing time was up.

No sooner had she steeled herself for what was to come, a rogue wave appeared from nowhere and slammed the side of the boat, sending them into a death-defying teeter. Swamped by the wave, the outboard stalled,

Aaron's body flung forward, landing with a thud onto the hull's surface.

With the outboard silent, their only means of survival lay at the mercy of the elements. The boat lurched, like the most enraged bull in nature's rodeo.

The Keeper's voice within her heart, melded with her own dark thoughts. '*Push him now!*'

As if to force her hand, a wave pushed the boat upwards. The bow reared high, forcing Aaron to tumble past her towards the stern. The weight of fate hung in that moment before the boat tipped at a precarious angle. She held on with all her might to the rope-hold and watched him flail in desperation. For a moment, he seemed to teeter, salt-and-pepper beard below boggle eyes full of fear, then a horrified cry, a splash.

There was no time to think, to scream. The dark mass, brought by the wind was sweeping its way towards the vessel. The Captain, in his expanded vaporous form, would soon be upon her.

Sticking with the plan, she felt The Keeper reach into her skull and tease the edges of her consciousness.

'*Come to me, wild dark spirit. Let us see you grow. You've been suppressed all these years. Come into the light, so that we can see you.*' The Keeper's enticement resonated from within Delia's heart.

The Keeper's surgical fingers gripped and pulled so hard she thought her skull would crack open like an egg. 'The pressure, I can't take it!' No sooner had she cried out, she heard a cackle on the wind, signalling the birth of her darkest nature – her shadow self.

Delia felt her shadow grow bolder with every passing moment. Wallowing in freedom, it squealed with delight, forcing Delia to steal a look at her manic alter-self. She gasped at the bold, bedeviled warrior at the bow. Her shadow self was a temptress vision, with flying medusa hair and laced corset. She rode the boat like a demented cowboy, hooting with glee at the savageness of the sea.

It was even more vivid than The Keeper predicted. Incredulous, Delia remained crouched low.

'I'm yours, at last! Come take me,' screamed her demon.

Delia looked to her left and smothered a scream. The dark mass was nearly upon them.

'Let me feed you the pathetic one's precious essence!'

The vision swivelled around the bow point, and discharged peels of raucous laughter on the wind. 'What, did you think I didn't see you, writhing like a coward?'

Delia scrambled across the pitching boat to get as far away as possible from her own shadow.

'I knew you were stupid, but without Aaron,' her alter-self pointed to the fast-approaching mass, 'don't you know you're to be the Captain's next host?' The vision leaned back and unleashed a spine-chilling hoot. 'He's going to eat you from the inside, Delia! And that will leave me to be his hero, his queen!'

She wailed like a banshee, a dominatrix of the sea. 'We will raise your old whaling crew my love. Come, come to me!'

With the imminent arrival of the Captain's vaporous form, Delia readied herself to fight with every ounce of strength she had left. She closed her eyes and strained to remember her protection symbol. The boat tossed wildly in the swell.

'Ha!' her alter-self hissed, 'do you think that all your stupid symbols will repel him? Remember, you are weak and pathetic! Here he comes, he has answered my call! It is too late for you.'

Delia turned haunted eyes towards the oncoming smog and willed the ferocious wind to blow the mass far out into the Southern Ocean. No sooner had she thought it the wind and rain dissolved, as if orchestrated by the invisible hand of God. The boat drifted into the eerie eye of the storm. Gaseous fingers found one edge of the boat, then the other, in seconds infesting the Zodiac with its malevolence.

The thick haze licked at the vision of her alter-self while the air crackled with an unnatural electrical charge. The smog settled and the Captain's face appeared, his thin lips curled upwards in victory.

The temptress flung back her head and screamed 'Let me be your queen! Let me help you feast upon her precious essence! Together, we will raise your whaler crew. See what I have for you, my king.' She swayed, as if under a spell, unlaced her corset, exposing her bare breasts.

Delia watched the malevolent spirit lick its lips and hovered close to her erect nipples. 'Yes, my king, I am yours, and together we will be invincible!'

From her huddled position, Delia mentally scanned her weak and freezing body, knowing she was no match for these twin forces of evil. Soon they would swoop across the bucking vessel and swamp her with their malevolence. She imagined them gorging on her precious essence or worse still, worming their way inside her, to torment her every moment. Their connection was too strong, too wanton.

She looked towards the smothering fog, the Captain's face closeted between bare breasts. The memory of Ronan's voice collided with the vision before her. 'Don't you know Delia that true art, it is about man's aversion to Hell, or his need to strive to befriend the Devil himself!'

Only then did Delia realise the truth; that they'd force her hand. Together they would blacken out kindness and the love of nature. She'd be forced to paint death and destruction, to paint scenes that tore her heart to shreds.

This wasn't how it was meant to end. The Keeper should have orchestrated nature by now, making the wind blow them to eternity. That was the plan wasn't it? How could she think when she was in so much pain?

She glanced over the side of the vessel, to the infinite black rolling troughs beyond. Aaron had just disappeared in the blink of an eye. Perhaps, after the horror of immersion, a few seconds of struggle, it would be over, and her spirit would find its way to the afterlife.

Delia closed her eyes, envisioned the luminosity of The Keeper glowing next to the emerald lake and Tāne's warrior face. 'Forgive me.' With tears spilling down her cheeks, she pushed herself upwards to sit on the edge of the boat. Her fingers kept a steel-like grip upon the side, while her legs trailed through frigid water.

She cried out, the ferocity of freezing water slicing through her legs, and looked down at her white-knuckled hands, still holding on tight. Only then did she see the monolithic shadow in the water below. A flash of white dorsal fins, a slipstream of ripples and blue water passed before her eyes. She gripped the side tighter, peering into the freezing abyss.

A torpedo of pure majestic might exploded from the depths, showering Delia and the boat in a great sheet of water. In a split-second Delia saw it, the vengeful eye, the barnacled mouth agape.

Delia's shadow-self shrieked and a bat-like screech emanated from somewhere deep within the vaporous mass. The sudden unstoppable force scooped up their shell-shocked images, sucking their screams deep into its belly before diving once again. A giant tail stood for a moment in silent testament to all that had been, before the creature vanished, taking its evil cargo with it.

Incredulous, Delia held her breath and waited for the magnificent creature to resurface. She strained her eyes to see beyond the rolling troughs. The ocean maintained its roar, either oblivious or all knowing, in its relentless push towards land.

Delia collapsed back into the boat, shuddering. Waves of relief and pain pushed sobs from her core. They were gone. Her twin nemesis had met their fate, all in the blink of an eye. The Keeper's plan had sounded insane, yet he'd been right all along. She curled up on the floor of the boat, freezing but thankful that she was intact, with her essence still safe in her veins.

Beneath her body, she could feel the vessel slide sideways down a trough. Through the veil of tears, way over the other side of the hull, she spied the outboard. If she could just catch her breath, maybe then she could crawl over there and start the engine? Maybe then she'd stop the boat from flailing in the waves.

She slipped her arm through the rope-hold and curled up next to the supply box.

'Keep fighting dear one. I need you, the planet needs you.' Was that Tāne's voice or just the wind? *I'm so cold, let me rest … just for a little while.* Her eyelids grew heavy. She felt herself slide towards a white sheet.

A distant buzz of voices infiltrated the fuzziness of her mind. In her mind's eye she saw Tāne's face in the dawn light and longed for his warm breath on her cheek, his large, tattooed hands pulling her close. Maybe she'd found the place of the shaman? The surge of hope in her heart made her flutter her eyes open.

'She's alive – get her into the boat, quick!' Hands pulled her up. 'God Delia – how on earth have you survived out here?'

'True love saved me,' she whispered.

CHAPTER 30

Deliverance

Whakarewarewa Forest, New Zealand, December 2019

The giant redwoods bore witness to Delia's final walk towards her destiny. The tapu of the Whakarewarewa Forest told her to step with great reverence. She breathed in the purity of the air tinged with ancient earth, pinecones and hints of sulphur and salt. Just ahead, water lapped on a pebble shore.

She emerged from the forest and crunched over pebbles towards the shores of Lake Rotokākahi, stretched out in all its jade green splendour. Her heart filled with knowing, that this was the right place, the right time.

'Follow your heart, my dear. Let happiness be your guide.'

Delia looked skywards. Athena was up there somewhere in the vastness of space, watching, cheering her on. She thought of Giovanni at the airport, the way his green-grey eyes had shone brighter for just a moment. *'Your happiness makes me happy, my bella. Thenie would be so proud.'*

She sat near the waterline, and studied sacred Motutawa Island in the distance, radiating a deep peace in the late afternoon sun. With no time to lose, she sketched the revered landscape cast in a bronze and golden glow before her. The pencil in her hand stopped. She felt the shift inside her, like a changing of gears, and readied her body to move into its most sacred journey.

She focused through her third eye on Motutawa, and allowed her spirit to soar up and up, until it merged with the kārearea flying overhead. At once she felt the beauty of the raptor's plumage as it soared on air currents high above the lake. Using the falcon's vision, her world expanded, filled with a kaleidoscope of gold and bronze and the sight of a canoe in the distance, near the shores of Motutawa.

Fuelled with ferocious desire, she flashed across the lake before descending in a spiral towards the canoe. She could see the man's face now, the sacred *tā moko* lines. Already alert, the man watched and waited, knowing an important message was coming to him.

She swooped low over his shoulder, readied her talons, and gripped the side of the canoe. Through the golden eyes of the falcon, his face looked more beautiful than ever. Gone was the haggard, haunted look of long ago. Here was a man filled with purpose, radiating a spiritual power and a great love of nature and life that billowed far beyond his mortal body.

Their eyes met, conveying an unspoken bond and eternal connection. She waited while his ebony eyes caressed her plumage, then stretched out her wings and elevated up into the sky.

Back on the shore, inside her body, her heart near pushed out through her chest. She watched the canoe approach with tears sliding down her cheeks and wondered what she would say. How could she put into words all that she felt, the relief of seeing him, the grief of the wasted years without him by her side? How she had yearned for this moment when their physical bodies would again meet.

Delia forgot to breathe as he beached the canoe and walked towards her, only the crunch of pebbles and the lap of water breaking the silence. For a moment she was lost in the truth and wisdom of his eyes until she felt his hands upon her shoulders, then nose to nose, forehead to forehead, they breathed each other in.

'My Delia, my Myo – at long last. *Kia ora*. Look how beautiful you are,' he said, stroking her hair.

With her throat choked full of utter joy, only her tear-filled eyes conveyed the torrent of things that needed to be said. She placed her head on his bare tattooed chest and slipstreamed back through time when the beat of his heart was her world. The sheer relief of that day flooded back, the feel of her essence back inside her veins. Crystal-clear words uttered from a long-ago canopy, rippled through her psyche.

Delia lifted her head off his chest. 'I think I remember that word Myo – what you just called me. In the forest that day ...'

His salty mouth pressed upon her soft lips pushed reality to the furthest realms of her existence.

'You are so special, Delia. My heart has bled and soared to the heavens and burst a thousand times for you. And now, here you are.' He looked upon her like the rarest of jewels then noticed the turquoise necklace hanging over the scarf at her throat. He brushed his fingers across the stone. 'Is this what you lost long ago?' The furrows in his brow deepened with confusion.

Delia nodded. 'This, us, we're together, where we belong. And now,' she looked into his glistening eyes, full of love and yearning, 'I think I know something else too. Tell me, what do you remember of that day in the forest?'

A startled expression crossed his face. 'I remember the great light, your skin drinking in emerald rain, the way the voice in the canopy called you 'Myo,' like it was your special name for you.' He brushed a tear from her cheek and went on. 'Your reaction to the clearing, your face registering love for the planet ... and the way that you felt pressed against me. You see, my dear one, I remember it all.'

'But you didn't tell me you'd seen them, that night, beneath the tree. And then you left ...' Her voice cracked and faded within the fissure of memory, too scared to continue.

'You don't know how sorry I am, Delia. I was younger then. You must understand, as a spiritual man, with a deep connection to the earth, to my ancestors, it was you who the higher power, the great light, or whatever you call them, wanted – not me. My pride and anger got in the way.' He averted his gaze to the darkening lake. 'And that has caused us so much heartache.'

He turned and looked deep into her eyes. 'I'm truly sorry. I should never have left you that day. I have regretted it ever since, believe me.'

He cupped her face in his large hands. 'So out of respect and love for you, and after meeting you in the realm of the shamans, I have called you my 'Myo' ever since.'

'I will always be your Myo,' she gasped as a strange sensation rippled through her body, like an electrical charge.

'Delia? What is it?'

'That's so strange. When I said 'Myo', she gasped. 'There it is again!' This time the feeling was undeniable. With her essence awakened, sizzling through her veins, she felt the turquoise stone at her neck become hotter and hotter. 'I think, I'm not sure ...'

'You can tell me anything, Delia. You know I will always be by your side.'

'Let's walk for a bit. Tell me about your life, I want to know everything!' They linked arms, crunched over the pebbles, and found the pathway back through the forest.

'I'm so happy, Delia. I've found my calling. Just like the vision of long ago, I'm now the most respected *tohunga tā moko*, the master craftsman I've always wanted to be.'

The sound of an axe cutting into wood suddenly reverberated nearby. Each step along the path took them closer to the sound of a sapling weeping beneath deep cuts. Delia stopped in her tracks and studied the large man swinging the axe, grunting with effort.

'How can that be allowed? Here in this ancient forest?' She scowled in the man's direction then grew thoughtful.

'What are you doing,' Tāne asked, watching her squat down and toss the contents of her backpack onto the ground.

She looked up into his quizzical face 'I have an idea.' *Could it be true? Had she found the missing element she'd been searching for all these years?*

She rubbed the symbol etched on the back of the blue stone, looked deep into Tāne's eyes and repeated the word Myo, like a mantra. In an instant, an electrical charge surged through her veins. She scrambled for a pencil and soon her hand moved with urgency across a sketchpad, as if channeling information from a higher source.

'Delia, you are incredible. Your hand – look at the speed. My God, it's beautiful!'

They stood back, admiring how the drawing near leaped from the paper, then turned in unison and walked towards the axe-man.

'Hello there!' she called.

The man placed his axe on the ground and leaned against the nearby girth of a giant redwood.

'Would you mind looking at this for a moment?' Delia put the sketch into the man's weather-beaten hand before he could protest.

Eyes that held suspicion only a moment before filled with tears. Blood drained from his face as he backed away from the tree then crumpled to the ground. Māori words of prayer flowed through his lips.

Delia looked into Tāne's ebony eyes filled with wonder and whispered, 'Because of you, I too have found my calling.'

www.ingramcontent.com/pod-product-compliance
Lightning Source LLC
Chambersburg PA
CBHW040017250626
47171CB00008B/29